I0597984

A Cursed Crow

# A COURT OF ONE

LANNE GARRETT

A Court of One
ISBN # 978-1-80250-575-7
©Copyright Lanne Garrett 2023
Cover Art by Erin Dameron-Hill ©Copyright October 2023
Interior text design by Claire Siemaszkiewicz
Finch Books

# A COURT OF ONE

# Dedication

For Cyn

*The subtle beauty of this day*
*Hangs o'er me like a fairy spell,*
*And care and grief have flown away,*
*And every breeze sings, "all is well."*
*I ask, "Holds earth or sin, or woe?"*
*My heart replies, "I do not know."*

—excerpt from *A Golden Day*
by Ella Wheeler Wilcox

# Elphame

- Alfheim -
The Golden Court

Spring Court

## SEELIE COURTS

Summer Court

The Court
of Blood
and Bones

Wildelands

The Gate

The Court of
Shadows

The Court of Less

## UNSEELIE COURTS

The
Hallows

- Tylwyth -
Winter Court

Autumn
Court

# Chapter One

We are all monsters here. Some have fangs and claws, while others have wings as dark as night and eat souls — innocent and evil alike. But there would never be a monster bigger than I had become, for I was willing, eager and had names to cross off my list before I was done. From my Court of One, I'd do wicked and vile things to save those who could not afford to be as awful as I could be.

I was told that this world ate warriors and bards alike. It drowned the babies of temperamental mothers and strangled those who flinched at their cries. Told that if I couldn't eat the monsters, I should stand back and wait for the scraps. But I had no desire to eat what was left after I burned this world with war. Monsters, after all, didn't love anything *but* war. That was the horrible truth of Elphame. Those who managed to survive the ugliness of this world were why Elphame was so ugly in the first place. And I'd learn that lesson in the same fashion as every other — on my knees, crawling through hell, tearing my soul apart and becoming comfortable with the monster within me.

From inside the frosted lands of the Winter Court, I was not the only vile creature that lurked, but I was the only one content with the darkness, wearing a mask crafted when I had first come into these cursed lands of the Fae. In the Golden Court, I'd learned how to wear that very mask. But from the war-torn fields of Elphame, I had realized I didn't need the façade. We were all hideous beasts here, and I blended in perfectly, with or without it. The only difference between me and them was our motivations.

Within my once-enemy's borders, I was covered in the smell of winter. My mask hid my broken soul, which yearned for darker places. *Monsters can cry, can't they?* And that's exactly what I was...broken. I was holding on for dear life, willing my heart to keep beating. A shattered soul felt like a childhood home burning to the ground and being the only one to have survived the flames. It tasted of ash, salty tears and burns that never fully healed. Willingly, I left pieces of myself scattered throughout a land that made no move to ease a single moment. I scrubbed off parts of myself from one end of Elphame to the other. I gave little bits of myself to the winds of a land that tried as hard for my death as I had for my life. But there was no room for wishes of better things in Elphame — only nightmares made of things that crept in the dark and attacked when your back was turned. Because that was what it took to endure Elphame — to survive *her*, the Caller of Crows.

With each passing minute I spent away from home, this new winter world became scratchy against my skin. The guise I wore chafed against every fiber of my being. It reminded me of the Golden Court, when I'd had to become a creature to be feared. I hadn't thought I'd ever have to become that Crow again. But here I stood, shaving away at who I had died to become, to survive another day.

I stood in unwanted moments in a place that wasn't my home. And Tylwyth was very much *not* my home. It didn't matter how breathtaking it was. The beauty of it was stained with my wish to be somewhere darker and more feared. Nothing would ever be as soul-settling as the Dark Courts. No smell was as calming as breathing in the wind of home. More than anything else, nothing could wrap around my heart as tightly as Solas could. Everything else held a taint and an edge of laughter from the Gods. From within enemy territory, now an enemy to every other land, I was on my own and trying to find my way back home. Each day, I inched closer to terror, lost in a world I didn't know and had no protection against.

I had left my home to find the truth and found my new path covered in shards of glass and new memories to stain my mind. Leaving Solas had been the most challenging part, even knowing what I'd have to do to get home. Since stepping into the Winter Court, running toward truths others would kill me to protect, I was torn between thrones—Fire and Ice, Dark and Winter, Truth and Lies, Life and Death, Blood and Bones. It was all or nothing. Final moves were left to play in a game I didn't know or understand. But this was what it took to survive in Elphame—become a monster or be eaten by one. Kill or be killed.

I was taken from my home in Whitwick, died to keep mortals safe and found my new home in the land of Fae. And now, I was on the run once again—only this time, I didn't want to burn everything or everyone. I only had one name on my list to hunt, and I'd focus my rage on the one who deserved the touch of a Soul-Eater—Solene, the Caller of Crows, the Lady of Blood and Bones, the blooded sister of Solas.

With my father tucked safely in Tylwyth, I breathed the air stained by my lies a little easier. I hadn't gone too far from him since he had stepped out of Whitwick Gates and into the land that had stolen his daughter. He was still healing from Fae sickness. Going through the Gate without a drop of Fae blood felt like walking into the middle of a war. Hell on earth climbed down your throat and made you wish you hadn't come. That my father was still alive was a surprise. On *my* first day here, I had hoped for death. And I remembered that day, regrettably...crystal clear.

Nix and Orrian, back from the Hallows, found me in my father's bedroom, helping him put his shoes on. He was feeling better—not perfect, but better. The healer encouraged him to walk around and get used to Elphame and the magick his body naturally fought against. It would take weeks before his soul gave in to this new world and accepted the energy of Elphame. The thought that any of us had weeks of life left was amusing, but I kept that laughter to myself. My father had slept for twenty hours straight before he had called out my name in a panic. He looked how I had felt on my first day here, so long ago it seemed like someone else's life I remembered, where everything hurt in a frostbitten and fire-burned sort of way. The air around me had smelled of seared flesh, scorched with flame and left rotting in the sun. Some things never changed. Even used to Elphame, I was still tired, scared and sore.

Once he saw I was okay, he calmed down and was ready for the mend. He had said he had too much to do to lie in bed all day. I, on the other hand, could have used a week in bed without the perils of Elphame gnawing at my insides. But I had only ever indulged in that luxury when my soul was near ruin and my deathbed called me by my full name, like a parent scolding a child.

"I've missed you," I cried as soon as Nix was in my arms. He looked happy and rested, the Nix I remember meeting, the friend I'd had before my Taking. "Your sister… I've heard you found her?"

"I have, and I can't thank you enough, Perdi. I feel — I don't know — thankful, grateful, at peace."

"You look it. You look like all the pieces of your soul are finally back where they belong." I hugged him a little tighter. "You didn't have to come back, Nix. There's only war here now. Gone will be your peace."

"My sister and every niece and nephew of mine are safe where they are. But you are my home now. Wherever you go, I will always be there." He lifted one of the tears off my cheek. "You are my home, wherever that may be. I will always come when you need me."

"So will I…for you," I answered. "Where's Orrian?"

"She's probably eating someone or something," he answered. It was only half a joke. "Now, what has happened to send you so far from home into Faolan's land?"

I shook my head and tilted my head to the door. I could smell Christmas carrying on the cool breeze that was Faolan. "I'll fill you in later."

"Nix, I see you've made it back," Faolan said as he stepped into the room.

"Almost didn't. Your forest isn't a walk in the park." Nix tried for a joke, then shuddered. "What the hell is out there?"

"Imagine if you hadn't had safe passage?" Faolan snickered. "And your little fairy is in the town center — *not* eating anyone, I hope."

"There are no guarantees with her," I answered.

Faolan searched my face for humor and looked to one of the guards in the room when he realized I wasn't joking. The guard moved quickly, no doubt to check on Orrian. I was pretty sure she wouldn't be eating the children, but I couldn't say for sure what she did when no one was looking. Even I was scared of her, and I considered her my friend.

"Sir, are you ready to see Tylwyth?" Faolan asked my father.

My father grinned while we got him dressed for Winter Court. Although he moved slow, he was the first out of the front door. Exploring a part of Elphame would be a dream come true for him. At a pace my father could walk, Faolan led us through the streets, pausing every so often to point out places he loved to visit. Each time we stopped, someone would step out of a shop and welcome us. My father was mortal, and I wasn't sure yet what I was, but no one seemed to care. They were as warm to us as they were their own king.

I couldn't help but notice how different it was in Tylwyth compared to the other places I had been unfortunate enough to know of and experience — how warm and kind they all were, regardless of who we were. My father tired after less than a half-hour and was led back to the house for rest and more herbal teas, very much against his wishes. This was his first time in Elphame, and he wanted to see it all in one day. Nix returned with him to settle in and snoop around, as I knew he was dying to do. Tylwyth was a mystery to most Fae, and Nix was nosey. I stayed with Faolan, curious about where he'd grown up.

"Your home is beautiful." I finally broke the silence as we walked. "It's not what I would have imagined."

"We are not the symbol of the rest of Elphame. We have no desire to gain more lands or courts. From here, we watch as the rest of Elphame fights and squabbles over inches of land. We're content just as we are," Faolan replied. "Here, in Tylwyth, it's home — not war, infighting or courts. It's just home — nothing more, nothing less."

"I can see why you love it here." I smiled on the outside, but on the inside, I felt homesick.

"I recognize that smile, and it's as fake as ever. As much as I enjoy showing you where I'm from, I'm sorry you're missing your home and wish, more than anything, you were home right now. There's a reason we never took part in the Taking of a Crow. It's barbaric and cruel," Faolan said. "Before you, I never went to the mortal lands during the Taking. I went to Whitwick before you, though. I wanted to see your realm, not conquer it. I stayed hidden and didn't meddle or interact with your people until you."

"What do you mean, until me? Why me?" I asked.

"Aoife," he answered. "She told me about you and that you would interest those who wished the Gate remained open, those who wanted more of the mortal world than was ever allowed. She told me that you would close the Gate and end this madness. I suppose, at first, I was just curious. The mortal lands have always been a place of interest for the Fae. But I found myself going back over and over. I was no longer only interested in the mortal lands. I wanted to go back to see you. With you, I could pretend I wasn't who I am. I could simply be Fao, without the throne or the demands and responsibility that came with it."

"How could you pass through the Gate, but no one else could without sounding every alarm?" I asked. "You came every day."

"I am not simply Fae. I am Daoine Uaisle, and my blood is Royal-born. My line is from the original Gentry, the original Fae. That alone gives me abilities others don't possess. It is how I got you home and you and your dad both back here in one piece," Faolan explained. "But I think it has more to do with my intentions. I never went to you with the purpose of harm. On days my temper was uneven or court business had me feeling aggressive or ill-willed, the Gate wouldn't let me cross until I was calm."

"I saw you almost every day. I imagine calm was a skill you learned quickly."

"That skill was born out of necessity and had nothing to do with the Gate. Under my father's rule, you didn't survive the Winter Court without learning to swallow every emotion."

My skin crawled thinking of his childhood, and I quickly changed the subject. "Solas and his father were from the original lines, weren't they?"

"Yes and no. Both were of the guard, part of the original Elphame Guardians. The Aos Si comes from that line. Solas and his father were not original Royals until they seized land and created their own court. They created their line. During the wars, my family was locked outside of the wall when we were fighting the rebels. We had no choice but to build our lives outside of the Court of Blood and Bones. We fought to protect this court, not for territory but for peace. We took in everyone we could and built Tylwyth to shelter them. Tylwyth is made of those from different lines. Very few of us come from my line through blood."

"His sister, Solene... She's still a Lady of the Court of Blood and Bones," I told him.

He squirmed a little at the mention of her name. But I think everyone did, not just him. "*My* cousin, Solene.

She's my cousin and more than just a lady of that court. She *is* that court. When her mother died, it all went to her. She comes from one of the original families, like Solas and me. The court began with two families, each creating a line — one of Royals and one of Guardians," he explained. "She is from the line of Seers, a Royal Seer at that, given who her mother was, while Solas was born into Guardianship, like his father. When a child is born here in Elphame of two different courts, there is a half-chance they'll have the powers of their mother or father. It depends on who is stronger. Solas and his sister were born into two different powers. Only the women of the court can become Seers. It skips males. As for Guardians, they are only male."

My mouth dropped. "Solas is your cousin? How am I only just now learning this?"

Faolan laughed. "All of us trace our lines to Blood and Bones, to one of the two founding families. We are related through blood. But we do not practice those relations as humans do."

"Weddings must be monstrous here." I joked.

"We don't have weddings here, not like the mortal realm. We don't have wives or husbands. We are oathed to each other for life. Consorts, we'll call them if we must give them a name. We are coupled, and we blood oath ourselves to them until the end of our life."

"Have you ever given your oath to another?" I asked and felt my cheeks heat. I didn't really have the right to ask him that question, but I couldn't help it. There was so much about him that I didn't know — and damn it if I wasn't curious now that the curtains had fallen. "Hundreds of years seems like a long time to be alone."

"No, not yet. Giving your oath is severe, Perdi, and not done lightly. No matter the circumstance, we cannot leave once we've given our oaths. Unlike in the mortal world, where you can leave your mate, we can't do that here. Here, that oath lasts for as long as your heart beats. Hundreds of years is a long time to be with someone you don't love or someone who treats you poorly." Faolan's mind was elsewhere. He'd grown up in a home with two people who didn't want each other, and it had played out over his mother's flesh, day in and day out. "There are times when the choice is not yours. And when that happens, those are very long years to be tied to them if you can't stand their touch."

"Like an arranged marriage?" I asked.

"That isn't as common anymore, but it still happens. Usually, it is done between courts to strengthen their ties. In those cases, most are not contested. But an arrangement is not permitted anywhere in the Unseelie Courts. Neither Solas nor I will allow it."

"Why not?" I asked.

"There is no tie I want to have bad enough to force two people into a lifetime together. We live too damn long to be saddled with someone we hate or that hates us."

"The idea that I'd be trapped with someone who hated me for all my days is scary." I thought of my time in the Golden Court, and my stomach flopped at the idea that I could have been stuck there on the arm of the dead King.

"When fate chooses for you, there isn't much you can do about it. You just try to make it work. But it is breathtaking when it is a good match, and there isn't much work to be done. You become one. It is everything we hope for, to be tied to someone we would die for, someone who will care for us in our final moments. Like mortals, we, too, crave companionship and love. It is everything one could ever want. But it is also terrifying. I'd suggest never coming between two

18

who are oathed. It can be deadly, to no real fault of their own. The men, especially, can be overly territorial. But the ladies? I'd fear them even more. They won't just kill you. They'll torment you first."

"Fate chooses for you?" I asked and let the rest of his comments fall away, but not before wondering if Solas was on the verge of insanity with me gone.

He nodded. "There are times when two Fae are brought together, and the oaths slip into place without much thought or notice. You forget, and the words just spill from your mouth, like saying you love someone. That happens more often than an intentional coupling. And when it happens, no force on this earth can keep them apart."

"I don't think I like the sound of that." I laughed. "Imagine waking up and being married?"

"This is why most kings keep multiple partners or none at all. It is harder to grow attached to one when you have many. Imagine a king lovestruck and with armies at his disposal? He'd wage wars to get to her."

I could imagine. Solas was one of those men.

"Do you have many partners?" I blurted out and instantly felt my face redden. "I mean, that's fine. I just want to know if I will run into them in the hall or hear you all night."

Faolan laughed. "No. I have none. I'm not one for bed jumping. Before all of this, your Taking, there was only you — and none since."

I squirmed at his comment. "Is there some oath between us that I don't know about?"

"No. I could never allow myself to get that close. It's not because I didn't care, but I have thousands of people who need a king and my love more. Unfortunately, when you sit on a throne, your life is very much not yours to live. Your people must always come first. Every choice made is for them before all others."

"Sounds like a bleak life," I replied.

"It can be. Often, it's just a simpler way to live. It's the only life I've known, and as lonely as it can get, it's not one I'd willingly give up," he replied. "Inside these walls, I lead a relatively normal life by your standards. My inner circle is small, which is how I like it. I work, cook and clean, fish, spend time with my community and participate in building a better world for my people."

"You work? You mean, as a king?"

"No. I teach at the school—history and arts. Being a king is my duty. We all must work here. We can't build a future for the next generation unless we all work toward it. I cannot lead from the back. I can't do what is best for my people unless I am one of them. I must make the same sacrifices, or I cannot ask it of them." His passion was almost physical. As his heart beat for his people, I could feel it move the air around us. "I couldn't imagine not being part of my community. It would be such a lonely existence. I'd feel trapped."

"It is lonely. Trust me," I answered.

Faolan took me to a small café for lunch, where we sat at the front window for me to see his world through his eyes. There, we were approached by one of Faolan's people, a guard who watched over my father. He didn't bow or kneel. Instead, he pulled up a seat and flopped down like a casual friend. But that was how everyone was in Tylwyth—friends and neighbors. It reminded me of the Dark Court and how Zephyr was with Solas. There was no show of power until others were watching. The thought of Solas and Zephyr pulled at something in my core. I missed them. I felt homesick...empty.

"It seems chance would have us meet again." His words rolled over my skin, cooling as they drifted by. "What a cruel mistress fate can be."

I stared at him a little longer, letting my Malice roll to the surface to taste the energy that rolled off him in waves of delicate snowflakes. I recognized him and fought not to squirm. "You were there the day Faolan came into the Court of Less."

He nodded. "The day you stole my king into your lands. Yes. I was very much there for that. Not the best first impression."

"Don't, Oisin." Faolan warned the man.

Oisin's face didn't flinch. Instead, he held out his hand to me. "I didn't get a chance to introduce myself on that fine day. I'm Oisin." He pronounced his name as 'O-Sheen'. His handshake was firm, and he didn't treat me as if I were breakable. I liked him more for that.

"Thank you for watching over my father." I tipped my head in appreciation. "It's nice to meet you again, Oisin. I'm Perdita, Perdi to my friends."

"And are we friends, Perdita? What do you plan to take from me today?" he asked, glancing up through his lashes. The look wasn't as friendly as he tried to make it. It reminded me of Zephyr and his warning glances.

I would never be the tough or bad guy, not when sitting at a table of men who had hundreds of years to practice and pounds on me. I let the amusement drain from my face and stared back with a smile that held only the fire within my belly. Those flames never went out and burned only for those who dragged me into war and chaos.

"I'll leave that decision to you, Oisin. We can be friends, or you can always wonder what I'll do to you when you close your eyes or turn your back to me." I let my friendly smile return. "I'll never win a hand-to-hand fight with you, but it's not beneath me to kill you in your sleep, poison your drink or push you off a cliff. That's the thing about witches. You just never know what end we'll choose for you, but rest assured, it'll be painful—and this smile will be the last thing you see. You may be Fae, and I am just a mortal, but I'm pretty sick of this shit and would caution your next words. This may be your last chance before choking on your regret."

"Interesting," he answered.

"What's that?" I asked.

"I had wondered how a little Crow could survive not only her Taking but the Golden Court, then the Dark Courts. But I think you've just answered those questions."

"We can be great friends, or I can start thinking of creative ways to tell Faolan of the tragic accident that claimed your life. Trust that I'll make it look like an accident."

"I think I like you." Oisin's smile widened. "Perdi it is."

"If you two are done grandstanding," Faolan interrupted. "Oisin, what can I do for you on this fine day? I thought you had the rest of the day off and were caving?"

"Caving?" Oisin rolled his eyes. "It's not caving when it stops to chase someone else."

"It?" I asked and felt the panic begin. "Chase?"

"Oisin here likes to drop into the caverns at the borders and outrun what is down there." Faolan's smile broadened. "It's what Nix was referring to when he crossed into Tylwyth. The dread you and they felt? Oisin likes to play with it."

"Dear God," I whispered. "Why would you chance it?"

"Live this long and see how you fill your time," he answered and chewed on a bread roll from the table. "I was down in the caverns, as I am on my time off, when the chase ended long before it should have. Someone had come to our border, and I'm not talking about that little gnome or the tiny-winged creature that bit me twice before I let them pass."

"She bit you?" I asked and tried not to laugh at him.

"She bit me, and he stabbed me. I tried to get out of their way. I knew they had safe passage, and I'm not stupid enough to get in the way of a gnome, let alone one accompanied by a fairy. But they were on me before I could step to the side." Oisin showed me his hands, which were bitten and clawed. Small slashes marred his flesh from Nix's blade. It made me grin. "Anyway, after I bravely fought them off—which was life and death, I'll have you know—I was doing my thing in the tunnels when the fun ended." Oisin pushed a letter to Faolan. "Zephyr came with a letter for you both."

"How brave of you." I teased, and he lifted his chin in pride.

"I'm surprised he waited this long. I was expecting him the first night," Faolan answered. "Thank you, Oisin."

He stood and looked from Faolan to me, then groaned. "I knew, from the first time Faolan went to the mortal lands, you would be nothing but trouble. I may have wondered how you could make it this far, but now I question if you're worth it."

Faolan cleared his throat. "Don't, Oisin."

"You have always allowed me a voice, Faolan," he countered.

"It's fine," I interrupted. "If he has something to say, I'd prefer him to say it now. I'd rather know if he'll let me die when he's supposed to be at my back. If that's the case, I'll make other plans, and he can stand behind someone else."

Oisin jerked back as if I had slapped him. "If I say I have your back, it would take my death to pull me away. My personal feelings about you have nothing to do with whether or not I do my duty."

"Yes, they do, and that's the bitter truth of our emotions. You will hesitate if you dislike me, do not trust me or even wish I had never stepped foot on these lands. A split second could mean my life. I'm not judging you. There are plenty I would let die while I watched. Hell, I would help hold several under water and drown the life out of them myself. The facts are the facts, and how we feel drives how we react," I countered. "Take this very moment. I'm not fond of you. This leads me to question if I'd protect you over myself. We protect most what we love — and you, Oisin, I do not love any more than you love me."

"I would give my life for my king. If you belong to him…"

I gripped the table and stood on the heels of a Horn that no one else could hear. My body shook with anger. It hummed with Elphame. "I belong to *no one*, Oisin. Let's get that straight. *No one* owns me — not him, Solas, you or any other bloody Fae in this fucking realm. I belong to *me*. This is not up for debate, *ever*. I don't care what the rules say about who owns who in this bloody world. Don't *ever* repeat those words. This is your only warning…end of story."

Oisin stood his ground. It irritated me, but I could respect him for it. Faolan didn't remain a king because he surrounded himself with those who scared easily. Fools, perhaps, but not cowards.

"If you are here, you put us all at risk. If we are going to die for you, I am ensuring you are worth it." His very tone was winter — ice cold and bitter.

"Fair enough, but I'm not asking you to die for me. I would never expect that from you. I'm asking you to give me a chance to run," I replied and took my seat.

"Running is weak."

"Running is all I have. Unlike you, I will die from a head injury. One good punch, and I'm out cold. A simple cut could turn infected and I will die. However strong I think I am, my body is not. I'm not Fae. I have no choice but to run."

Oisin breathed me in and shivered. "You're more Fae than you care to admit."

"Go to hell," I snarled.

He smiled. "Keep that anger with you, Perdi. You'll need it when we meet with the darkness who stole you into the lands of slavery."

Faolan finally stood. "Oisin, are you done making a mess of my day?"

"I told you, Faolan. The first time you stepped through that Gate, I warned you of this day. Is it worth it?" Oisin asked.

"Love and peace are always worth it," Faolan answered. His words made me fidget with discomfort.

"It's the only worthy death," Oisin answered and patted his friend on the shoulder. "You, Perdi, I will see on the field. I hope you can run as fast as you think you can. No one can outrun the dark."

"It is not those who lurk in the dark we should fear. It's the one who hides in plain sight."

He tipped his head. "Ain't that the truth."

Oisin left as he had come — casually, laughing, the friend next door. But I knew, under his calm exterior was a blizzard that rivaled the greatest of gales. The moment he was gone, I missed him. He reminded me of Zephyr — a storm that cared nothing for your feelings and tore your house out of the foundation as you begged for mercy, but he secretly grieved when he was the cause of your pain.

"Who the hell was that?" I asked.

"Oisin is my Commander. He heads my armies."

"I don't think he likes me," I answered.

"I think it went well, considering."

"Considering what? I'm human? I'm a Crow? I come from the Dark Courts, your enemies? I helped jail you? I could continue. The list is long."

"No. Oisin doesn't care about that. And, for the record, he told me I'd be imprisoned the day I came to offer you freedom from Solas. But, considering his sole purpose is to ensure I live a very long life, that my people are never forced into combat and that Tylwyth never feels the pains of war, it went well. His job is not to trust you, Perdi, for no other reason than that is his duty."

"I shouldn't be here. Oisin's right. I cast war and death with my shadow." I felt guilty. It had been a good idea to come until I got here and saw what my being here could do. When I considered him a tool I could use, I didn't think of everyone else who would suffer for it.

"Oisin will come around. Don't worry about him. He's an honorable man. He's a good one to have on your side."

"For you, maybe," I mumbled under my breath. "What's the letter say?"

Faolan snapped the black seal, its crack echoing in my ears, and unfolded the letter we both knew was coming. He didn't try to hide it from me or read it first. But I leaned away from it as if it could touch me, and I'd be gone before I could read the first sentence. "Solas requests an audience tonight. We can select the location."

"Why?" I asked, then raised my hand. "Never mind, why else? I'm gone, you have me, he wants me, the Gate, the power, the ego, war, death, horror. Did I miss anything?"

"No, that pretty much sums it up. Do you want to go?" he asked.

I shrugged. "If we don't play the game, things will only get worse."

"Likely. Whatever the reason for your being here" — Faolan glanced around the room and brought his finger to his lips. We wouldn't speak only about it, not in places where ears hung too closely to our lips — "Solas is honor bound to ask for your return. It is the way of Elphame. But more than that, his heart, love and ego would never allow him to stand by and watch. No Fae, dark or light, could swallow this pain. He'd be…pushed to come for you. He won't get to you, but it'll take many to stop him. In truth, my concern is not Solas. It is who he will send in his stead."

"Zephyr." I groaned. There'd be no hiding from him. He'd eat this world to get to me. "Let's see what he wants before he comes to your door with his demands."

# Chapter Two

We stood on the edge of Faolan's territory, his most prized possession, Tylwyth, and my legs quivered — fear, anticipation, dread from whatever lived in the caverns. My emotions acted as a magnifying glass and brought everything into hyperfocus. My skin wanted to crawl off and run to safety. It itched in places my nails couldn't reach. It felt like I was allergic, not to the fabric or the grass at my feet but to the bedlam that was now my life.

The panic took root like a cluster of hornets in my stomach. Tension grew in my shoulders as my mind replayed every attack prior. My breath came out jagged, rapid, like I could do nothing to get the air I needed. I closed my eyes and rotated my shoulders. I told myself I wasn't trapped. I was free. No one would touch me. I was protected. I knew Solas wouldn't take me against my will, not because of the war it would cause, but because he wanted me here as much as I wanted to be here. If I told him I wanted to come home, I knew he would let me, and he'd torch everything between him and me. We'd both die in those flames, but he'd willingly burn for me, and I knew it. But it wasn't Solas I was scared of. It was Zephyr. He didn't play court games, and he didn't give a damn about the consequences. He was a kill-first, ask-questions-later kind of guy. More than that, I was afraid to see the hurt in his eyes that I had left behind when I'd fled. Whatever my reasons for going, a person's soul didn't give a damn about court games.

Oisin stood at my back while Faolan and a few men went ahead to scope out what mess we were walking into. I could feel the frost twisting off him, like snow blowing off a hill and hitting my back. Little frozen spiders danced across my body, touching every part of me. I could feel his eyes on me, like ants dancing across my skin. His glances only added to my discomfort.

"How the hell can you stand this feeling? I couldn't imagine crawling into a cave with it." I twisted in my clothes and tried to rub the feeling from me.

"You get used to it. It helps when you're not scared," Oisin answered. "Is the wee Crow scared?"

"I'd be stupid not to be scared. Fear has kept me alive longer than anything else," I answered.

"What are you afraid of?" he asked.

"Why, Oisin? What does it matter?"

"Fear is a great motivator, Perdi. I'll give you that. But fear can also steal your power. I ask to help you take it back," he replied. "What we're walking into? Fear won't help you there."

"You sound like a friend I had before all this." My mind went to Zephyr again, who I knew would handle this worse than Solas. Oisin sounded a lot like him. "I'm scared to see Solas. I'm scared I'll have to go back to having no control and fearing my death to save a war from coming. I'm scared to see Zephyr, the Aos Si and the Sluagh. And just standing here, with this sinking dread, I'm scared of whatever the hell is in those caves."

"That's a longer list than I was prepared for." He laughed. The sound of it made me smile. "First, your fear of Solas is misplaced. You'd already be dead if that was what he wanted. How many chances did he have and not take? If death is what he craved, you'd simply be dead. That is the truth about the Dark Courts. Hell, that is the truth of every court in Elphame, including the one you're standing in. What we're doing now is merely a play to the gallery, showing off. It is nothing more than the dance of kings. It's irritating but nothing I would fear to any great extent. His ego and heart are broken, and he will lash out with that pain. As much as I dislike the man, I'd do the same. We all hurt those around us when we feel powerless or hurt. And he, Solas, is a broken man. But he won't kill you tonight. And if we're being honest, I doubt very much that he would kill you at all, for any reason."

"No, Oisin, I don't fear Solas, not in the way you may think. I dread how I'll feel when I see him. I fear I'll have to go back. I'm not scared of him. I fear what he may be forced to do."

"Noted. But you can't run from how you might feel. Bringing your fears about tomorrow with you today won't help you, so don't bother. The war is already on the way and has nothing to do with whatever went on or is going on with you and Solas. There's always a reason for war, whether you played a role in this or not. Adding another to the litany of 'whys' and 'wherefores' won't bring the war here any faster or keep it at bay any longer. So, like I said, don't fear seeing him. The small army he'll have with him — Zephyr, the Aos Si, Sluagh and whatever else he drags out of the dark pits of hell —

you've seen them all before. You know how they will behave. You know most of it will be bravado, save maybe Zephyr, but I have a feeling he won't harm you or you wouldn't be here. Why fear what you know is not real and just a show of force? We wouldn't be having this conversation if they wanted you that bad. You'd be dead, and I'd be wine-drunk at home, never having met the Crow."

"You could have simply said I had nothing to worry about. I think I just aged a year listening to that story." I smiled.

"Yes, but we've also eaten the time you would have spent worrying about that which you do not control and calmed much of the unrest in your soul," he replied.

I smiled. "Thanks for the pep talk."

"Do you love him? Faolan?" Oisin asked, close enough to feel his breath on my neck. It made me step away, uncomfortable to have him so close.

"Why does that matter to you?" I replied, my voice hot with anger. For me, fear always twisted into fury. I swallowed it begrudgingly. I wasn't angry with Oisin. He hadn't done anything to deserve what I had pooled in my stomach.

"If he is willing to die for you, I'd like to know if you are willing to die for him? Let us leave the song and dance for kings and speak honestly between us. You and I will be the only ones who lose. Kings never suffer their losses as great as the rest of us."

"Truth… How out of place that will be in a land of lies." I turned with a sigh and met his heavy stare. "Faolan wouldn't die for me any more than I would die for him. But he would die for his people. I know that to be true. Today, for this, I would protect him, but not to my death. I'd never have the chance to. But I will do what I can for him not to suffer for my actions."

"I'm too old and too tired to dance around your riddles. You didn't answer my question. Do you love Faolan?"

"Once, yes...very much so. Now, I don't know what I feel for him. I'm twisted inside and don't know a lot anymore. I don't even know if I can trust Faolan, let alone love him." I answered and paused to give Oisin the truth he asked for without trying to hide behind the mask I'd pulled on when I stepped out of Solas' territory. "I love him, but I'm not *in* love with him, if that even makes sense. The love was always there, but I don't know how much of it is real or how much is just a memory of how I once felt. It's complicated and simple all at once. I wish I could give you more, but that's the only truth I have."

"I appreciate your honesty and can see the struggle in your eyes. I'd have left you for dead if you had lied."

"If it comes down to Faolan's life or mine, choose his, because I will be the only one there with friends." I rubbed the middle of my chest, where my pain met my anxiety and knocked continuously on my heart. "If I could save everyone by going with Solas, I wouldn't have even left."

Oisin nodded. "Let us hope it never comes to it. But if it does, I will hold you to your word. I will drag Faolan off that field and leave you to die, to save him. I will always choose him over you. It is not merely my duty. He is my friend, and you are something else to me."

"I'd expect no less," I replied and turned back around. "This is going to hurt."

"Love is a cruel bastard, isn't it?" he asked. "It doesn't matter where that love lives or who we give it to. We suffer for it just the same."

"How can something that feels so good also feel so bad simultaneously?" I asked, not for any specific answer, but to curse the world for making it so.

"Balance." Faolan breezed to my side. "If the Sidhe has taught us anything, it's that you'll never know joy without knowing how to suffer for it. Without balance, it could never be real. You cannot know true happiness unless you've tasted misery. Love is much the same. How can you know love unless you've known hate and suffering?"

"Ignorance is bliss, and I'd love nothing more than to revel in oblivion," I answered.

"Wouldn't we all." Oisin laughed. "So, what did you find, Faolan?"

"Solas has Zephyr with him, which shouldn't surprise anyone. A hoard of Sluagh are tucked away in the trees, and the Aos Si are scattered throughout the field. It looks like Solas has come with a small army."

"Sounds like him," Oisin answered. "How do you think this is going to play out?"

"He looks as sure as he usually does," Faolan answered. "But he's not the one I ever worry about. Solas is war, but he's usually the rational one in the mix. Zephyr looks pissed off. I don't think I've ever seen him angry. Aggressive, yes—but emotions on his face for the world to read, never. Even in war, before he was locked away, I had never seen his emotions. The Aos Si are mirroring his anger—and that's never good."

"Zeph is always pissed off," I spoke up and was ready to be shut down, but they both turned to me. Oisin motioned for me to continue. "Zephyr won't interfere unless you touch Solas or he senses I need help. If he thinks I'm here against my will or being harmed, he'll kill everyone to get to me. He really won't care about the fallout it'll cause. He doesn't answer to courts or crowns. But, of anyone in the Dark Courts, Zephyr is probably the one with the most honor. He commands the Aos Si, and they won't move unless Zephyr orders them. They wouldn't dare go against him. I think he'd kill them all for it."

"Solas doesn't command them?" Oisin asked, and I shook my head. "That's news to me. Solas has always behaved as if he did."

"He might as well command them. The Aos Si are as devoted to Solas as their Commander. And Zephyr is fiercely loyal, to the point he would kill us all for Solas, just to save Solas from having to make that decision or carry our blood on his hands. If it came down to it, Zephyr would take my life so Solas wouldn't have to suffer that grief," I answered. "Worse than the Aos Si, Solas commands the Sluagh, which are scary enough on their own. Aos Si have honor and a code to follow. Sluagh? They're a hungry bunch and don't give a shit about a white flag. They'll use your surrender to wipe your blood from their lips."

Oisin grinned. "I wonder if they like caving?"

"Let's hope you don't have the chance to find out," Faolan answered and turned to face the trouble that was the Dark Court.

I leaned into Oisin. "I bet you wouldn't dare cave with the Sluagh."

"I'll take that bet." Oisin smiled.

"If I wasn't so scared of what's down there, I'd come and watch."

"I bet you couldn't last five minutes down there," he countered, and I almost took that bet just to prove I wasn't a weak little Crow.

Faolan held out his hand to me, and we ran through the trees. Our feet barely touched the earth, and I tensed when the river came into view. I could swim, but no one climbed into the waters of Elphame and survived. There were things in those waters that no one liked to talk about, and I didn't want to find out why. But our feet didn't even graze the water. Faolan wrapped around me and misted like a snowstorm to the other side, pulling me with him. On the other side, I drew away from Faolan and dry heaved. My body felt scattered and cold, as if I were still waiting on pieces left frozen on the other side. To say it was disorientating was an understatement.

Oisin crouched in front of me. "Breath through your nose. It'll pass."

"That's awful. I don't want to do that again," I grumbled.

"You can swim back if you'd like?" he teased, and I laughed. "I heard you and the water nymphs are great friends."

I stood and shrugged. "They like trinkets and gold."

"They like meat," he countered.

"Yes, but they like to eat in style." I grinned.

Faolan cleared his throat, and I turned to see the pitch-black fog roll through the field and snake across the water. Seeing it made my stomach want to heave again. Solas' darkness was a sight when standing on the other side. There would never be a time when I didn't look at fog and question if I was safe. I was born to fear it, and no amount of time would save me from that fear. The darkness stopped twenty feet in front of us. Solas and Zephyr walked from the nightmarish murk, pulling the shadows back into them as if it were their very souls. I tried hard not to flinch at Solas' sight but shook in my boots just the same. Oisin's pep talk had done nothing but kill time.

"Perdi, how wonderful to see you again." Solas smirked. He looked at Faolan and dismissed him with an expression that said Faolan was beneath him. "I feel like we've done this song and dance once before, and over the same piece of Crow."

"Allow us to skip to the end of our posturing. We've been here, done that. It's old, it's boring and we'll be here all night. What is the reason for this invitation?" Faolan spoke, although Solas had ignored him.

"You make friends everywhere you go, little Crow," Solas taunted and finally turned his attention to Faolan. I knew his bravado was soon to follow. As he's always been, Solas was a smug bastard in the face of uncertainty. He glanced at Faolan's hand holding mine. I watched a flicker of jealousy roll across his face. It was enough for me to pull my hand away. "A night in bed with her, and you're willing to give away the freedoms of your people? She's good — I'll give you that — but I've had better."

I laughed. I couldn't help it. The amusement filled my face until tears came to my eyes. I dabbed them with my sleeve and shook my head. The song and dance of Elphame were tiresome, and he played them well. There would never be a time when games weren't center stage — not here, not ever. The realm could be calm as a summer's day, and they would pick each other apart for entertainment. Mask or no mask, we were no exception.

"Solas, come now. I had been a prisoner of Elphame for months, tortured and abused. I admit I may have been off my game a little, but what was your excuse?" I smiled as if we were friends, not talking about life and death. "We've both had better. Let's just leave it at that and get on with it." I waved him off with my hand. "You should be used to me wanting to just get it over and done with by now."

Oisin shifted behind me and cleared his throat. Zephyr shook his head. He knew goading Solas was not in anyone's best interest, no matter the reason, as did I. I left my needling alone. One slight jab was all any of us could afford. It gave me the bravery I needed to face him and whatever it was that controlled us all. Not enough to make me stupid, but just enough to make my jitters leave.

"Not everyone's bed is worth climbing back into, silly Crow." His warning was heard by only me. "Do you really think you're safer with him than me?"

"Yes, I do. I'm safe here," I answered. Solas would understand what I meant without having to tell him I'd found what I was looking for. The truth lay with Faolan, and I was as safe as I could be.

Solas stepped forward. Wisps of dark mist leaked from his body and twisted in the breeze. "Little King, you'll return my property, and I'll forget all about this insult. This will be the only time I will make such a gracious offer. You appear to be a favorite of Perdi's. For that, I'll let you live another day."

"She's not mine to return, even if I wanted to, which I can't say I do. Perdi belongs to no one and owns her own property. She has made that abundantly clear. Of anything she's ever been, her own person is who she would like to be. You, Solas, should know this better than the rest of us." Faolan turned to me. "Do you want to go with Solas?"

"No, I don't. I will die there," I answered and stared Solas in the eyes.

Faolan shrugged. "What's a king to do? I control her as much as any other does. The lady has spoken. I will not force her from my lands. She has been granted sanctuary. And we do have plans over the next few days, which I'd hate to cancel because you're sulking and can't deal with the situation you created."

Solas glared at him and reached for me with the speed of night. I stepped back before his hand could wrap around mine. Oisin stepped forward, mirrored by Zephyr. Oisin leaked frost from his fingertips, and Zephyr's eyes darkened with the promise of shadows. They eyed each other, but neither moved another muscle. The tension rose to a palpable level. You could almost chew on the very air, ice and all. They were of equal size, identical in nearly every way. Oisin might be brave enough to throw the first punch, but Zephyr could eat his soul before Oisin could think of striking out. I wondered if Oisin knew that a fight between them would never get to the physical point and would end before he had the chance—if he were lucky.

"I wouldn't do that if I were you," Faolan warned Solas and Zephyr. "This very spot was chosen for a reason. Solas, you couldn't possibly believe that we could drag a little Crow into our kingdoms and not have her learn what it takes to survive this cursed place, could you?"

"The Seelie Courts aren't going to protect you, Faolan—not against me. It's best you remember that." Solas motioned behind us. "They will only ever do what is best for their crowns."

I smiled, and Zephyr's look did not go unnoticed by me. He showed me the very land we stood on and wasn't surprised I had picked it. I watched realization flash behind his steely eyes.

Faolan grinned. "Perhaps, perhaps not. But we do not stand on Seelie land. We stand on Wildelands, the undisputed neutral territory in all Elphame. This land cannot be claimed, as agreed upon by the kings of yesterday. When Elphame divided, it was decided to have a neutral place to come together, to disagree and to make treaties. All court laws, including your own, still state that to harm another in the Wildelands is to forfeit your court and all that comes with it, including your life. You, Solas, may be willing to die today, but are your people?"

Faolan wasn't the only one smiling now. Oisin grinned ear to ear. Solas, of course, was not happy, but he rarely was now that he was nothing more than a puppet. Although he held an unreadable face, Zephyr wasn't impressed by my tactics. His eyes lit up for the briefest moment, then landed on me with the force of eternity. He shook his head slightly as if to curse me without the words.

"This is the original Courtless Lands," Oisin spoke. His voice rattled my bones. It was deeper than I remembered. Each word puffed out white fog, frozen from the winter storms within his soul.

"There will be war between us," Solas' voice held warning beneath all his anger.

"And there will always be war, Solas." Faolan echoed the very words Solas had once said to him. "It was coming long before today. But we both knew that, didn't we?"

"Solas." I pulled his attention back from the brink of oblivious rage. I couldn't afford him stepping forward or killing the only person with my answers. "Stop what you're doing to the Gate. This will be the only time I will make such as gracious offer."

"There is nothing you can do to stop it. The Gate rests on my lands. If anyone enters, they will die. You got your one free pass, Perdi. You will not get another," Solas said matter-of-factly.

"So be it," I answered.

"I'll see you in hell," his only answer.

"I'm already there, and I'm getting mighty comfortable with it," I replied.

He looked me dead in the eyes. "The Gate will fall shortly. War is coming. I trust even you can feel it in the air. I hope you're ready for this. I hope you know what you're doing, little Crow."

"I was born for this," I answered.

"Unfortunately, so was I." Solas nodded his understanding. He turned and left in a fog of darkness.

Zephyr took a moment to look each of us in the eyes. When his stare focused on me, it was hard not to take a step back. "You and I aren't done, Perdi. I'll see you soon."

"I didn't think we were," I answered, and he shook his head before he, too, was gone, wrapped in shadows. I felt the tug in my stomach and, for a moment, could feel Zephyr's fear on the other end.

"Well, that went well," Oisin finally said, breaking the silence. "Let us go and enjoy the moments we can before we can't."

I wasn't laughing. I knew Solas would bring war for whatever reason he had. War rested in his bones as marrow rested in mine. He was all violence and rage and now hunted for any unfortunate soul to unleash it on. I truly pitied whoever crossed his path next. Conflict was all he knew and all he'd ever know. It was the way of Fae. If they couldn't have it, they destroyed it. If they couldn't kill it, they always found a way to own it or the person who had it.

Solas had warned me right then and there, but I was the only one to take it as such. It wasn't just any war coming. It was Solas, and he was much more than just war. He was death. And I had very little time left to find his reasons. But I knew nothing, and now, I was outside of his protection to find the answers.

That night, I dreamed of following the Horn to the Golden Court while stepping on bodies to get there. Even here, in my dream, the smell was impossibly strong. But unlike every other time I had struggled in the nightmare of the Golden Court, the stench blew away in a breeze, replaced with lavender. I closed my eyes and smiled. It smelled like home — the Dark Court.

*"Solas," I whispered and turned to face him.*

*To my right, Solas stood at my side. A mischievous smile formed on his lips. "Little Crow, that was quite a provocative display this evening."*

*"I could say the same about you."*

*He pulled me into his arms and breathed me in. "I didn't like seeing you standing on the other side. Neither did Zephyr. You're going to have to talk to him eventually."*

*"As if I could stop him from coming?"*

*He pulled back and shook his head. "He's waiting for you to call him. He doesn't just think you left me. He believes you left him. I think he's scared to come in case you send him away, proving you don't want him."*

*"I'll call on him tomorrow after the Golden Court," I replied. "Faolan is meeting with the other courts about the coming war. I don't want to go there."*

*"You didn't want to the first time, either. The second time will be worse and better. Your memories of the place will hurt." He tucked my wild hair behind my ear, pinching my cheek playfully. "You've killed to leave there once before. You can do it again. Take that with you when you sit at their table."*

*"Why did Faolan ask me to go with him?"*

*"I don't know. Let Faolan lead you to the answers he can't speak out loud. Pay attention, not just with your ears and eyes, but also with your Malice."*

I nodded. "I miss home."

"And home misses you, little Crow." He kissed my forehead.

"I love you," I whispered, tucking myself into his arms as deeply as I could. There, I stayed until the sun rose and forced me from his grip.

# Chapter Three

The smell of flowers hit me first and dragged with it the memories of the first time I had walked up the gravel path to the Golden Court. I was assaulted with the need to hold my breath, vomit and run, all at once. My stomach twisted, and my legs felt like jelly. I was once again in Alfheim, the Golden Court. It was as I remembered, right down to the bones that made up the path we stood on, and the unrelenting perfection of it all gagged me. It wasn't real. It didn't match the horrors I knew it to be. Putting lipstick on a monster didn't make it less of one.

We had stepped through the trees and onto perfectly manicured lawns, and, just like before, I wanted to tear it all up. The flowers were as bright as ever. Their scent butchered my senses and left a taste coating my mouth like only bile and memories could. My eyes watered, both from the stench and nerves. What bothered me most was that I was free and still felt like I was being marched to my death. It was as if these months hadn't happened, and it was my first day. I tried to push the fear down, ignore it and focus on anything but the emotions this place dug up, but my brain wasn't wired that way. My brain was very much mortal, and we were driven to survive. Fight or flight. I knew the answer as soon as the blood rushed down my legs, preparing me for a run I knew my gut would tell me to take.

The magick of the shining court was the next thing to touch my shaking body. It snaked up my legs and scratched at my flesh as it slithered. I wiped my arms to get it off, but it clung to me like the smells did. It felt like the days I had spent trapped within those gold and white walls. It reminded me of every tear I'd cried, every time I'd begged and every pain I'd felt. More than that, it reminded me of the monster I'd had to be and those I'd had to kill. I couldn't do it. I didn't want to do it. I shouldn't have to.

"Get it off." I scratched at my arms and panicked. Each time I stopped, the Horn blew, pushing my feet one more step. "Oh God, get it off me, please."

Oisin spun me to face him. He squeezed my arms just enough to get my attention. "It's not there, Perdi. It's magick. It's here to scare you and turn away those who wish harm on the court. It will pass. You have my word."

"No, no, no…" I shook my head and tried again, in vain, to pull the sticky webs of magick from my body. "No. I can't do this. I can't come back here. I can't. You don't understand what they did to me, what I had to do. I can't. I'm sorry. I'm not that strong."

Oisin shook me once, hard enough to snap me back from the brink I teetered on. "I won't lie to you. Coming back to a place like this, after all that had been done to you, would scare the shit out of even me. But you *must* go in. You must do this, or your fear will always own you. You don't have to do a damn thing in there, but you need to face it, or it will control you forever. Don't let them own you again. If you leave because of fear, they own you. Trust me, Perdi—not even I want to be in this place. I feel the horror of this court in my soul. The thought of stepping onto this land disgusts me. But we must face our fears every chance we get, or they will own us to our deaths."

"I killed the king, Oisin. I stabbed and cursed him to sleep so he'd bleed out and die. I looked him in the eyes and smiled."

"Rest easy. I've done worse."

"Perhaps, but I enjoyed it. When I killed Aelfdene, I was angry I didn't have more time to torture him. One of my last thoughts was of regret for not being able to make him suffer for longer." I leaned into his ear. "If I could go back, I'd do it slower and damn being caught."

"There are times we all have wished that," he answered.

I pulled back from his grip and looked him in the eyes. "The shame I feel for being afraid of being caught still haunts me. If I could do it again, I'd have let my Malice out and would have killed them all. I'd have burned in that court with them, just to make them all suffer as I did."

His mouth fell open in surprise. "You'd have risked being captured to torture him?"

I nodded. I didn't go into details. I didn't know if I could trust Oisin with my dirty little Soul-Eating secrets.

"I'd keep that little bit of news to yourself. Not exactly something you'll want to talk about when you meet his son," he answered, then grinned. "You are the deadliest creature here. I can feel it in my bones, and I'm rarely wrong. Nothing they can show you compares to what you could do to any of them. Remember that as you walk in. They may have caused you pain, but you can make them pray for death should they try it again. You've already taken one of their kings. What's another to add to that list?"

I smiled and felt tougher in some way. "Thank you."

He tucked his sword back into his back sheath. "I doubt I'll be needing this, since we brought you."

I laughed. I knew Oisin was only trying to pump up my confidence, but I appreciated it. "Glad to be of service."

"Is everything okay here?" Faolan walked back to us. "We can leave at any minute, Perdi. You don't have to do this. I don't care what Oisin has said. You do *not* need to walk in there if this is too much for you. I can go in without you."

"She's fine," Nix barked from our feet. "Move it along. We're eating daylight, and this isn't a place I would like to be once the sun sets."

"Is your little friend always so rude?" Oisin asked.

"My rudeness is the least of your worries," Nix replied. "And who is the rude one? When referring to me, you can direct your questions to me. I speak for myself."

Oisin had enough respect to blush and walk away. I waved Faolan off and walked the rest of the path with Nix and Orrian, as we once had. The manor was as sprawling as it had been the first time I had seen it. In terms of beauty, it was nothing now that I had seen the Court of Shadows, the Court of Blood and Bones or Tylwyth.

"This place is a dump," Nix joked. His mind had gone to the same place as mine. "Did you know, when I went to the Hallows, they call this place 'The Tarnished Court.'"

"It *is* tarnished," I replied.

"The place is, Perdi, but not those who have left it," Nix comforted me. "You are not this place."

I nodded. "It feels like the first time. My body still remembers the fear. My stomach remembers being twisted in knots. I may know I'm safe, but my body is ready to run."

"I feel safer today than I did the first time. That should tell you something," Nix answered.

"I'm glad one of us isn't scared." I groaned through my discomfort.

"This has nothing to do with them and everything to do with you. I'm not scared because I have you with me. I know you won't leave me behind, so walking in, I can swallow the fear."

"Thanks, Nix." I smiled at his kindness. He always knew exactly what to say and when to say it.

I darted my gaze around the property and counted the guards, still dressed in gold and white. High-Fae walked the grounds, and creatures on leashes ate at their feet. Beasts I had seen before stopped to look back at me. This time, there was no snarling or growling. They dipped their heads as if to say hello, and I nodded in return, as if to ask them not to try to eat me this time.

Once, I swore I wouldn't leave this place. I'd never be free. I'd live out the rest of my mortal life within the confines of the Golden Court. I had barely escaped and now was back of my free will. That proved how utterly foolish my decisions were. Or, as Zephyr would say, stupid. If he could see me now, skipping my way up to the stone manor, that's precisely what he'd call me. I scanned the trees again, wondering why I'd think of Zephyr at this very moment. At the edge of the property, I watched the shadows move and pull back.

Zephyr was nearby. He had probably felt my fear and panic the moment the sticky webs of magic clung to me.

Nix had seen the same shadows and inched his way up my side to sit on my shoulder. "What's he doing here?"

"He has one of my pearls," I answered.

"I thought he gave it back to you?"

"I gave him another. He paid the cost for it by never bringing harm to me."

"Oh, that must really tickle his fancy right about now." Nix laughed.

I laughed with him. "That's a polite way to put it. So much happened after you left."

"Obviously, since you forgot to mention that entertaining nugget. Why do you think Zephyr is out there?" Nix asked.

"He probably felt my fear and came to check — or maybe he's spying for Solas. I don't know. I haven't talked to him since I left."

Nix nodded. He didn't have any answers, either. "It seems that all roads lead back to this godawful place."

"Let's burn it down on our way out," I suggested, and he agreed.

The balconies of the stone manor were filled with Fae, both the curious and the hateful. And I wondered if the new king would be as inquisitive or if he'd hate me for taking his father's life. The weight of their stares at the return of the Crow, made my skin prickle and itch. I had once teased Solas for having no friends in this court, and now, I faced the same fate.

"Who needs friends when you have enemies?" I whispered to myself. Those were the exact words I had once said to Solas. "Me," I answered myself.

I stopped at the place on the path where I had pulled a whittled butterknife from my pocket and stabbed

Solas with it—a knife Orrian had chewed into a point. I should have known then that my little creature knew not to trust any Fae completely. I had surprised Solas on that day and again and again since. I had done exactly the opposite of what anyone thought I'd do. I'd survived. I'd fought back. I brought war with me wherever I went. Even knowing I could and would strike against any who tried to harm me, I slowed my step.

"Breathe." Faolan stepped to my side and offered his arm. "No one here owns you or ever will."

I nodded and gripped his arm. I walked the last few feet to the manor and up the massive staircase that protruded from the rocky earth. Two golden doors opened as we reached the enclosed balcony. My heart pounded as my feet touched the white marble floors of the Golden Manor. The same floors my blood had stained. My body went rigid. I forced myself to step forward, but my muscles cramped in protest. I could push my mind to endure, but my body wanted nothing to do with it. My body remembered, even as I tried to forget.

"You bite back," Oisin whispered at my side, then took the lead.

Again, I was bombarded with colors and smell and the sounds of swishing of gowns. "This place stinks."

"Try being me," Nix whispered from my shoulder. "I almost puked in your hair. Orrian has been sick twice now. She's filled your pocket."

Orrian poked her head from my pocket, vomit fresh on her chin. Although I didn't understand her, I knew she was sorry. I smiled as she flopped back down and heard her squish in her displeasure at the bottom. I felt bad for them but had been grateful the moment they'd volunteered to come. Nothing I could say would change their minds. Although I didn't say the words, I was relieved I wouldn't relive these moments without them — not because I wanted them to suffer with me, but because I wouldn't suffer as much with them.

Faolan led us through various rooms, Oisin at his front. I mentally prepared to kneel before the Golden Court throne but was led to a table instead. I glanced around the empty room, save one man at the table. I had expected this to be a spectacle, as all things in Alfheim had been under the rule of the maddest of kings, Aelfdene. Instead, the room was stripped of the tables and paintings and artwork. It was a meeting room, no longer a throne room.

"Faolan!" The man who had taken the throne after I'd killed his father stood. He was dressed in the Golden crest, adorned with the jewels I had seen Aelfdene wear the very night I took his last breath. The sight of him, decorated like his father, hitched a breath in my throat.

Faolan smiled and moved toward him. Faolan's arms opened for a hug that made me flinch to watch it happen. "Theo, allow me to introduce you to Perdita Darkmore." Faolan motioned for me to join him. "Perdi, this is Theofanis, the Golden King."

I stood close enough to him to feel uneasy. "It's nice to meet you."

Theo grasped my hand. "Rest easy, Crow. You're safe here."

I flinched. "Please don't call me that."

"Perdita, you are safe within these walls," he corrected himself.

"I don't feel safe," I answered and inched closer to Faolan.

"You've done as so many, including me, have tried to do for decades — end the rule of my father. You have done my people and me a great service. I give you my word when I tell you, you are safe here."

I nodded but didn't believe the word of a man I didn't know — a man who had buried a father I killed, then climbed onto a throne responsible for the slaughter of many.

"The others, have they come?" Faolan asked.

"They are here. I've asked them to wait until you are settled before they join us," Theo answered and led us to our seats. "Do you care for food, drink?"

Nix jumped from my hair and landed on the table. He looked to my pocket, where Orrian stayed, still sick. "Myself and my friend could use food and drink...and a wet cloth."

Theo nodded, and within moments, Theo's people flowed in with trays of food and drinks. I didn't touch anything. My stomach wouldn't have been able to handle it. I sat silently and stared at the room I had been in for banquets. To my right, a small stage once sat, where the entertainment would be displayed and ceremoniously ended in death. The floor had been cleaned and the scene was gone, but my memories showed me where each and every innocent had lost their life. I swallowed hard and closed my eyes. Faolan grasped my hand and squeezed it.

Soon, I watched as the rest of the table filled with Royals and their consorts, families and guards. I looked into the eyes of their ladies, their wives, mistresses, daughters and sons. Some of them were once human. I could feel it, like seeing someone you vaguely remembered from a time you couldn't. They stared back, as curious as I was, but for different reasons. All of Elphame had heard of the Crow and the ruin she had left in her wake. And here the very Crow was, at the same table they were. The only missing king was Solas, who hadn't been invited.

We hadn't invited the man we were meeting about. Faolan had called a meeting to discuss protecting the mortal realm and another war with Solas. Given that all had shown up, it was safe to assume that no one wanted to war against Solas or his darkness. Only a madman stood against the very pulse of war. But I knew from the comments and questions that no one here cared what happened to the mortal realm. I sat silently as they bickered among themselves. I watched the reactions of those who'd come with the Royals. Each of them shuddered at the thought of war, of the mortal world invaded. Some blinked away tears, forcing themselves to remain stoic and not show their outrage at the very discussion that maybe nothing would be done to save mortals, that it wasn't worth a war against the Dark Courts. I bit my tongue until my mouth tasted of blood, which I preferred over the taste of roses and lilies.

I'd finally had enough of talking in circles. It was all they ever did. It would be why they'd always been weak in the eyes of the Dark Courts. "This is why none of you are a threat on your own. Solas washes over you in hours because you waste your precious time hoping someone else will save you. No one is coming to save you."

From the static in the air, I knew their fear was misplaced. Yes, they should fear Solas and his armies, but they should be more concerned with who they put their faith in—the one no one was willing to speak out loud about. Solene, Solas' sister, the Lady of Blood and Bones, wouldn't save them. The cocksure look they all had told me they thought she would. *Fools...all of them.*

"The only reason war with Solas has lasted days is because he uses it to train his men. You bicker and whine while he plans every movement to the finest detail. He and his army have planned out this war to be ready for every possible inevitability. There is no move you could possibly make that he isn't already prepared for. That you're still alive is not a win. He just doesn't see you as worth his time or resources. He, like me, likely knows you're waiting on a miracle that isn't going to happen, waiting on a savior who isn't coming."

All eyes were now on me, and their focus wasn't as uncomfortable as it had been just moments before. Anger always did that for me, shielded me and dredged up the tiniest scraps of bravery.

"Would you allow armies to kill your partner's descendants, King Killian? Because, when the war comes, it won't care who she is." I looked at the King of the Spring Court. His wife had flinched moments ago when Killian said he didn't care about the mortal world. "She once was human, even I can see that. She's bound to have a bloodline outside of Elphame. Would you not protect them as you would have everyone else in this room protect her? Or would you allow her family to taste death that you could prevent?"

"Who and what my consort is, is none of your business, Crow," he spat back.

I was still nothing here, not to them. I was the lowly Crow, undeserving of the same respect served to others at the same table. I nodded and chewed back my instinct to lash out at him, to match his hate with my own. I could approach this in one of two ways. I could come in like a fire or gentle like a breeze. As tempting as it was to sit gently at their table, I was never the delicate type and wasn't welcome there.

"Very well, and when they come for you next, what would you have this Crow do?" I asked.

"What can a simple Crow do? Nothing." Killian answered and dismissed me with a flick of his hand.

"I'm sorry." I glanced at Theo and winced my apology. He nodded. "Killian, it wasn't *nothing* that I did to gain my freedom. And it won't be *nothing* I do to ensure I remain free. And rest assured, it won't be *nothing* that washes over all these lands when the war is done and gone. This is only the beginning. This war is merely a warmup for what comes next, and I think we all are dancing around that truth. You all can sit with your lies until they blister you and burn down your courts, but we all know the truth, whether it's spoken out loud or not. You will not be saved in the end. There is no winning unless you take a stand now."

Killian shook his head. "I do not fear this war nor the outcomes. This war does not come for us. It comes for you, for your people. Do not ask us to put ourselves in the middle."

"Does he speak for you all?" I glanced around the table and only received blinks in response.

No one spoke up. They didn't have to say the words for me to know. They were still counting on someone else to save them, someone who would never come for them. It wouldn't matter what I said. They'd live and most certainly die for their misplaced trust. I shook my head and wondered how they had lived this long on lies alone.

"With all due respect, the war will come whether you want it to or not, and it doesn't come with only my name on it. I'm merely the only one standing in its way right now. Soon, the attention will be gone from me, and your courts will be put in my place. You are fools to think you are safe. No one is. Your families will die, just as mine will. Your people will burn, just as mine will. Does it really matter who dies first when we all die in the end?" I blurted out and didn't bother hiding my anger. I unleashed it rather than keep a death grip on it, as I usually did. I had spent too many nights in this court to swallow another bitter taste of it.

They really thought they could choose whether they'd have to fight or not. That choice had been made for them as it had been made for Solas. And while they sat thinking on it, Solas was already prepared. He had been born ready. He would come and blot out the sun with his darkness, and it would be the last any of these kings would see the light of day. Because after Solas, what came next would steal away their freedom, and they'd never feel the sun on their skin as free people.

"Do not underestimate what you are asking, Perdita Darkmore," Parrish of the Autumn Court finally spoke after hours of sitting in silence. "My territory borders with the Court of Less. Once Solas finds out, he will come, and there will be nothing I can do to stop him. My court is small, my army even smaller. You're quite literally asking me to risk all my people."

"Your territory also borders on mine," Faolan added. "We will come, we will take in your people and we will help to protect you."

"You can't protect us, Faolan," Parrish muttered. "When my court falls, then what?"

"That is the question, isn't it?" Nix finally hopped back onto the table from my shoulder. "As you said, Parrish, your court is small. It is very much not worth Solas' time to invade your lands. He will ignore you because you're no threat to him. You're missing the point of what Perdi has said. Solas is a threat, and he will decimate all in his path. And you should be thankful for that. What you should fear is not the darkness swallowing you whole. You should fear still being alive when he's done. Because what is coming next will be our end, the end of life as we know it."

"A gnome?" Killian sat back and grinned. "You've brought a gnome to the discussions on whether Elphame or the mortal lands burn?"

"The question is not about who gets to live or die. The question is, do you want to live for who is coming next?" Nix glared and turned to Theofanis. "My name, to be entered into the record, is Nix Lubdan of the Ulster Territory, the descendant of King Lubdan."

"And so shall it be added, Nix Lubdan, of the Ulster Territory and Lubdan line," Theofanis spoke up from the head of the table in the chair his father once sat in. "I knew your uncle well. I am honored the wee folk are at my table."

"Thank you." Nix stood proud. His voice was steady. "Killian, the fact that you underestimate the gnomes is why we've killed so many of your people without sending more than a dozen. We have never once lost a battle we have fought. We've entered no war where we've not been the victors. Do not make today the day I remind you."

Killian blanched at the words.

Nix grinned at the man's discomfort. "More than what you should do and shouldn't do, that's not why I am here. It is not you, the kings of courts, I worry about. It is your people. I am not here to tell you to pick a side. Let's move beyond the lies we came here with. I can smell them in the air, and they stink more than the roses. I am here to tell you that whatever side you pick will be the side your people will die for. I don't care which side you choose. I didn't come here to convince you of either. I'm not so foolish as to think we could remind you of your stakes and have it mean anything to you. You move for power, riches, titles and land. You don't move for anything less. And I'm not here to bribe you into doing what I know is right."

"Then why *are* you here," Killian asked, "if not to sway our decision?"

"I am here for your people, since clearly, you are not. I care about those you will leave at home to defend your lands while you're not there. You all have talked circles around protecting your land and your throne. What about your people? I don't give a shit about your crown or your throne—or your trinkets. I care for those left unprotected." Nix walked the length of the table and eyed every lady. "I hope they can protect themselves from whatever choices you all make, because they will suffer those decisions, not you. And suffer they will, because no one escapes the wrath of war, and your people will always pay that cost."

"I will not have my consort fight alone against the Dark Courts," Killian barked.

"Then they will die, as they always have and always will," Nix said plainly. "When the war comes, and you are not there, they will die unless they are able and willing to fight for their freedom. Nothing is free, not even freedom. If you do not allow them to protect themselves, it will be seen as a weakness within your walls, and they will be conquered. If you think Solas is your only enemy, you are bigger fools than I thought. Even as we sit together at this war table, each of you is thinking of what you can pillage from the other. And as we point fingers at the Dark Courts, there's a greater threat than him, and we'll all burn gloriously together under her thumb."

Killian nodded after his wife cleared her throat. "Very well. If, and I mean that, *if* we were to join your cause, I would ensure they have what they need to defend their homes."

"Whatever cause you join has nothing to do with Perdi or me. But all your people should be able to always defend themselves. You damn them, otherwise." Nix may have been small, but I watched Killian shrink under Nix's words. "Think long and hard about who you oath yourself to and what comes after that oath. Do you really think you will remain safe once the mortal lands fall? All will be conquered. If you do nothing to stop this from happening now, it will be too late later. You curse your lands, crown and those you are oathed to protect, for power. I hope it was worth it, because you will pay tithe in the end with that which you are desperately trying to protect. If you think payment to Elphame is great, fate is going to kick your ass when it is she who comes next. And there has never been a soul alive to escape fate's debt."

Orrian finally crawled from my pocket to the table. She braced herself on my wine glass and puked on the table. We all turned away from her show. She looked paler than usual, almost gray from sickness. She glanced around the table with bloodshot eyes.

"Orrian of Fairy, welcome." Theofanis looked at her questioningly. "Do you need aid?"

Orrian shook her head and stood straight. She didn't speak as she walked the table. She stopped to look at each person long and hard, as if committing them to memory. Once she had seen each and every person, she returned to Nix and whispered. Nix nodded, then she crawled back into my pocket to be sick again.

"What was that about?" Killian asked.

Nix smiled. "She wanted to make sure she would remember who sat at the table."

"Why?" Killian asked.

"When the war comes, she will see who came and who did not. She will see which side you fought on. She doesn't want the Gate to fall and wants to know who let it happen. She does not want the mortal world to be invaded, and she wants to know who crossed over when it happens," Nix answered.

Killian sat back with wide eyes. "I thought we were able to decide of our own accord? Yet, you threaten us?"

"I'm not threatening you. You asked a question. You just don't like the answer I gave you. The truth often works that way when you've built your kingdom out of blood and bones." Nix answered. "If you think any of us can control what Orrian does or doesn't do, you'd be placing your trust in the wrong person. Orrian is her own kingdom, and her alliance is with Perdi. And unfortunately for you, no court controls either of them."

"What is wrong with her?" From one of the ladies at the table.

"The smell," Nix replied. "She doesn't like it."

"Nor do I," the lady replied.

"It's not like I enjoy it." Theofanis laughed. "It won't go away, but you get used to it."

"No," I spoke up. "You never get used to it. You merely get used to having no choice. You either breathe it in or hold your breath until you die. Once you leave, anything that smells even remotely like this place will remind you of it. Believe me when I tell you, when you go home, you'll throw out any flowers you may have, and you'll never enjoy a bubble bath as you once had before without thinking of this fucking place and its stench."

"Why did you come back if you hate this place so much?" Morrow, King of the Summer Court, asked.

"You know, I asked myself that very question on my way here," I answered. "Against every fiber of my being the little voice that kept telling me to run, I still came. But I want to save lives more than I want to be able to enjoy a bubble bath."

"Mortal lives and your own life," he countered.

I shook my head and tried to hold back a glare. "If that was all I wanted to save, I wouldn't be wasting my time here, arguing among kings who think of themselves and their thrones before the weakest members of their kingdoms. I'd simply collect who I could and wait it out in the mortal realm for you all to come. And if I wanted to save myself, this is the last place I'd be. I'd have waited it out in the Dark Court, knowing it'll be the last to fall." I replied with the same rudeness. My tone was as harsh as I felt. "Do you really think I wanted to come back here? You all, every single one of you, saw what happened to me here. You all watched as this place broke my people and me. I watched your faces as smaller Fae were plucked of their wings, horns sliced from their heads. You delighted in the torture of others. Each of you makes me sick to even look at, let alone be in the same room with. I recognize several of you who actually cheered while the flesh was lashed from my back. You called for more, one after the other. Why would I ever want to come back here and face any of you if not to save as many as I could?"

"You left this place and ran to Solas, then caused a war. Then you left Solas and ran to Faolan, causing a new war. Why should we listen to you?" Morrow matched my tone. "What's to say you won't run to another and bring with you more war?"

I laughed at the horror of it all. "It won't matter, will it? We'll all be dead if this war plays out to the bitter end. Even if what you say is true, there won't be a court left standing for me to run to." Faolan leaned forward to answer, but I lifted my hand. I would speak for myself. "For the sake of argument, what you're saying is partially true. I did run from here. I killed to leave, and I'd do it all again. I wish I could say I was sorry for what I've done, but I'm not, and I won't add to the lies the rest of you speak. And when I ran, I was running from hell. Nothing about this place was or ever will be deserving of my guilt." I tried to straighten myself but felt the pressure from their stares. "I tried to close the Gate. To keep this, what happened to me, from happening to others. I would do it again if I thought I could save someone from the fate of being a bloody Crow in Elphame. I left Solas when I had no other choice. Do you really think I enjoy running for my life, to feel like, at any moment, I could die? Tell me, oh great kings, what the hell would *you* have done? What would you do if I took one of your children into the mortal world and beat them every day until they finally died? If I took your ladies into Whitwick and allowed the men to do with her as they pleased? How far would you go to protect them? Think of that for a moment and know I will do so much worse than your mind could ever create. I would bring hell down on this realm to stay alive. Are you willing to do the same for your people? Because that is what it will take to save you from who we don't speak of."

Morrow's face twisted into something painful, like a memory you tried to fight against. "There are other things to fear besides my death and the death of my people. What you ask is bigger than you or I or any of us."

"But it is you and I and everyone else who will suffer," I replied.

Faolan's calm exterior finally fell. His magick rolled off him in cold waves, sending shivers up my spine. "Respectfully, Morrow, you don't know what you're talking about. You, in your tower, have never suffered a day in your life. You were born into gold and power, into a lap of luxury. You never once had to fight to keep it. You speak of Perdi as if she were given choices in this world. We, all of us here, gave her the option of death and war only to punish her for what we thrust upon her. Put down your stones unless you're willing to spend a day in the life of those you throw them at. You don't have to like her or what she had to do, but you won't judge her when I've seen you do worse."

I swallowed my hate for Morrow. It was a larger meal than I had in ages. "I understand your position better than you think I do. Both of our people will suffer. It matters not what side we stand on. They all will fall in the end, and we're both looking for any path that could bring them protection and safety. And both of us are willing to tie ourselves to the devil for that safety. I'm not asking you to trade your people for mine, because I wouldn't trade anyone's people for yours. But I am asking you, when you're no longer sitting at this table, to tell yourself the truth."

I looked him dead in the eyes and didn't feel the pressure in his returned stare. With a sliver of courage, I also found a common understanding. *Our people. Our willingness to cleave the heaven to anger the Gods into notice, to buy the safety of those we love.*

"What truth?" he asked.

I huffed a soft laugh, a slight smile curling on my lips as if to say we all knew that answer. "The truth none of us are willing to say out loud. Ask yourselves, what will be the payment if your people are allowed to live? So far, it is only me who has paid, me who has risked."

"You have risked nothing for me." He leaned back in his chair and his smug look returned and looked at home on his tanned, summer-kissed skin.

"There, you are wrong. I freed six of your people in the dungeon. I did what you wouldn't do. I risked my life for them. Not once did I ever see or hear of you trying to bargain for their freedom. I spent months freeing those fated for death, at great risk to myself. Every day I spent nursing them back to health and buying their safe passage put my life at risk. And I did it without asking a soul for anything in return." I motioned to the others. "Each of you, sitting at this table, I have freed your people and have never asked for a thing in return. When I risked my life for them, I never thought of what you'd owe me. And I still don't. I am *not* your enemy."

"Whose enemy are you?" Morrow asked.

"Anyone who gets in my way," I answered.

"Who will protect my family? Who would help my people if I die?" Morrow asked, not to me, but to the table.

"You don't protect them now, so what does it matter?" Nix muttered.

"I will," Theofanis answered. "I would guard your throne until your son is old enough to take it. You have my word."

I leaned back as they continued to go back and forth. Scenarios that could never possibly happen were questioned. Circumstances that would never come to fruition were feared. They thought up the craziest of situations and asked who would be responsible. It reminded me of Solas, who would have asked the same questions but would have already thought out every possible outcome and how to win. My mind reeled from the bickering. More than that, I watched them all worm their way into favor with each other. The games never ended, no matter the reason for coming to the table.

I allowed my Malice to roam the room, sipping the magick in the air but never touching a soul. She blended in with the panic and confusion and show of power. They were not noble, no matter what they said out loud. I could feel it like a sudden clammy fever as my Malice rolled their disloyal flavors across her tongue. And they were traitors in every sense of the word. The Horn had led me here to witness who would come for me next. One by one, I could feel their intent, like tiny cuts against my flesh, with each glance they risked in my direction.

With one final draw of hot air, I drank their truth like soured wine. All of them balanced their lies in front of the Crow, but they would all fall together if they came for me. Their fate, hanging in the air over their heads like a noose, was tied to the life and death of a Crow. They would kill the Crow if given a chance. But when Solene came at the end, it wouldn't matter what side the kings stood on. I was to die at their hands, and they would die at hers. Hints of deception filled my stomach like long-rotten food, and I felt full. One more bite of it, and I'd vomit.

By the end of the conversation, I hated them even more than I had when I'd arrived. When we left the table of the Golden Court, Faolan walked away without any guarantees. But I left their lies behind and carried with me more truth than I'd had on my way in. I listened to Oisin and Faolan discuss the particulars. Those who stood against Solas would receive support from Faolan and the others. But no army was endless, and no army could stand against Solas for long. But perhaps those who came to Faolan's call would stand against Solas long enough for me to find the last slivers of truth. I felt weighed down by the daunting tasks of my path and wished, more than anything, that I had Solas to talk to about it. He would know what to do, had his hands not been bound by oaths and others. Of all things I hated about Elphame, playing these games was now at the top of my list.

# Chapter Four

We stood at the edge of Faolan's territory. Behind me, the Dark Courts. In front of me, the illusion of safety and warmth, the Winter Court. But behind, even in the shadows and terror that gripped any who strayed too close, was everything I needed to calm my nerves. And death? There was also that in those hills. Although Tylwyth was temporary and false, it looked much more appealing to my weary bones than running for my life in the Dark Courts. Along the way, I mulled over every possible outcome of a war with Orrian and Nix. Orrian suggested I called on Zephyr and try to talk to him, be honest with him and stop holding my cards so close to my chest for once. Perhaps he knew something I didn't, which was more likely than not. Zephyr knew more than he ever let on. If anyone could help who wasn't bound to stand against me, it would be him. And even if he came with wrath on his tongue, I missed him as much as I missed the Dark Court. I would suffer willingly just to touch a piece of home.

"Faolan." I grabbed his arm and held him back from the others.

"I'm not going to like what you're about to say, am I?" he half-joked.

"I need to speak to Zephyr."

"Why?"

I shrugged but thought twice about telling him the reason why. The longer I thought about it, the less I trusted Faolan or anyone who sat on a throne. "I need to talk to him about what's coming and see if he knows something I don't."

"Yeah, I don't like this. Will Zephyr try to take you?" he asked.

"No. But full disclosure, if Zeph wanted me, there's nothing anyone here could do to stop him. If Zephyr really wanted me back, I'd be back already. Hell, I would never have gotten away." It made me wonder why he hadn't taken me back when it would be so easy. He, like Solas, had let me leave, even if he didn't want me to go.

"Do I wait here or come with you?" Faolan asked. I was grateful that he wasn't making demands. This was hard enough to do without having another king nipping at my heels.

"You can wait here if you'd like, but don't follow me. The shadows won't allow you in, anyway. And if you try, it'll be a painful experience for you," I continued. "Think, having your soul pulled out of your nose."

"All right," he answered. "Do you still have your stone?"

"No. Orrian ate it." I laughed. Faolan raised his eyebrows.

"She eats everything anyone puts down, damn it. She ate my birds, Perdi. I found her sleeping in a bed of feathers at the bottom of the cage. This is why no one allows a fairy into their lands." Faolan shook his head, an exasperated look on his face.

"Sorry?" I replied and tried to hide my smile.

"If she touches my cat, I'll rip the wings off of her." He handed me a new rock. "Just in case. And keep this one away from your fairy."

I walked to the edge of the territory. I looked back at Faolan once, who stood with Nix, Orrian and Oisin. I turned around and called on the shadows. I closed my eyes and called them as I had done hundreds of times before. Like whispering a name, I felt them in the back of my mind before they flooded around me. They were scared and panicked. I knew who was coming on their heels without them needing to tell me. I could feel it in their uncertainty.

"Zephyr is coming," they whispered.

"I know. I can feel his anger," I answered and waited.

Inside the pit of the darkness, Zephyr stepped forward. The shadows rolled away from him and pushed up an inky wall around us, blotting out the world and prying eyes. The heat of Zephyr rolled up my legs and burned my gut. "You're either brave, stupid or wishing for death."

"You said similar words before I released you," I answered. "Zeph…"

"Do *not* call me that!" he snapped at me. His temper lashed out at me, and I cringed at the sour smell it left in the air. His anger dried my mouth and throat. "You have no idea what you've left for me to clean up."

"I saw you today," I started to say and stopped when his hands gripped my shoulders. I turned my face away as if I were preparing for his wrath. I readied myself for a world of pain but didn't step back. I whispered to myself, pulling bravery from every corner of my soul. "I can take it, Zeph. It's okay."

"What?" he sputtered. "I would never do that to you. *Never*." He let me go as if he sensed what I had pictured. He screamed his frustration, wordless anger and hurt.

"You could have fooled me," I countered.

"Shake some sense into you, always, but I'd never hurt you like that," he said calmly, but I knew his anger was just below the surface like a sea monster, waiting for the perfect moment to breach. "You've left one hell of a mess. What do you want?"

"What do *I* want?" I asked, my voice finding that bravery I had scraped my soul for. "You could have stopped me from leaving at any minute," I answered and glared through the darkness. He could see me as clear as a summer's day. And as the mist cleared between us, I could see the hurt look on his face, hidden behind his temper. "And I'll call you whatever the hell I want. Stop with your posturing. You have the power to take me, willing or not, but you have not flexed those muscles. Why? Why would you not drag me back? Solas claims I belong to him, that I am his property. If I am, you are within your rights to grab me right now and take me back without consequence. Right now, Zeph, you could snatch me this instant, and no one could stop you. You could even blame me for calling you into these lands."

"You know why."

"Because you can't bring me to harm? Oh, please." I rolled my eyes as I crossed my arms. "I've been in harm's way since I stepped through that bloody Gate. You are the master of oaths. The very second we had made that pact, you had a dozen ways out of it. You wouldn't have ever made an oath with me that you couldn't worm your way out of. You haven't taken me because you know I was right to leave. You know this was the only choice, the only way. You don't have to like it, but you don't get to punish me for it."

"Is that why you called on me, to tell me why you left? To rub it in that you are with Faolan and not Solas?" He paused. "That...you don't want to be with me, either?"

"I didn't want to leave you," I said.

"But you did!" he yelled, and I staggered when the ground moved under his anger. Each word bounced around in my chest like a thunderbolt. "And now everything is out of control. *He* is out of control."

"Did you really expect me to stay?" I asked, almost surprised.

"You left us both!" His voice staggered me.

"You left me!" I finally snapped back. "When I needed you the most, you left me. You did nothing to help me or stop any of this from happening. And now my people will suffer for it. As you help Solas, you damn all my people to death. Why the hell would I stay for that? Why would I not try to help them? You must have known I'd do everything possible to protect the mortal realm. Zeph, you, of all people, should understand why I did what I did."

"I never left you once," Zephyr replied. "I've always been there. I've stood between you and my king. I have threatened death upon the only man I've ever followed or trusted to protect you. I would have stood with you and only you until my final breath." His voice held the edge of decades of unshed tears. "I would burn the world and everyone in it for you and only you — and you know it. Don't you dare blame me for this. I *never* left you."

"Zeph, listen to me," I spoke over him. The shadows twisted tighter. They were scared and had every reason to be. One of us angry was bad. Both of us being angry would level the world. He was hurting, and so was I. But it served no good to keep cutting each other up. "I never wanted to leave you. You have my pearl. You know what I'm saying is true. It would take death to keep me from you, and it kills me a little each day that I'm gone from you and Solas. But if I didn't go, I would have died there. We all would have. Whether you tell yourself differently doesn't take away the truth. Your loyalty is admirable, and I love you for it. But it blinds you from the truth." I released a long, shaking breath, trying to calm myself. "Solas knew I was leaving. He told me he'd leave if he were me, then pointed me in this direction. He was out of moves, so I made one for us. Now, I need you to listen to me, please. I need your help."

"Did you call on me so I'd leave Solas and fight for your side?" he asked. "Don't even try it. Did Faolan send you to ask?"

"No, he didn't." I frowned. "And why would I waste my time with that? Why would I ask you to leave Solas? Zeph, I don't want you to leave him. In fact, I want you to stay as close to him as you can possibly be without climbing into his pants. Do *not* leave his side. If you don't have one of his pearls, I would ask you to take one. My gut tells me that you may need it."

He smirked. "Of course, I have one. But you didn't call me to talk about his pearls. So, what could you possibly want? What more do you want from me?"

"There's a lot you need to know, and we have little time to talk. I know you have listened in on my conversations with the shadows, and you've seen me sneaking around. But there is so much more that you don't know," I answered.

"Such as?" he asked.

"I don't even know where to start." I mulled it over for a moment, what information I could share. I glanced around at the wall of shadows and wondered if anyone could hear. "Is it safe to talk in here?"

Zephyr pulled his darkness so tightly around us that it staggered me. "Now is not the time to keep your secrets, little Crow. No one can hear us."

I smiled at the Crow comment. Hearing it meant he wasn't as angry anymore. Although Solas had told me to say nothing and I knew I should keep it all to myself, it wasn't just my life on the line. My secrets could take countless lives. Innocents would die unless I shared with the only person I could trust. I started at the very beginning, including what I had already told him about Solene meeting Solas and me meeting with her at Blood and Bones, of my spying on Solas, the Gate, of every secret the shadows had brought to me that I knew for a fact he didn't hear. I told him of my dreams, what I saw play out in them and what I believed to be true. I told him about the gargoyles, every conversation I'd had with Solas, the little hints he'd dropped and the truths he'd managed to tell me. Then of my meeting in the Golden Court and those who would choose to stand with Faolan, and how I had been guided by the Horn from the Dark Court to Winter and to the door of the

Golden Court. I left nothing out and put it all on the table for him to sort through and question. I had no more secrets from him. I told him why I was in the Winter Court. It was there that I'd find the answers. With Faolan, I would find the truth. The part that hurt the most was that I admitted to keeping the truth from him.

"What takes the cake is that it doesn't matter who wins the war. I am to die on that field. One of them is going to kill me in the end," I added.

"And what am I supposed to do with this? Why tell this to me now?" he asked. "Jesus, Perdi, what the hell do I do with this information? It's a little late now, don't you think? Had you come to me sooner before running into enemy territory, I could have done something with it."

"I tried to come to you. The day you dragged me in my underpants for training, I tried to talk to you about it. And I tried to tell you again the day you took me to the Wildelands. Over and over, I've tried. But you're still not listening to me any more than you did when I first came to you with it. You're so focused on your anger that you skipped past all the important parts." I knew he'd reflect on the conversation later and remember every word I'd said. There was no point in repeating it. "I tell you all my secrets, so you can tell Solas, to warn him. He needs to know. Then maybe we can find a way to end this. But do not tell him in the open. You will be heard, then there will be no saving him, me—or any of us."

"I think it is you who will need saving," Zephyr countered. "If they're going to try for you, then it is you who we need to protect."

"Not this time, Zeph. They will come, they will try and they will fail. But I can't protect everyone," I answered. "Just tell him what I told you and do it in private. He warned me, and now I must warn him."

"Why? Why do you even care?"

"You're still not hearing me. I never left because I hated Solas. I left because I love him, and he let me go because he loves me. I've always loved him and always will." I finally said the words I had been holding in as I played a game without room for love. "You are the only way I can save him — from himself, from *her*. I can't protect him from the Winter Court."

"He already knows of your meeting at the Golden Court. It's a meaningless warning, Perdi."

"That's not the warning that I mean. But Solas needs to know who sat at that table in case they come to him begging for protection," I replied. "He needs to know that they're all on Solene's side. They will fight against Solas for the Gate. He needs to know of their plans."

"Solas isn't a fool, Perdi. Parrish has already called on him."

I smiled. "And I'm not the foolish little Crow you think I am, Zephyr. Did you think I went there for nothing? I didn't only go there to see who would show up. I picked up a few things while watching you and Solas. I knew what to listen to and look for. I did pay attention when you and Solas spoke of potential threats. The first thing either of you did was protect our people and secure the court and territories. And that is what I warn you of, not a war Solas can win in his sleep." I smirked and felt a little taller, prouder in some way, that I was able to help. "You know who was there, but do you know what they were thinking? Do you know what they were scheming, hidden from the others?" Zephyr's stare became heavy, prompting me to spill what I knew. "When my Malice roamed the room, I picked up bits and pieces from everyone. They have moles within the Dark Courts. I could feel it like they knew more than they should. They're not as scared of Solas as they should be, and it isn't just their belief in Solene's protection. I'd check your armies and court for moles and change whatever plans are already on the table. Specifically, the Autumn Court and the Golden Court. The others wish to be a fly on the wall to protect their people. But Autumn and Golden have had moles inside for weeks. I caught the name Caraway, but that's the only name I could hear before Parrish started to squirm, and I had to pull back my Malice."

Zephyr finally nodded. His anger grew, but it wasn't directed at only me now. "If we have moles, they'll be taken care of. It would explain why Solas is hesitant to speak out loud."

"No. And we both know that isn't the reason. Solene is around, always. If she's not physically there, her ear is never far away. Be careful with what you say out loud," I answered. "I wouldn't doubt she also has her own moles kicking about."

"This doesn't make us even, Perdi."

"I don't care," I answered back. "I didn't do this to hurt you or him. Solas allowed me to hear him and Solene. He can block me out whenever he wants, and when he does, I can't even feel him. But he always let me hear her and the bits about me. He warned me that he would have to kill me. The day I left, he knew I was leaving and didn't stop me. Think back to that day. He took all his guards from the manor and let me leave. He knows what I'm doing but needs to know what I know."

He laughed, but it was strangled and frustrated. "There's no stopping this now. Don't you get it? I can't do anything about it now. The wheels are in motion. Nothing can stop this from playing out now."

"Then it is absolute war?" I asked, and he nodded. "Then we'll all meet on the battlefield, and I haven't much time left."

"I pray we do not meet on the battlefield. It would kill something inside me to take your life." He hung his head. "But I will protect Solas and our people, whatever the cost."

"As will I." The words stung, unlike anything he had ever said to me before. Instead of stepping back, I inched toward him and rested my hand on his arm. "I have loved no one as I've loved you. You are part of me, and I am part of you. And if you force me to take your life, Zeph, to save my own, I will mourn you for all my days. I will grow old with regret, but I *will* grow old."

"I have never loved before you, Perdi. And I will never love another after you're gone." Zephyr pulled away and took his darkness with him.

I stood in the trees and wondered if that was how two Soul-Eaters said goodbye to each other. My heart broke open, and I screamed my sadness into the forest. I knew Zephyr would sense my pain. Even though I couldn't feel him as he could with me, I knew he echoed my screams on his end. The earth trembled under our feet at the agony of two Finis — world breakers. And the one man I wanted to curl up beside, the only man who could have put my brokenness back together, felt a world away.

# Chapter Five

My father was moved to the front lines with the rest of the army. No amount of begging could convince him to remain back behind the walls of Tylwyth. He would inform the Elphame troops where the Guardians would need the most help, their strengths and weaknesses. Those who oathed themselves to Faolan would go to Whitwick Gates to protect those who remained behind to fight for the mortal realm. My father, who lived for Whitwick and its protection, would give his life for both Fae and man alike. Like many others on the field, he would sooner die than allow this to continue. I doubted any of these men would live long enough to help save my people, even if they wanted to. Those who stood against Solene would die at her hand. I was hopeful, but I wasn't a fool. It wasn't lost on me when I watched Faolan chart the field and place men where they were needed. His court would be the only one to go straight to the Gate. At first, it made me nervous. But after listening in, neither he nor Oisin trusted the others to protect the Gate or mortals. And unless I found a way to end this, it wouldn't matter which side of the field anyone stood on. We'd all die in the middle when Solene finally left the deadly walls of Blood and Bones.

The armies began to call this the Last War, the war to end all wars. It didn't matter who was still standing after the battle. This one would be the deciding war for us all, mortal and Fae alike. If we failed, there would be no more wars, no Guardians, no free mortal or Fae realm. It all would become Elphame. And if the mortal world was invaded, it would not be a war. It would be a bloodbath, a grand Taking of souls. Fae would conquer Whitwick, then bleed out into villages far and wide. The communities beyond Whitwick had never tasted a Taking since halflings had never been welcome, for fear we would bring the Fae. For as long as the oath had been in place, anyone outside of Whitwick Gates had been safe from the horror. If we failed, they'd feel it by the following dawn and choke on it, unprepared for the carnage that only Fae could bring. At one time, I had been jealous of those who lived well beyond the borders of Whitwick. Now, I pitied them. They'd never known horror like the rest of us. It would be a baptism by fire.

Nix and Orrian had left to scrounge whatever support they could find and had secured the Hallows, gnomes, goblins, fairies and everything in between. They would return in a matter of days with those who would fight for the mortals, to stop a war that had never really ended since the courts divided. They may have been small, but I couldn't wait to see the faces of the opposing army when the leprechauns showed up with Orrian and Nix, their hordes in their wake.

Seth had landed on the rail of my small patio the day we had gotten back from the Golden Court and hadn't left. The gargoyles had perched in the trees of the field where the battle would take place and had been there before Faolan's men arrived. They sat and watched as they had for every other war of notice. They would bear witness to the death of many. When I had asked Seth about Solas and what was coming, Seth had told me of his plans, which were what I had already suspected and what I had warned the others of—complete and utter carnage. The only difference at the Dark Court since I had left was that Solene hadn't been seen since the night Solas and I had met in the kitchen and spoken the truth before I fled my home for the Winter Court. The Court of Blood and Bones was locked down tight. No one was coming in or out. Seth didn't know why but suspected it was due to the coming battle, and the Seers didn't like dirtying their pretty white garbs. What I wouldn't have given to drag Solene through the mud, just once.

Faolan had come in the morning and asked to spend the day with me. It was cute at first, then uncomfortable. It hadn't dawned on me before that he and I had never gone on a date or done anything in the open that hadn't ended in death. Back in Whitwick, we'd had to sneak. He had been my secret for so many years that we had never risked being seen together. In Whitwick, his kind was as hated as my kind was in Elphame. Here, I was the one who was hated. It was a strange and unsettling twist of fate for us both.

I dressed and walked with him from the house into the city. We sat in the city center, had lunch on the grass and watched a play by the children of Tylwyth. We strolled through the streets, eating handmade sweets, and he told me about every building and bench. He knew the history of Tylwyth, but more importantly, he knew every person by name. He knew their stories, where they came from, who their parents were and what their dreams were. Faolan told me stories of where he'd kissed a girl, where he'd got his first black eye for kissing the wrong girl and where he used to go when things at home were hell. He didn't dwell much on home as a child, but I knew enough about it and heard the sadness in his words not to ask questions.

Sitting and laughing with him was almost enough for me to forgive many of his actions and the lies he'd told. But the moment I edged my willingness to forget some of it, the soft hum from the Horn pulled me back. I wasn't here to forgive him. I wasn't here to know him in that way. I was here to save my people, to save those I loved and to have a home to return to. I wondered, for a moment, how Fae had friends if they were always on the brink of devastation. How did you build a life with others when families could be on opposite sides of a war?

"I want to show you my deepest secret." Faolan held out his hand. "You must swear never to tell a soul, because no other person currently alive has been to this place. Outside of a select few priests and myself, no one has ever stepped foot there. Not even the threat of death could get this secret from me."

"Your deepest secret that I can never tell?" I lifted my eyebrows. "Are you about to show me a basement full of bodies that you either want me to join or help you hide?"

He laughed. "You'll have to trust me."

"That's a tall order," I joked. "But I suppose if you can guarantee that I'm not going to be hiding dead bodies, I'll come."

"I'll save that for date number two," he joked back.

"A second date? Aren't you a confident man?"

I finally nodded and followed him. He led me up and down flights of stairs through the city until my legs burned from the climb and my heart hammered in my throat. I was in great shape from all the running for my life, but stairs had never been part of those escapes. Faolan led me through the trees and twisted root paths until we stood at the cave entrance with a boulder at the mouth. It looked similar to the ones carved by the Sluagh, and my imagination tried to take root. His cool magick chilled the air around us and morphed the boulder into a metal door.

"If no one has ever stepped in there, why are you showing me?" I asked, my heart in my throat. "What's in there?"

"I can see your curious mind is as good as ever. There are no monsters in there, Perdi. Nothing beyond this door will harm or hurt you," he said. "When I became king, many oaths shifted from my father to me. This place was one of them. I was oathed never to reveal it to anyone unless I deemed their need greater than the need for secrecy."

"And you deem my need to see it greater?"

"I don't know what it is you'll need, so I give you everything I have to give. Some secrets, Perdi, I can give you freely. Whatever I'm free to give, I will." He pushed open a thick steel door, and I followed him inside.

"There are dead bodies in here, aren't there?" I asked and ducked into the darkness.

"This is the sanctuary, old as Tylwyth. But yeah, it could use a good airing out." He chuckled. "This was the first building on this land. My mother used to say that this place was the bringer of our power. Today, I think she was right. Information is power."

"It smells like old people," I mumbled. "Old dead people."

Faolan led me through tunnels, lit by globes of light that hung suspended from the ceiling. It was the same light I had seen Faolan call once before. I could feel us descending slowly. It reminded me of the tunnels of the Golden Court, the caves of the Sluagh and all the horrible places I had been since becoming a Crow. I breathed deeply and calmed myself.

"If there's a monster down here, you'll be the only dead body I'll be hiding today," I whispered. I tried to make it a joke, but it came out shaken with fear.

"No monsters, I swear," he answered and squeezed my hand. The tunnels finally opened into a massive room of glittering stone, as if the walls held thousands of diamonds. Rugs covered the floor, seating and tables sat against the edges, and in the middle, massive bookcases. "All the records of Elphame are here. Family lines, treaties, births, pledges, titles, you name it. Everything you wish to know about any family, line or magick is held here."

"This is your secret? A library?" I laughed. He shook his head and led me to the rear of the room. There, in a small bed, lay a plump black cat. "A cat? That's your big secret?"

"Perdi, Elphame doesn't have cats or dogs. Well, we do, but they're wild and will eat you. I brought him here from Whitwick."

"Wait! Is this one of the barn cats we found ten years ago?" I asked as I stared at the little furry beast.

"I took him the night we found him after you begged your father to keep it. He was cold and hungry, so I brought him here. He never seems to care that he's surrounded by Fae. He's always been my reminder," he answered. "To me, he is the visual soul of Whitwick. It's a reminder of you. I've been coming here a lot more since your Taking, praying I'd find a way to see you again, to explain."

"I don't know what to say. I'm sorry," I replied. "I feel like I failed in some way. Most of this could have been avoided if I had listened to more than the fear and anger in my bones. But I ran the first chance I got."

"I don't blame you. I'd have run if I were you. I'd have done pretty much the same exact thing as you did, probably worse. I've been that scared before, and I've done things that stain my soul to this day because I've been more scared of doing nothing." Faolan hugged me the way he always had, with his entire body. "We can't go back, only forward. You're here now, and that's what we focus on. There are no more apologies to be made. We both took paths we thought would end in the least amount of pain and lives lost. And those paths found their way back, so I think we were meant to make those decisions. It's led to the Last War and, hopefully, the end of this great madness."

"What do you think will happen? Do we have a chance?" I asked and pulled back from him. I wandered the room, running my fingers down the spines of long-forgotten books.

He sighed. "I'm hopeful. But hope will only get us to the battle. It doesn't win wars, unfortunately."

I closed my eyes and felt the leftover emotions that stained each page, oils of men and women from days long before the Gate. My Malice flowed softly, not the storm I was used to unleashing. She, like me, was curious. As she slipped in and out of the pages, she brought back impressions of love and hate, death and birth, times when the world stood on the brink and final moves that should have ended in utter disaster. But each time, the world kept turning.

"The history of your people, as well as my own, sits down here." He pulled me out of memories that weren't my own.

"Why do you have it?" I asked.

"We always have," he answered, as if that were enough. My look said it wasn't. "When there is war, it is absolute. Courts are destroyed, and every memory of who they once were is burned to the ground, wiped off the face of this earth. But we've always taken their history and added it to ours. Since the start, we've always collected and saved what we could. You never know when it'll come in handy."

"Why?"

"You ask a history teacher why he protects history?" He laughed and gave me a look that said I had asked a silly question. "Simply put, how can we be sure we won't repeat the worst parts in history unless we understand it? I thought you should know if ever you had questions about Elphame, you would find the answers here. You are welcome here whenever you'd like, with or without me. Everything, from the beginning of Elphame to now rests on these shelves. There are many truths here, Perdi — ones the rest of us cannot speak out loud."

I nodded. "I'll look if I'm still alive after the war."

He paused and looked as if he thought of his words carefully. "I think what's held down here is what will ensure you see the end of this war."

I tucked that information away for later. Whatever was here would take me years to read, and I only had days left. "Do you think this will actually be the Last War?"

Faolan led me to the edge of the room, to a heap of pillows and blankets, where he had obviously spent many nights. He poured us a drink and we sat on the floor, curled in furs and cushions.

"You asked what would happen and if we had a chance. There's always the chance. How it plays out is a different thing. The mortal realm has always been something Elphame has wanted to take since the day we could no longer take from it. But there are more of us who want it to end than Fae who want to keep Taking mortal children from their homes. The Taking was never…" He paused and thought about his words. "Those of us who had to do the dirty work were never the ones who wanted it to happen. Unfortunately, until now, we haven't had the chance to stop it. There have always been greater powers who made those decisions and forced our hands."

My body shivered from head to toe, and I braced myself. He sensed my unease and froze beside me. We scanned the room and saw nothing more than the cat and documents older than paper and written on leather hides. I looked behind us, toward the door. We were alone to the naked eye, but so much more hid in the dark than the eyes could see. I let my Malice roll from my hands and search for prying ears and eyes. There was no one, but I wouldn't put it past Solene to test her reach.

"Did you feel that?" I asked.

"I don't feel anyone other than us in here, if that's what you mean," he replied. "There is no one listening in if you're worried about that. Those we worry about cannot hear this far from their walls."

I half-laughed and half-groaned. "I think maybe I'm just nervous."

"Same for me, I think. I feel jumpy at shadows," Faolan answered.

I looked once more. Shadows, in my experience, were something to fear. "There's nothing uncomfortable about this at all."

"I may not have thought out my plan very well," he replied. "I didn't think of this place as a deep, dark basement until now."

"I've missed this," I said. "I wish we could go back to the days when the biggest worry was making it home before my dad knew I had been out later than allowed."

"I've missed those nights." Faolan breathed deeply and pushed himself closer to me. "Being with you like this was the only time I didn't have to hide. It was the only time my mind relaxed, and I didn't protect my soul. You have no idea how peaceful it is to drop my walls around you. Whenever I'm with you, I'm not guarded as I am with everyone else."

I searched his face for the meaning behind his words. I watched him calm his nerves and nod his head. He closed the last little gap between us, and my body reacted to the familiarity of his touch. My face heated and a shyness grew like butterflies in my stomach. It was an unusual feeling to be nervous around him after having known him my entire life. I steeled my will and focused. If I were to ever get the truth, there were things I knew I'd have to do that would stain me. This would be one of them. I wondered how badly I needed the truth compared to how desperately I needed a clean soul. Could I give myself to a man I didn't truly love? No. But I could do this for a man I did, for my people, for all our people. I could do so much worse for all of them, mortal and Fae, and I had. This wouldn't stain me nearly as much as what I had already done to live this long.

I leaned in, tentatively, for a kiss. In my mind, I told myself it would be chaste, just enough for me to feel that connection once again, just enough for me to worm my way into his head. In my mind, I told myself it wasn't wrong. I had to do this. I had come here to right the wrongs, to find the truth. But my heart told me to stop. It was a war within.

Instead of fighting, I gave myself over to it. A hunger from deep within burst from me. When Faolan's mouth had found mine, a clash of right and wrong, we kissed like it was our first and last. Desperation is a heady thing and drives decisions to be made before anything else can make them. I had decided to come, to follow the horn, and now I'd do what I had come to do. Eat his truth like it was my last meal.

He rolled onto me, bracing himself above me. As we kissed, we pulled at each other's clothes. The fabric of our clothes stretched and ripped under our touch. With his mind occupied, I allowed my Malice to slowly find its way into Faolan's soul, picking through his thoughts carefully. When Faolan slowed, I knew he could feel my Malice. I pulled him greedily to me, and his attention fell back on me. I eased my Malice through the surface of his thoughts. I felt like I was tiptoeing down a dark hallway, with monsters hunting my every movement.

Snippets of Faolan inched their way from the stronghold of his mind. He guarded his soul as I did, using the same force as when going to war. The bits I managed to feel told me I couldn't trust him, but at no fault of his own. He wouldn't betray me without being forced to. He, like Solas, was at the mercy of another's whim. As I dug deeper, he could feel me and started pushing back against my Malice. I forced myself a little deeper and saw flashes of Solene, her laughter, her punishing Faolan with a lash and her threatening to kill his people if he tried to protect the mortal world. I eased from his mind as he moved his body closer, my pulse sped back up and I froze. I couldn't do it, no matter why I needed the information. This was not something all of me wanted. My heart, soul and mind all screamed for something different, something not here. I needed the truth but wasn't willing to pay this price, being with him, to gain it.

"I've missed you," Faolan muttered into my mouth. The power that was Faolan began to whirl around us, blocking out the world.

"Wait," I whispered back. "Fao, I want you to stop."

He pulled his mouth back and hovered over me. His entire body lifted from mine, uncertain if he had done something wrong. Not an inch of his body touched mine as he rested above me on the tips of his toes and hands. "Are you okay?"

I shook my head. "No, something is off. This doesn't feel… I can't do this."

"I'm sorry, Perdi. It's okay. You don't need to explain." He lifted completely off me.

"No, you haven't done anything wrong. It just doesn't feel right. It doesn't feel like I should be doing this," I answered. I couldn't explain the twinge I felt, but I knew I needed to listen to it. "I'm sorry, but this isn't what I want—not entirely and not for the right reasons."

Faolan pushed himself a little farther from my side and put enough space between us that I didn't feel the heat from his body. I felt the slightest draft crawl between us, dampening any fires that had blossomed. "Don't apologize, Perdi. It's okay. You've been through a lot, and your emotions have been twisted. I understand. Please don't apologize for it. There are no expectations and never will be. You own your body, no one else. If this doesn't feel right, then it isn't, and there are no apologies needed for that."

I nodded slowly. My eyes still scanned the room, looking for whatever had caused the uncertainty within me. But not even the shadows stirred. At first, I thought Zephyr had come, but he wasn't there. I wondered if it was the Gate, and that was the energy I felt shifting. But it was different this time. I closed my eyes and used my other senses. The only sounds I heard were our hearts beating and the cat breathing. I smelled only us, with the backdrop of the musty library we sat in. Nothing physically felt wrong or different or as it shouldn't. But my Malice wouldn't rest. It turned in on itself, over and over, until finally, I stood.

The feeling was familiar, but I couldn't place it. I racked my brain and thought of every place I had been, willingly or not. I thought of every person I had met, creatures I had run from and spells I had spun, but nothing came to light. My Malice, on the other hand, knew the feeling well. She knew something was off, not only in my soul but in the room itself.

"We should go." I picked up the sweater I had been wearing.

He stood and held out his ripped shirt and laughed. "This didn't fare all that well."

He tried to change the subject to something lighter and didn't dwell on my ending the night. I appreciated that and let him. He didn't look the least bit upset, which I also valued. Perhaps I was ashamed for enjoying myself while we stood on the brink of war, guilty for lying with Faolan after having just left Solas' bed. It was a new flavor of guilt. One I wasn't accustomed to.

"It's all right, Perdi. Truly. I am content with knowing you again, but I don't need to know all of you as I once did. Whether you say the words or not, I know where your heart is, and it isn't with me anymore. That you've found love is wonderful. It doesn't have to be with me for me to be happy for you." Faolan kissed my hand. He breathed in and laughed. "I doubt we will be allowed in here again."

I laughed and playfully slapped his arm. "At least it doesn't smell like old dead people in here anymore."

"I don't think they'd appreciate it smelling of lust, either." Faolan winked. "But now you know of this place — and I think you'll like coming back here."

I followed Faolan out of the library and into the streets. We walked home in the middle of the night, having eaten the daylight in the library, him in his tattered shirt, my arm slung through his and a black cat in tow, no longer a secret. Whatever I felt, I carried it with me in the pit of my stomach. But for a moment, as the sun climbed from her slumber, I felt like I wasn't dragging the world behind me.

Oisin passed us on the street and wagged his finger at us both. "Is this good night or good morning?"

"Good night," we both answered and didn't stop walking.

Inside, we stood in the hall and stared at each other. He looked from his bedroom to mine and shrugged. The cat walked by us and inched into Faolan's bedroom, as if he already knew he had moved permanently.

"Good night, Perdi," he finally said, a slight nervousness in his voice.

"Good night," I answered with a forced smile and watched his shoulders relax. I leaned in and kissed his cheek. "Thank you for sharing your secret with me."

"If you play your cards right and learn better control, you'll know all my secrets." He kissed me back and watched me walk to my bedroom. His whisper crawled across the floor like fresh frost. "I tried to show you. With you is the only time I don't protect my soul. I felt you in my mind, Perdi. You cannot afford to be that clumsy. The truth needs to be coaxed out, not forced, or you'll be felt every time. I will give you everything you need, but I cannot willingly give you the information I'm oathed to protect. Learn to steal what you're not given freely."

I closed my door without looking back. Faolan had felt me prying the truth from his mind but hadn't tried to stop me until he had no choice. Although he had offered me a warning, I wouldn't give the same in return. I wouldn't destroy his mind for those secrets if *he* played his cards right. Inside my bedroom, I showered and climbed into bed. I tried twice to call on the shadows but received nothing. I knew Zephyr would be preparing for the war and wouldn't allow them to come unless I was in actual danger. Me wanting to talk to them wasn't danger. It was loneliness and homesickness.

I tossed and turned until I finally drifted into a restless sleep, torn between dreams of my death and the end of those I loved, neither of which could I stop. And when I couldn't relax, when all that was left of me was rage, I screamed inside my head, never daring to let it out for anyone else to hear. I cursed Elphame, the war, and Solas and Zephyr. I cursed Faolan for his lies. I cursed the very Gods who built a realm of trials and death sentences. I swore until I couldn't breathe, and all that was left was me, in enemy lands, without a friendly territory to run to, suffering in silence.

All the pain rolled inside me had lit a small fire waiting to catch on dry brush. What I had felt in Faolan's mind twisted in my gut and fueled my fire. He was a pawn. He could only be trusted until his life, or the lives of his people, came under the magnifying glass. From the shallowest parts of his soul, I knew he didn't love me, not how I had once loved him. Although I had already known he didn't, hearing it echo in his soul had stung. I hadn't stayed in his head long enough to know what he was planning or his part in all this, but I had read enough to know that I was a tool he needed to save his people, just like he was mine. The same person who pulled Solas' strings was pulling Faolan's. The only difference between Faolan and me was what we would offer on a silver platter. He would hand over anything and anyone to save himself and his people, and I wasn't willing to give just anyone.

"Little Crow, calm yourself." Zephyr was there, in between heartbeats, curled around my back, his shadows tucking tightly around us.

"I don't want to. I want it all to burn," I answered back, my grief strangling me. It felt like a hand was gripping my throat. "Why are you even here? Shouldn't you be planning my killing blow?"

"We're not on the battlefield yet, little Crow," he replied. I turned to face him and tucked my face into his chest. His very smell reminded me of days that didn't hurt as badly. It was still painful, but it didn't cut nearly as deep when he was around. He smelled of home, of Solas. I held on to him like a raft in the middle of a raging river. "Let it out here before you burn all of Elphame to the ground, and there's nothing worth saving."

"There'd be no more wars," I answered. My voice came out in one long, ragged sob.

"This is true, but there'd be no more victories, either. No more love, no life, no home, no nothing that makes this place bearable. Your pain would become the grief for all."

"They'd all deserve it."

"No, little Soul-Eater, they wouldn't."

I groaned at his truth. "I want them to."

"Your wanting it wouldn't make their souls taste any better."

I cracked open like an egg and screamed until my voice was raw. Tucked in the safety of Zephyr's shadows, I cried for everyone that I knew would die. But the most tears fell for those I loved—for me, for where I was, for who wasn't beside me.

"I miss home. I miss you. I miss Solas," I cried. "God, I miss him so badly. Every breath burns without him. It smells awful here, like every day is Christmas, and the only gift I keep waking up to is pain. My heart is breaking, and I have run out of string and glue to keep it together. With each day that passes, I'm pulled farther away from him. I'm scared I'll wake up one day, and he'll be gone — and I'll still be alive without him. I don't want to be here without him."

"Perdi, if things do not go as planned, I want you to call on the shadows. They'll bring you home."

"Zeph, if things don't go as planned, I won't have a home to return to — not here and not in Whitwick," I replied.

He tensed and relaxed in the same breath as if I had said something he didn't like. If I hadn't known him, I would have missed it. "Tylwyth won't fall. It never has. If this is where you are, this is what I will die protecting."

"I'm not talking about the Winter Court. This isn't my home any more than Whitwick is," I answered. His body relaxed completely at my answer. "Did you really think I considered this place, of all places, my home? You haven't listened to a bloody thing I've said for months. This, what I'm doing, is using the tools I have to protect my home. I did everything you told me to do. I climbed out of my wounds and faced the decisions I had to make, and you will kill me for it. I'm here with my enemy, *our* enemy, for you, Solas and all our people. I'm in this territory, alone and afraid, to save us and *our* home. But all you saw was me leaving you, and you never asked yourself why I would do such a thing. I followed that damn Horn to protect Solas, but you only saw me as a deserter. Zeph, *you* are my home. *Solas* is my home."

Lanne Garrett

"I should have listened. I'm sorry. I just don't understand why you did this, why you're still doing this. You don't have to do this. Come home, Perdi."

"Yes, I do. You have no idea how badly I want to come home, how many times I've had to stop myself from running back. But I can't leave...not yet. And I can't tell you what moves I have left or why I must stay because you'll stop me. And if you stop me, all of this, the pain, the agony, will be for nothing. I won't save anyone. I won't save Solas or our people. I can't risk it."

"I won't stop you. I hate that you're here. It kills me inside every minute you're gone." He kissed the very top of my head and breathed me in like a favorite smell. "You were right about the moles, about the sabotage. They were carrying Solas' plans back to their courts and back to *her*. Now, she'll only know if she's brave enough to come and ask for herself. And I doubt, very much, she'll ever knock on my door."

The muscles in my shoulders relaxed. I had saved someone, at least. "It was worth it, even if I only saved a few."

"Saving a life is always worth it. Too many people die here as it is for power and lust, and greed. But, Perdi, if you find yourself at a wall, no escape, nothing left to give, call on my shadows. They will bring you home to my court. If you can't do this or find you can't go on, come home. No one, not even *her*, can get to you there. There will never be a safer place in either realm than the grounds of the Finis. I don't care if we're in the middle of a war. Call the shadows. I don't need them to win. I need them to protect you."

I pulled back and stared at his smile. "You have a court? When did that happen?"

"Population one. It's only been me since my...*our* people were slaughtered. No one else, who isn't Finis, has ever stepped foot on that land. I suppose I just doubled the population to two now. We are the only Soul-Eaters left, Perdi. The land is as much yours as it is mine. Whenever the rest of this world becomes too much, or you fear for your last breath, go home. You will be safe there, with or without me. Whoever comes for you there will die before their feet touch our soil. Not even the Gods or Goddesses would survive an unwelcomed trip to our court. The magick is different there. It will protect you, and you'll never want for anything. You could live out the end of the world on that island."

"What if the shadows don't come when I call? I tried earlier, but they didn't come."

"They'll come when you need them, Perdi. I swear."

I nodded. "If it all goes to hell, won't they come for me next? Won't *she* come for me?"

"They will try, but they will fail. If they come, they come for us both. Together, we can outlast, outrun and outlive any army that is brave enough to try to invade *our* lands. Together, we will burn the world before we let them take us. If she comes for you, she comes for her death, and we will unleash hell and damn the consequences. I'd rather sit alone with you until the end of time than allow anyone to take another Finis life."

"Please stay, just for a little while?" I asked, and he pulled me in tighter.

"I'll stay until I no longer taste your tears."

"You'll be with me forever," I only half-joked. The rest was a wish.

"You are not the only one who has scheming to do, little Crow. You dropped a bomb on me earlier, and now I must find a way to keep it from blowing up and taking us all with it."

"Tell me about home until I fall asleep, please." I pushed my face into his chest and breathed in the smell of safety. "You smell like Solas. God, I miss home so badly. Everything here hurts. It smells awful here, it doesn't rain at all and the stars look wrong."

"The stars look wrong because you see them from a place you don't want to be. But they're still the stars you see from home." I curled into Zephyr while he ran his hand through my hair. Nothing about him was soft except for the moments he stopped the world around us to love me a little harder. "I think you would love it at home, where I'm from. You've spoken about the mortal world, and each word felt like you were describing not just where you were from but where I am from. It's never been touched by war or fights for power. No one, other than a Soul-Eater, has ever stepped foot on that soil, and no one ever will unless we invite them in." He lowered his voice to a calm whisper. "It's a small island off the coast of Blood and Bones. It's where I was born and raised until I joined the others." When I stirred in his arms, he held on tighter. "Close your eyes. Sleep."

"Don't stop, not yet. Let me build your memory in my mind. It'll give me somewhere to drift off to." I closed my eyes and began to imagine a place that was so special that Zeph had never spoken of it before — a place he had guarded against even me until now, when I needed it most.

"It sits in the middle of an island but feels like an entire world. It's very much like how you described the hills of Whitwick — forests and gardens and wildflowers. There's a pond in the middle, where you can swim. It's the only water in these cursed lands that isn't filled with creatures that'll chew on you. Creeks surround you on all sides, and they drown out the noise you go there to escape from. If you're quiet enough and allow yourself to settle into the flow of the island, you can hear only life — no death or war. You feel the hum of peace, and it calms even the scariest moments. Soon, after you settle into the land, time slips away and carries your worries and doubts away with it."

"Do you go back often?" I asked.

"When I felt you, tonight, that's where I was. Whenever I'm not with you or Solas, that's where I can be found. I go there to remind myself why I keep fighting and will always keep fighting. It gives me purpose."

"What is that purpose? Why do you keep fighting?"

"Peace, love, family, honor...now, you."

I jerked to pull back, but he held me tighter. "Why me?"

"So long ago, Perdi, I knew I would fight for you. Before you were born, before Aoife, before Solas, I knew. I've seen you in my mind since I was a child. Solas may be my king, but you are my queen. You are my destiny."

"That's not even close to being true — not now, not ever," I countered.

"It is and always will be. Your belief in it doesn't diminish its truth."

"Don't leave me yet. Zeph, I'm so bloody scared. I'm down to final moves, and they are getting harder to make."

"Stay in my shadows until you fall asleep. They'll eat your fear as they always have," Zephyr answered.

"It's really you, though, eating my fear. How can you stomach it?"

"I've eaten worse things than fear, little Crow. For you, I'd eat the world. Good night."

"Zeph, tell Solas…" I called out. "I love you, both of you."

I heard nothing back, but I could feel his love. The shadows rolled around me and lifted me into their cocoon, as they had done so many times before. "I've missed you."

"We've missed you as well. Zephyr loves you. But his heart is broken, like yours."

"How is Solas?" I asked.

"He is as he was when you last saw him in person."

"Broken?"

"He is like you…lost. But, like you, he does not like to be controlled, and someone will suffer greatly for thinking they can control either of you. He misses you, and it's uncomfortable to be near him when he's thinking of you."

"Does he know what I'm doing here?" I asked, then swallowed my shame for how my date with Faolan had ended.

"Yes. There is not much Solas doesn't know. He knows what you're doing and knows you will do what you must." They swirled tighter around me until it felt like nothing in the world could get to me. "Rest easy, Perdi. Solas has eyes here, as he does in every court. Never has there been a day, since coming into Elphame, where he hasn't had someone watching over you in his absence. Although he can't come to you, there are those here who will fight for you."

I nodded. "I feel like I've been here before, between decisions I have to make and ones that'll be made for me."

"It seems you have lived between decisions since you got to these lands. But no greatness comes without teetering on the edge of suffering. You can never truly appreciate life unless you've walked the brink of death."

"That truth gets harder and harder to swallow," I muttered. The reality was often more difficult to stomach than lies.

"But you'll find more truth here than anywhere else. Even the dread that blankets this land can help you more than anywhere else."

"Tell me about Zephyr's home, just until I fall asleep." For the first time in a long time, I fell asleep with a smile and a dream worth holding on to. Come tomorrow and the next day, I didn't think I'd smile much.

# Chapter Six

A war inside the Sidhe was no different than war across the mortal lands. We were all descendants of those who had fought and survived a battle that changed our realms. We, the ancestors, were born of armies who had marched before. Now, we would be the ones to fling ourselves into the arms of war. We had never evolved beyond our need to take whatever we were not allowed, kill for what we wanted and starve for power not our own. And, with each new fight, we fated the next generation with the same bloody fortune. This perpetual cycle, hated by all, was needed by most. The irony was thick enough for me to choke on. I wanted peace and would fight for it. I wanted survival and would kill for it.

The battlefield, where the Last War would eventually end, was eerily quiet. It reminded me of a graveyard, which it would soon become. Those who muddled about, making final preparations, just hadn't been buried yet. The sun still rose, and the wind still carried the smell of mossy earth, but somewhere, mothers and fathers waited in vain for the return of their sons and daughters. The hopes of each family would become nothing more than meat for the creatures who would come after all was said and done. And that was the cycle of Elphame. That was the cycle of every realm with a pulse. As much as I hated the reality of our worlds, I wouldn't have been alive without others falling before me.

The battle had been planned, by each side, to the finest details. We camped miles apart, awaiting the final moment. We'd come together for the ultimate dance. This field would see each side wield magick without mercy, until that, too, was exhausted. Swords and knives would decide the war, not magick — not in the end. The wounded and dead would lie thick over the Courtless Lands, brought down by the strongest, those more schooled in battle. There would be no room for the weak or scared. They would be the first to fall. And when the dance cards were full and the song finally ended, without a doubt, Solas and his men would be the only ones alive, and there wouldn't be enough men to fight in the war no one was brave enough to speak of. The mortal realm wouldn't stand a chance and would fall next.

In the center of Elphame, the Court of Less. From both sides, war would flood the lands of Solas. It would be in the Courtless territory that all fates would be decided. Solas had selected that land for a reason. It was from within those borders you could see all of Elphame. Trees lined the edges, but there were no routes for an ambush. Anyone foolish enough to enter the forest would find certain death at the hands of creatures no one else chanced in their territory. There would be nowhere to hide and no place to survive.

Solas stood between this world and the next, guarding the Gate. I was new to war, but not new to the games. With unspoken truths, I watched as two enemies, Faolan and Solas, worked around an oath that bound them both to the Gate and Solene. Within those oaths, Faolan had only sent traitors from other courts to face Solas, and Solas did not move against Faolan. It was a juggling act that would soon come to an end, and when that time came, Faolan and his people would die at the hands of the Dark Court. I had little time to work with, but soon time would no longer be on my side, and I would side with Solas. I prayed that I wouldn't fall with Solas as well.

I stood on the hill, overlooking where the last stand would be, and couldn't shake the feeling that no matter the outcome, I would never be the same again. If I lived, this would harden me in ways I'd regret. If I died, I wouldn't care. But I was not the only one contemplating their futures. I could feel the pressure building around me. It prickled the air like static and rubbed the army into angry men. The pending doom made us all teeter on the edge, lashing out at each other — venting, hating and fearing. On one of the last eves of freedom, we didn't hold each other closer. We pushed until we had only ourselves to worry about. Friends and neighbors became nothing more than people to step over on the battlefield. I left the bickering to the men and understood why they needed it.

As I walked the forest of Tylwyth, I feared nothing that could drag me into the caverns and caves. There wasn't a creature or monster that could bring me the fear I already felt in my twisting and cramped stomach.

The feeling from the past night hadn't left. I still carried the dread around in my bones. I watched as clusters of Fae made their way from the surrounding mountains, ready to fight for Faolan. While they moved to the front, others moved to hide. Mothers and their children took refuge while they left their husbands and fathers to fight for another day.

"I can feel you, Zeph," I whispered to the shadows I watched slink unnaturally over the ground.

"And I can feel your fear. It's hard not to come and check on you." Zephyr stepped from behind a cluster of trees at my right and pulled the shadows around us. "Your fear came through your pearl. It was rolling off me in waves. Even Solas felt it, thick enough for him to rub his chest. He called out your name, and I came."

"If you are waiting for the day I won't be afraid, you'll be waiting a lot longer than you have days," I answered.

"I felt you call out as you dreamed, over and over. It didn't stop until you woke this morning."

"I don't remember calling out to you again," I replied.

"You weren't calling for me. You were calling for Solas. It took a lot to keep him from coming," he answered.

"I'm sorry, but thank you for coming."

"I came when you were asleep, dreaming, crying. And I stayed until you would settle, only to start back up the moment I left. Eventually, I had to leave the shadows with you. You wouldn't be calm without them or me," Zephyr replied. "I always come when you're dreaming like that. Bad things happen when Soul-Eaters dream too deeply. Last night was different, though."

"Sometimes, when I'm dreaming and scared, I can see the flicker of shadows in my dreams. When I'm in a fight and want them to die, I can smell you."

"Without training and control…"

I mimicked his voice and repeated the exact words he had once said to me. "*It's a lonely road to walk and one you must walk with absolute care and attention to every single detail. One bad dream, one loss of control, one wish, and you could be the cause of countless deaths and not even mean to do it.*"

"Smart ass." He smiled. "I'm glad to see you've not forgotten how dangerous we are, even as we sleep. I will come until you learn control — or I'll be hiding bodies until the day you die."

"I'm fated to die in the next few days, so I doubt there will be many bodies for you to hide between now and then." I winked, and he rolled his eyes at my dark humor. "How can you enter these lands and not signal every alarm?"

"There are no borders that could keep me from you. And if I couldn't get to you, I'd send my shadows to drag you across hell back to me. Faolan knows every time I come to check on you. He's just not bold enough to face me or tell me to get out. But I suspect he fears your wrath more than mine. So, he gives me — and you — a wide berth. One pissed-off Soul-Eater is bad, and two would mean certain death."

"He knows what I am?" I asked.

"He suspects it, but isn't sure. Something in the back of his mind tells him to run, but he doesn't know why."

"Making friends as a child must have been hard for you," I teased.

"You, little Crow, are my first real friend."

"Solas is your friend," I countered.

"This is true, but he was and is my king before anything else. It took decades for him not to step back each time I entered the room. Whereas you never did, not once. You knew what I was and still released me. The first time we met in person, in Solas' dining room, you went toe to toe with me and didn't flinch...and you still don't. You've always been willing to look me in the eyes. You've never feared me like the rest, and it has nothing to do with *what* you are but *who* you are. You, little Crow, are my friend before anything else."

"I'm happy for the trip down memory lane, but why have you come today without me calling? Shouldn't you be terrifying villages or something equally as shameful?"

Zephyr grinned at my comment, then shrugged. "I'm always around. You just don't always see me. But today, I don't know... Something feels off. Perdi, I'm scared for you."

"You're always scared for me."

"I was rarely scared for you until you left and came here. And before you bother with the whys of it all, I don't care right now. You're in danger. You're in more danger than ever before. I can feel it in my gut, and it's eating me." He raised his hand the moment I went to open my mouth, and I closed it. "I know, you're always in danger. But today is different. It's not just danger I feel. I'm scared for you. I'm used to feeling your fear, but today, the strongest fear I feel is not coming from you. It's coming from my own soul. I had to come and see you, make sure."

"Yet, you could kill me if you had to," I said. I instantly felt awful for being spiteful. Zephyr was stuck between Solas and me and all of Elphame. That was not a good place to be. I looked up through glittering vision. Tears threatened to fall. "Zeph, could you really kill me? On the battlefield?"

"Why? What are you planning to do now?" he asked. "Should I start looking for another kingdom to call home, or should I just kill them all now and save us the trouble of sorting through the bodies later?"

"I'm not planning anything. But I do wonder how deep your loyalty is to me. Could you kill me, as you said you could?"

He turned his eyes from mine. "At one time, I could have answered that question without hesitation. I'd do it just to prove I would. Before, I'd hunt that person and take their life simply because I said I would. Those who stand against me are my enemy. It's always been very black and white."

"And now?" I asked.

He squinted, then finally shrugged. "I don't know anymore. You're in this gray area. I care for you deeply, but I care for Solas and our people. I come when you call or when I feel your sadness. I've given you the keys, so to speak, to my home. Yet, I feel the same way about Solas. If he allowed it, I would kill everyone the moment they stepped foot on the battlefield. That's not ego. That's just how deadly Soul-Eaters are and how deep my loyalty runs to him. And at the same time, I find it hard to prepare, because I know you are on the other side of that war. I'm torn between love and duty. It doesn't help that Solas has threatened to cut off certain body parts if you come to any harm during the war. A fucking *war*, Perdi. I am to ensure you walk away without a bloody scratch. Death happens during war. How the hell do I ensure he wins *and* protect you from getting, as he says, not even a hangnail?"

I laughed at this comment and could see Solas saying those exact words. "I see the dilemma. But you haven't really answered my question."

"It's because you won't like the answer, and I don't want to argue with you today," he replied.

"I need to hear it just the same. Today, I want the truth without having to fight for it."

"With Solas, I am utterly loyal, and you know this. The things I would do to save him, I won't speak out loud. But with you, it isn't just loyalty. It's love. I thought I could sacrifice you over Solas, but I can't. Solas knows, whether I'm ordered to or not, I will let him die to save you. I would drain him of pearls to save you. I would let everyone die on that field for you. I would damn my own pearl to Hades for you — and that is the truth." His face softened to the man I knew he was when no one was looking. The face he had when he held a butterfly or when I watched him mend a pixie wing.

I felt bad for him — not pity, but my heart hurt for who he had been forced to become. He was war and death, but he was a million moments in between each war of love and compassion. I saw those moments — but rarely did anyone else.

"Did you talk to Solas about everything I told you before? About Solene?" I asked.

"Yes, and he absolutely lost it on me. He completely destroyed the dining room, using me as the bat that broke the windows. He, as politely as only Solas can be, reminded me that I was not to meddle."

I stepped to his front and squeezed his hand. "Are you okay?"

Zephyr laughed a sharp bark. "I came to see if you were okay, not the other way around. I've lived through countless wars, battles where only Solas and I were the survivors. This little fight with Solas isn't anything I'd lose sleep over. We've had worse, and I'm sure we'll have more. But I'm stuck between heaven and hell, and I'm about to reach out to purgatory and see if they have a room for the night."

"Is he okay?" I lifted an eyebrow. I had seen them fight before, and Zephyr was a force not even Solas could survive.

"He will be." Zephyr grinned. "He's wounded, hurting, and there isn't anything I can do to fix it. He wins wars but loses at life. Everyone he's ever cared for either dies or leaves."

"Can you blame me?" I asked, suddenly defensive. I didn't want to argue with him. I had my reasons and wasn't about to hammer them home yet again.

"No. And like you said, Solas doesn't either. I believe you when you said he wanted you to run. He knew you'd come here. Before you left, when I had suggested we warn the mortal realm, he already knew you'd be the one to do it. I didn't even have to tell him I let you through the Gate. He already knew and had let you and Faolan get to and from the Gate safely," he answered. "Whenever I bring you up, he tells me you won your freedom and to leave it at that."

"I don't feel free," I whispered. "I feel trapped, and those who hold the key won't tell me a damn thing."

"Perdi, do you trust me?" he asked.

I laughed. "Every time someone asks me that, they kick my world out from under me," I answered, and his silence forced me to give him an honest answer. "Yes."

"You're not asking me the right questions of those who are bound not to speak."

"What do you mean?" I scowled at his vagueness.

"As Solas' Commander, I cannot tell you his secrets. I'd choose death and torture before I sold him out to anyone, even you, little Crow. As you know, I don't share your secrets with him, and I don't share his with you. But my oath to you demands that I answer any question where the outcome could harm you." He winked. "Those who want to tell you will, if given a way around what stops them."

"And?" I asked and laughed. "Do we play twenty questions now?"

"Now you're catching on. If the answer could help keep you from harm, I can speak freely and suffer no consequence. I'm just not able to volunteer information."

"Why did Solas let me leave?" I asked.

"Love, I suppose."

"Love?" I laughed. "I was not expecting such an interesting answer from you about Solas."

"I find it more interesting where you ended up, where Solas led you," he replied. "Don't you?"

"Solas told me this was the only place he hadn't invaded," I replied. "He basically packed my bags and pointed me in this direction. Hell, the day I left, I found winter mittens in my bag, and I don't even own a pair."

"Did you ever stop and ask yourself why here? Why *this* court?" he asked. "When Solas couldn't answer, he sent you to someone who wouldn't stop you from getting what you wish to know, to someone whose mind is much weaker than his, to get the truth. He sent you to find answers, to bring this to an end. Who in all of Elphame holds the truth of us all?"

I nodded, but my mind struggled to keep up with the movement. I put a hand to my forehead and tried to focus through the wave of dizziness. The Horn, which had lived in the background of my mind, was now an ear-splitting pitch with very little respite between blasts. "I was in Faolan's mind last night. I don't know what he's done, but I know Solene is behind his decisions. I could see flashes of her lashing him, but I don't know why. He's scared to death of her."

"It's the same reason she's trying to control Solas. Think of where she'll least expect an attack and what you need to do to stop her. You're in the only place that holds those answers. You must put yourself five steps ahead of her, with the last step, her ending." Zephyr stepped forward when I swayed and touched my elbow to steady me. "What's wrong? You feel off."

"It's...Horn...Gate..." I tripped over the words in my mouth. I squeezed my eyes closed and tried to shake off the vertigo. The world tilted on its side and took my brain with it. The Horn blew a pitch higher and higher, and I couldn't think beyond the piercing pain.

My legs faltered, and I grabbed on to Zephyr. As my grip fell away, he wrapped his arms around me and pulled his shadows tighter around us both. I couldn't breathe. I couldn't think. I crumpled to my knees in his arms and screamed. My body ached as if I had been shot with fiery arrows, one after the other. I burned and cramped and twisted. Everywhere he touched me, it hurt. My skin felt raw, like being in hot water for too long.

I couldn't string a sentence together enough to tell Zephyr what was happening. I dug my nails into his arms and screamed. Flashes of brilliant white light flooded my vision—dark to light, dark to light. I couldn't see Zephyr. I couldn't feel him. I couldn't feel anything beyond my pain.

"Breathe." Zephyr's voice whispered through the darkness. "It'll pass. Now would not be a good time to burn down the forest."

"Not me." I shook my head. It wasn't me. I wasn't doing this. I twisted into a ball and screamed with each breath. I couldn't do anything more than yell out in pain. I couldn't lie there and let it pass. I told myself to let it come and roll back out. But my body didn't care for what my mind knew, so it twisted under its power. With each lungful of air, I ate down the shattered force of the Gate. It filled me and ate me back with as much intensity. It was burning a hole through my middle. The fire I had kept deep within was blazing, and I had nothing within me to stop it. I couldn't control it. It wasn't mine to hold.

"Die... I'm going... Death..." I screamed. "My spell..."

"What's happening?" Zephyr asked, shaking me in his arms. "Did you use your Malice to weave a spell? Is this a payment? It smells worse than when you have to pay for your magick."

"No...not mine... Gate." The words burned up my throat, and I screamed around them. "It's gone... The Gate is gone."

I felt my spell peel away from the Gate, and it felt every bit like my own flesh pulled from my meat. The spell I had used to close it was gone. The magick used to protect the mortal realm was stripped away like aged paint. I felt it shatter against my soul. Solas wasn't just damaging the Gate. He was shredding the Darkmore spells used on the Gate. It felt like he had sliced off a piece of my soul and set fire to it. The combination of an assault on the Gate and on my spell left me wishing death would come quickly. It wasn't often I willed death to my door, but today, my door was wide open, and I had set out tea and cakes.

"Fight, Perdi," Zephyr's voice broke. "Please, fight it."

"Can't..." I screamed again and twisted in the shadows. I couldn't control it. I wasn't strong enough to eat it down. There was too much energy for one Crow. All the power built up to break down the Gate hit me at once. Every drop it took to ruin the Gate had rained down on me, and I was drowning in it.

"Give it to me," Zephyr called out to me. But each time I tried, the power didn't want him. It didn't recognize him. I tried to push it out, but it didn't budge.

"Won't leave..." I screamed.

"Hold on." Zephyr pulled me into his arms. Wrapped in shadows, we left the forest of Tylwyth. I knew where we would land before I smelled the lavender gardens...the Dark Courts.

"Help her!" Zephyr's voice boomed in a room I couldn't see. "Goddamn it, Solas. You did this. Now you fix it."

"Perdi," Solas whispered through the darkness, and I rolled away from it, "breathe."

"No!" The burning pain racked my body and branded me with its hot touch.

*Traitor*, the pain whispered.

*Deserter*, it screamed.

*Witch*, it accused.

*Death dealer*, it screeched.

The pain took over my reasoning, leaving my brain to think only of my death at the hands of Solas. He would no doubt let me die. Whether by choice or by force, he wouldn't save me. I'd escaped but been brought back anyway. I had gotten away, fearing I'd die if I stayed, and been carried back into the waiting arms of the man tasked with ending my existence. This was how I'd die. This was how my people would die. My soul screamed with me as I realized I had failed in such a monumental way that we all would die. Was it a blessing or a curse to be the first to go?

"Perdi." Solas grabbed my hand and fought against my lashing out. He pulled me from Zephyr into his arms and held me until I could think. Wave after wave, a barrage of agony slammed down on my bones. "Give it to me. Give me the fire, as you have before."

"Gate..." I shook my head. The pain hadn't yet stolen that part deep inside my soul that didn't want to cause pain in others just to spare myself. And although the agony felt like someone held blistering fire against my flesh, I didn't want anyone else, including Solas, to suffer from it.

"I know. Give it to me. I can take it. Whatever has caused the fire, I can take it." He whispered. His cool touch against my chin made me relax in his arms. "This is going to hurt."

"Everything...hurts...in Elphame," I replied.

"I never meant to hurt you," he answered. "Now, though, is a different story. I plan to hurt you a great deal. Close your eyes, little Crow, and think of freedom. It's so close. You're almost there."

There were two types of screams. One came from the body, the mouth and lungs. The other from the heart and soul. I screamed from the pit of my soul as Solas' cold touch wrapped around my fire and squeezed it tightly. His cool touch was ice in my veins. He wasn't as gentle as he usually was, and I felt his nails claw away at my insides as he tore the flames apart. My mouth stayed open, frozen in pain, wordless, as his touch ripped through me. He took it all and didn't utter even a peep. And for the briefest of moments, I pitied him for not even flinching, for being so used to the pain that he hadn't recoiled from it in the least.

Lying soggy in his arms, I could finally breathe without feeling like I was gulping down hot coals. The fire inside me left, replaced by the cold touch you could only find in the darkest pits.

My Malice slinked in and out of me, touching Solas as it had in the past. With it, she carried bits of his soul — not for keeps, but to know. I could feel what he felt in this moment, hidden behind the pain he ate from me. Although I sensed love within him, I also sensed so much rage that it stole my breath away, and I screamed again. It was a furious fire of anger and hatred that rivaled mine and Zephyr's. Solas pushed my Malice out and shut that door in his mind. He had allowed me a glimpse, but that would be all I'd get.

"Do not venture where you'd not like to be trapped," Solas whispered. "My head is not a place you'd want to stay for too long, little Crow. Not even I like it in there."

"Why?" I finally asked him. "Why are you doing this? Won't this make things worse?"

"Why help you?" he asked, and I nodded. "There isn't a power alive that could stop me from helping you. I never wanted this for you — not now, not ever. I didn't want to involve you. I tried to get you away from here, from all of this. But you were too stubborn and held on until the bitter end."

"The Gate, my people..." I whispered. I knew that was the cause of my pain. It was all too familiar, only worse than anything ever before. "Why did you destroy the Gate?"

"Your mask is slipping, little Crow." He leaned into my ear as he passed me back to Zephyr. "The Gate, that was not me. I fulfilled my oath and rebuilt the Gate, but it was not me who destroyed it. No oath could force me to sentence your people to the death that's coming. You cannot save them here. You cannot save any of us if you're here and not seeking the end of *her*."

"How do I end her?" I was gone from Solas before I could get an answer.

"You won't find those answers from anyone's lips," Zephyr whispered through the darkness. "But here, you will find what others cannot say."

Zephyr returned us to the forest and sat with me, wrapped in the shadows. We sat silently until my legs and arms worked of their own accord. Zephyr could sit quietly for days, watching, listening and enjoying not having to be anything more than part of a world that wasn't asking something of him.

"You cannot kill Solas, no matter what." Zephyr finally spoke. "I can't let that happen, no matter your reason. Please do not make me get between you both, because you'll need to kill me to get to him."

"Do not come for Faolan—at least, not yet. I need him alive more than you need to kill him," I replied. But it wasn't out of love that I said those words. Faolan held truths that I needed. I needed to know how to stop Solene or all would be lost. For that, I'd play the game and protect the one person who probably didn't deserve my protection.

"I cannot agree to those terms," he answered.

"Then all there will be is death, and we'll be the only ones left alive." I sighed. "I won't kill Solas, no matter what, no matter the cost. But you won't kill Faolan until

I get what I need from him and his court. Neither fall at our hands, or there is no deal."

Zephyr stared at me longer than was comfortable. Whatever he saw in me, he nodded. "I will agree for as long as there is peace between his court and mine. When that peace fades, I will come, and you, little Crow, *will* not and *cannot* stop me."

"Agreed," I answered.

"And so shall we make this oath," he finally said.

"And so shall the oath be written in our blood," I agreed, but I knew Zephyr would find a way, just as I would, to get out of the oath. He wouldn't make one, not even with me, unless it served some bigger picture where Zephyr won in the end.

"The Gate is gone." He said what I already knew but didn't want to face.

"Protect my people, Zeph." My chin quivered as I spoke. "Please. I can't do it alone. Please help me. I'm begging you, help me."

He leaned into my ear. "No one will step foot through that Gate until the war is over. After that, Perdi, I won't make you promises I can't keep. But rest assured, little Crow, neither Solas nor I will let you stand alone."

"Thank you."

"Faolan is here," Zephyr hugged me against his chest. "He has Oisin with him."

"Has Oisin tried to invade your darkness yet?" I joked.

"Of course. He got a little too close and touched that which he does not understand. His hands are probably hairless now." Zephyr laughed softly. "But he wouldn't be the Commander of an Unseelie Court if he wasn't plotting an invasion and testing every power around him."

"Faolan is going to be mad," I grumbled.

"No. You won't find a lot of anger in Faolan, especially not with you. His childhood gave him the skill to swallow his temper. Anything else, and he wouldn't have made it to adulthood. I may fear for your life here, but it wouldn't be at Faolan's hand."

"I always seem to find and draw out the absolute worst in others. If I die, I suspect Faolan will play a part in it." I pulled back from Zephyr.

"If you die, he will soon follow. That, little Crow, is a promise." He answered and kissed my forehead. "Two days, Perdi, then Solas invades. You have until dawn, two days from now."

"Thank you," I answered, then tilted my head. "Why two days?"

"There are things we all must do, including you," he answered. "If you're going to find your truths, you have two days before I strike Faolan down with the vengeance he deserves. You have no idea how much joy it will give me, to wring the life from his body. So, if you are going to pick through his brain, I suggest you make it quick. Once the war begins and the truce is gone, no oath will keep me from him. You know he will not step off that battlefield should things not go as planned."

I nodded. "Zephyr, you said you'd answer my questions if it meant I would stay out of harm?" I asked, and he nodded. "Then tell me about the Gate? Who brought it down?"

Zephyr smiled and tapped his nose. "You're catching on, and you already know the answer to that question."

"Did you know the Gate would come down today?"
I asked.

"No, I didn't. I knew eventually it would fall, as did
you. But I felt something off. It is why I came to you."

"I felt it last night when I was in Faolan's library."

He smiled again. "No. That was me."

"Why?" I asked.

"Because of our oath, I'm forced to intervene to keep
you from harm."

"How would me and Faolan lying together bring me
harm?" I asked.

"That is a silly question, little Crow."

"Are you going to answer it?" I asked.

"How do you think things would go if you bound
yourself tighter to a man who is only a puppet? More
importantly, how would you have felt after if you had
done that which you did not want to do wholly?"

I nodded. "You're right. It's the reason I stopped."

"Every question you have resting on the tip of your
tongue leads to one common thread."

"Solene," I answered.

He raised his eyebrows but didn't answer out loud.
He couldn't—just like Solas could never answer any
question that would lead back to her.

"Are you oathed to her in some way?" I asked, and
he smiled. "Can she force you to kill me?"

"Not the same oath all others have with her. All Finis
and Aos Si were oathed to protect the original court.
And no, she can't force me to kill you—not because of
my oath with you but simply because she's not strong
enough to make me kill for her. But she can force me to
protect her secrets."

I signed with relief. That was one less monster hunting me down when this came to an end. "What does she have to do with Faolan?"

"As I said, you should be as interested as I am in finding out how you ended up here, why Solas picked this place for you to find your answers. What does Faolan have that no one else has? Once you find that out, you'll know all we know," he answered. "One last question, Perdi. Solas is calling me home. He isn't happy that I dragged you there. It puts him in the same position I'm in, between a war and a little Crow."

I opened my mouth to ask what I needed to do before the war, how I'd find out the truth of why I was in Unseelie territory, but I knew I'd figure that out on my own.

"Was Solas going to kill me? Would he have really done it?" I asked. "He may not have wanted to, but we all must do things we don't want to save the rest. Sacrifice the one for the many."

He rolled his eyes. "You wasted a question on that?"

"If I'm to find the truth, I need to know if it's worth the risk. I won't save a man who would let me die to save himself."

"Did you ever see me guarding your every movement? I am oathed to protect you from harm, and the only time you've ever seen me checking in on you is now. He wouldn't kill you, even if you deserved it."

"You were always checking in on me," I countered.

"No, Perdi. I was visiting a lonely friend. I was spending time with someone I cared deeply for — not to protect you, but to love you."

"But you came once to protect me." I thought back to that day in the dining room, when Zephyr stood between Solas and me.

"Oh, foolish little Crow." He laughed. "Wrong. I came to protect *him* from *you*. Remember, you're a Soul-Eater. He is just a king. You were scared enough to eat his entire world in one gulp. I could feel it, as could Solas. He dared you to take your best shot. He kept pushing in hopes you would do it. He was cruel in hopes you would be just as cruel. Only with his death could he save you from all of this. He thought that the rest of this wouldn't play out if he were dead. Had I not come, you'd have eaten my king. And how could I show my face at court again if I let a fledgling Soul-Eater eat my king? I couldn't be bested by a little Crow and still have my pride, could I?"

"I'm pretty sure I could take you." I smiled.

"You're a dirty fighter." He joked in return. "Little Crow, get your answers then come home. You are our home, and we're getting awfully homesick without you. Spending my days with only Solas is growing old."

I thought for a moment, rolled his words around in my head and returned to the same thoughts over and over. Each time I whispered them, my gut told me it was the purest truth I'd ever find in a land of lies. "Zeph, I need you to really listen to me now. When we have no moves left and we are at the end, one pissed-off Soul-Eater is bad, but two would mean certain death."

He grinned ear to ear and nodded. "Find a way, Perdi, and I will stand at your side."

The shadows faded into the forest, along with the scent of my pain and fear. My time of peace and quiet was up, curled into Zephyr and the smell of home. I turned my head to find Faolan waiting for me with Oisin. Zephyr walked me to the arms of Faolan. Neither of them exchanged a single word, but the look on Zephyr's face said more than enough. I scooted to my feet as fast as I was handed over. Zephyr was gone in a mist of inky darkness, swallowed by the shadows that rolled along the trees and shrubs.

Faolan smiled. He looked relieved, like he had held his breath the entire time I had been gone. He held my face and looked me over for injury. I was covered in blood, crusted from my nose and ears, and dribbles had stained lines from my mouth.

"Are you okay?" he finally asked, as if scared of the answer.

"I am," I answered. I left out the *now* part. I would have died without Solas.

"We all felt the Gate fall. I came for you as soon as I felt it, but you were gone. Nix said Zephyr would have you, that you're tied to him."

"That's a long story." I stopped and looked at Oisin. "Don't you have somewhere else you should be?"

He smiled. "Nope. War will be here any day. I can't leave Faolan's side until the war is over."

"Dawn, two days from now. You have until then," I answered.

"And how would you know that?" Oisin asked, his eyes questioning me with the weight of his entire army.

"Zephyr told me."

"Just how deep is this tie you have to him?" Oisin asked.

"Don't." Faolan's voice was stern. Oisin had overstepped. "Perdi doesn't answer to you."

My spine went rigid. "Who is it that I answer to, then? You?"

"Yourself, Perdi. I don't own you," Faolan answered. "I'm worried and would rather you not go into enemy territory, but I can't stop you. I *won't* stop you. You will make your own choices, and I know those decisions need to be made for reasons we can't say out loud."

"Solas isn't the enemy here, and I think we both know that," I answered and lifted my hand when Oisin let out a shocked gasp. "I think he, like the rest of us, is caught between his freedom and a fate decided by others. I don't think this war is of his making, and if it is, it's not for the reasons we think."

"What the hell does that even mean?" Oisin asked. "Will there be a war or not?"

"Calm down, warmonger. There will be a war. But also know, you won't be fighting the real enemy on that battlefield," I answered and waited for a reaction from Faolan. I saw nothing on his face. He knew the truth of the war but held it for himself. From the look of confusion Oisin had, he hadn't been told the truth, either. What dangerous games did kings play when they held their cards away from their closest advisers. I wanted to shake the stupid from Faolan but thought that well ran deeper than I had time for.

"Why would Zephyr tell you this? What does he get out of it?" Oisin asked. "And before anyone climbs up on some high horse, understand this. I can't protect my people without the truth, and I'm not going to shut it down because it's personal."

Before Faolan could answer, I did. "I agree, Oisin. The truth is the only thing that will save any of us."

"You agree?" He was surprised.

"I do. But would you mind if I changed my clothes first? It's a very long story, and I'm covered in my own blood and vomit," I answered.

"I'll see you for dinner, then," Oisin answered and left me with Faolan.

"I'm sorry I left without saying a word," I finally said to Faolan as we made our way back into Tylwyth. "I'm not a traitor, if that's what you're thinking. I mean, yes, I went into *your* enemy's territory, but not because I'm selling you out or anything like that."

"I wouldn't ever wonder those things about you. Oisin? That's his job. He suspects everyone, including himself. He wouldn't be the best if he didn't ask the questions none of us are willing to ask," Faolan replied. "I know Zephyr comes here, and I also know that he is your friend, regardless of who his king is. He is in the same position all our people are in, fighting a war they played no role in creating. They follow their king. That is their duty, even when they'd rather not."

"That is an interesting way to put it, fighting a war they played no role in creating. Did you play a role?" I asked.

Faolan raised his brows. "That's a hard question to answer. I knew, just as you did, this was coming and the reasons why — which is the reason you are here, is it not? To find your truths?" I nodded, and he shook his head when I tried to answer. "Your thoughts are better left unsaid on that matter. Some things are better left in the dark. I cannot speak of what I don't know for certain to those who will ask."

I thought about what Zephyr had said, how people would talk if you asked the right questions. "Are you hiding something from me?"

"Yes," Faolan answered and smiled.

"Am I safe here?" I asked.

"Until the war is over, yes."

"Does *she* know I'm here?"

He nodded. "But she does not know why."

"Are you going to tell her?"

"No. No oath could force me to sell you out twice. But I would caution you to hurry along your scheming before the war comes to a final boil. I cannot help you, but I will not hinder you."

"The Gate is down. Will you invade the mortal lands?"

"No, and no oath will force me to."

"Will you protect my people?"

"I will do what I can, but you need to know, the best I can do is not invade. I can't go there and protect them, not from *her*."

I nodded. At least I got a little truth out of Faolan. "Do you know how to stop her?"

He flinched at the question. I knew he couldn't tell me. "I can't answer that question, but you're on the right path. I've given you the tools you need but can't do much more than that when it comes to her."

"How come no one can tell me how to stop her?"

"The same reason Oisin would never tell you the quickest way to kill me. Oaths upon oaths protect thrones. Without them, we'd never have a king long enough to remember their name."

I sighed and followed Faolan back to his glittery kingdom. The riddles and puzzles were frustrating, but I had gotten more truth today by simply asking than I had by trying to play by their rules.

# Chapter Seven

The small table was uncomfortable, like dining with the dead, and no one wanted to point out the rotting body parts on the table. Dinner came and went, none of us touching much on our plates. Oisin shifted in his seat. He wanted to start the interrogation, but one look from Faolan at the start of the evening had stanched Oisin's plans to roll me on a spit over a fire until I spilled all the secrets he thought I had.

"It feels like decades have passed since I first stepped foot in Elphame." I finally broke the awkward small talk with the reason we were all together.

"I have walked this realm for over seven hundred years." Oisin looked happy not to talk about pointless things and joined me. "But this last year has felt like eons all slammed together. And these last few weeks have aged me unlike any battle could."

"This last year has aged my soul in ways I can't even put into words. It's all a blur. But I remember my first day like I just stepped out of it." I heaved a sigh like it was stuck in my chest, right next to the regrets I carried around with me.

"Everyone remembers their first day here," Oisin added, and I nodded.

"On my first night here, I was lashed until I could feel it against my bones. That was my first taste of how time could stand still and age you all at once." I risked a glance at Faolan, but he was staring down at the table, reliving that night with me. He looked guilty, but he hadn't been the one holding the lash. I didn't forgive him for the part he'd played in my coming here, the lies, but I didn't blame him for what had happened once I got here. I had, at one time, because it was easier to put a face and name to my anger and hurt...but not anymore. "They put me in the dungeon after. Although I was only down there for five days, time moved differently. Every minute stretched to impossible lengths. If it weren't for Orrian, I'd have died of infection."

"The Golden Court dungeon?" Oisin asked and cringed at the thought. "I don't think I'd have made it down there. I've heard stories. I don't think I'm that strong. I'd rather move into the caves of Tylwyth and be hunted by that which haunts those hills, Oberon and his people."

"Be thankful your knowledge is second-hand," I replied. "Even though I'd do anything not to go back there, my experience doesn't compare to the depravity within those cells. That is what haunts me—not what was done to me, rather, what I heard happening to others."

"Don't," Faolan whispered. His voice shook. "Oisin doesn't get to have your truths just because he wants them. You don't need to talk about this."

"Yes, I do. That dungeon is where my story begins, not in Whitwick. The mortal realm is where I come from, but I became who I am today in those bloody cells of the Golden Court. I have so many regrets, but the dungeon isn't one of them," I answered. "On my first day in the Golden Court, while sitting in the bath, I saw the shadows. And when I was down in the dungeon, the shadows tried to help me. They were pieces of Zephyr. As you've seen, Faolan, they're not to be trifled with."

"Did you piss off Zephyr's shadows?" Oisin asked Faolan, and he nodded uncomfortably.

"They've been protective of me since day one. They, like me, were prisoners. From my very first night in the Golden Court, his shadows followed me and did what they could to protect me. They helped and loved me. They kept me from going insane and held my soul together when I couldn't. They were there when I was alone and scared and didn't know how to survive in a world not meant for mortals. And they never asked for anything in return. They never tried to bargain or force me into oaths. They never once asked me to free them or Zephyr. They simply wanted to help me. I wasn't scared of them. I think I was the only one who never feared them." I smiled at the memory, one of the very few good memories I had of that court. "Then, I found Zephyr locked away. When I released him, I unleashed hell on that court. I did it and asked nothing for myself, only that he and his shadows save as many as they could during their escape. And since that day, Zephyr has always been there. He's never that far away.

"You all may not understand this, but he was the only friend I had here. Sure, I had Nix and Orrian and, for a time, Elswyth. Nix and Orrian would eat their way through a court to get to me, but Zephyr is the only one who would breach the treaties, oaths and things that bind kings and kingdoms because I am the only real friend that he's had. He would kill everyone, every soul, to save me. To this day, with all due respect, he is the only one who will risk everything for me and wouldn't care for the consequences. Everyone else has a court of people to protect. Zephyr only has me. He truly would burn this world down to get to me."

"You are friends with the enemy," Oisin blurted out, and Faolan growled his irritation with Oisin's comment.

"He's not *my* enemy. He's *yours*," I countered. "Zephyr is my friend, and we've both been pushed into opposite corners. I understand you see him differently, Oisin, but he is someone I trust and care about."

"And if he comes for our people, or me or Faolan, where are your loyalties?" Oisin asked. "With your friend?"

I shook my head. "All truth here, Oisin. Zephyr doesn't kill for pleasure. He does it because he has no choice and sees no other options. I hate to say this, but I wouldn't stand between him and you or him and Faolan. If he came for you, you'd have deserved it, and I'm not about to die trying to stop fate from collecting her dues. But for your people, I would kill him if he came for them. It would hurt, but I would take his life. No amount of love for anyone could keep me from doing what is right. I do not follow anyone blindly — not you, not Faolan, no one. But know this... If I did nothing to protect you, if I didn't even try to talk him down, it would be because letting you die was the right thing to do."

"Cold," Oisin muttered.

"No, it's just the truth," I answered. "Right now, Zephyr and I are at a stalemate, an impasse. If he comes for Faolan, I'll stop him. If I try for Solas, Zephyr will stop me. Until the battle, there is an oath between us."

"You oathed yourself to the enemy?" Oisin asked, surprised.

I glared. His comment was weak-minded and hateful. "I oathed the strongest power in all of Elphame from ending Faolan."

"He is not the strongest power in all of Elphame. Solas' sister is," Oisin countered, and Faolan's face paled. Faolan cleared his throat, and Oisin dropped it. But I didn't miss it, and I was all the more curious.

"She is powerful, I'd agree. But I oathed the only one in this entire realm who would stand against her with me."

Faolan's eyes darted to me. He understood what I meant. At the end of this war, two Soul-Eaters would do what they could to stop Solene. Win or lose, Zephyr would stand and fall with me.

"And in return, he oathed the strongest person in the Unseelie Court from ending Solas and this bloody war," Oisin's voice rumbled like a growl. "You. He bound your hands."

"No, I'm not the strongest. I cannot kill Solas and live," I countered, and Oisin disagreed. "I'm not selling myself short. I know who I am and where my strengths lie. Killing doesn't come as easily to me as it does to Solas. I will flinch. I will hesitate. Killing him would not be easy for me. I love him far too much for it to be that simple. I'd doubt his threat, and he'd kill me a dozen times over in that gap between my uncertainty and my love."

"Solas is and always will be the nightmare of Elphame," Oisin replied. "Do not hesitate, Perdi, whatever you do. He deserves the death he will have."

"He deserves the same fate all of us here at the table have earned. But I will not be the one to dole out that punishment. I think that will be hand-delivered by someone else," I answered.

"Such is the way of this fucking place." Oisin groaned.

"As much as you hate him, Oisin, he helped me survive my Taking. He kept me alive, kept me fighting and protected me when everyone else came to his door for my head. You can hate him all the way to your grave, and you probably have thousands of reasons for that hate. But I don't. I can't, and I won't." I felt the first pull of a smile at the thought of the man I had grown to love. "Solas said he didn't break the Gate, and I believe him. I also believe he played a part in it, but not as willingly as I had originally suspected. I think, like many others, decisions were made for him."

"You were with Solas?" Faolan asked, surprised. "I had assumed you were with Zephyr."

"I was. Zephyr took me to Solas when he thought I was dying," I answered.

"Why would you believe the word of Solas? He isn't known for being truthful," Oisin asked and took the heat from Faolan's glare.

"Your hate blinds you." Faolan's voice was harsh, and his heavy stare was all for Oisin. "It keeps you from seeing the strengths in others, which will undoubtedly be your downfall. If you cannot see him for the man he is, rather than the monster you want him to be, you miss the parts of him that make him the warrior he is."

"Whatever his strengths, the truth wouldn't be high on that list, Faolan," Oisin countered.

I shook my head, as a parent would. "I disagree with you, Oisin. Solas is sly as a fox. He can talk circles around the truth. He's even blatantly withheld the truth, but he's never outright lied to me. As for Zephyr, he's trying to protect his king, but he wouldn't lie about this, not to me."

Oisin leaned forward. "I'm curious as to how you and the Soul-Eater of Elphame have become so close."

"The journey I took to get where I am, this moment, is not for you. It's not for anyone. That story and that pain are mine to carry," I replied. "You all watched me close the Gate and know that I paid with my life. I'm linked to it as a Darkmore. Our spells, my spells, keep the Gate in the back of my mind. Today, when the Gate came down, I was talking to Zephyr. When my life began to leak out of me, Zephyr tried to help me, but I was dying. He brought me to Solas because..." I groaned. I was nervous to say I needed Solas. Building my web of lies was a deadly game of balancing on those wires.

"For help." Faolan finished my sentence. He let go of any remaining anger I had just seen him direct at Oisin. Zephyr was right. Faolan didn't have the same endless pool of rage that I had, or Zephyr or hell, even Nix had. "It's okay to need help and to go to those you trust to save you. It doesn't matter how I feel about him. It only matters what *you* feel."

I wanted to tell them I was Finis, a Soul-Eater. It would have explained so much more than words could ever do, but my gut told me to keep my mouth shut. He could suspect all he wanted, but saying the words out loud gave them power. Soul-Eaters had been hunted to near extinction. There were two left in all of Elphame, and I wouldn't be able to stop an army that decided to come for me when I was alone. Hearing Zephyr's words rattle around in my brain told me to side with caution. Faolan himself had told me that my truths weren't safe with him.

"I am a Darkmore Witch, filled to the brim with Malice, Magick. It has certain cravings that I can't sate. The payments are too great to even try. I used it to escape the Golden Courts and almost paid with my life for that freedom. No spell is free. That's where Zephyr comes in. He has one of my pearls. It's a drop of my soul. I once traded it to him to get me to safety. And when I had closed the Gate, it killed me."

"Malice... That's a deadly magick to have," Oisin replied. The look on his face said he was still hesitant to believe me. "What kind of dark magick brings back the dead?"

"The kind of magick that saved my life. Dark or light, I don't care. I'm alive because he saved me," I answered. "Do not comment on things you know nothing about, Oisin. I'm trying to explain, and you won't shut your mouth or stop with your groaning long enough for me to speak. Perhaps you should be elsewhere if you're not here to listen."

Faolan glanced at Oisin, who then lifted his hands in surrender. "Sorry... I just have so many questions. It's my job to ask questions."

"Not tonight. You're not going to get the answers you want from me. If you're so curious, go ask Zephyr yourself," I replied.

His face paled at the idea. He shook his head like a smart man and motioned for me to continue. "Sorry. I'll stop."

I nodded. I could appreciate the curiosity, but Oisin wouldn't get Zephyr's secrets from me. Like Zephyr with Solas' truths, I'd pick pain and torture over selling him out. "It took everything I had, all of my Malice, to close the Gate, including my life. It was painfully brutal and beautiful all at once. And when my heart finally gave out, exhausted of energy and the will to beat, Zephyr saved me, as only he could."

"When the Gate shattered today, did it kill you?" Faolan asked, his eyes wide.

"Close. I was with Zeph, though, when it happened. Had I been alone, I think it would have killed me," I answered. "As I said, I am a Darkmore Witch. My Malice pools in my stomach like fire. I can usually control it. I've learned ways to let it out safely. But when I'm threatened or can't control my emotions, it eats its way out, literally. I can't breathe. I can't move of my own volition. I just burn until there's nothing left to burn. When I felt the Gate fall, my entire body was ablaze from the inside out, with more energy than my soul could handle. I truly was certain I would die. It didn't just feel like I was dying, in the sense that the pain was too great for me to handle. I could taste death on my tongue, mixed with blood. Zephyr did the only thing he thought he could do. He took me to Solas."

"Why to him?" Faolan asked.

"Solas' touch is cold inside my burning pit. He's able to stop the burn. He can eat all of my pain and calm my fires."

"And Solas helped you freely?" Oisin asked, no accusation, just curiosity.

I nodded. "Solas doesn't hate me any more than he wants to watch me burn. He cooled the fire within me with his touch."

"If that is all you needed." Faolan grinned and touched my hand. "We are Winter Court, after all."

His magick was like snowflakes falling on my skin. I could feel where each one landed and shivered against it. I closed my eyes and invited the snowstorm into my core, like standing on the banks of an ocean, snow drifting off the frigid water and washing over me. It wasn't the storm I had experienced before. It was a calm Christmas morning around a fire. It was family and hope and memories you treasure.

"I didn't know your magick could feel this calm." I finally spoke. I opened my eyes to Faolan's ice-blue eyes and tinted blue lips. "You feel like a snowfall on Christmas day, where everything you need is already here."

"Each court calls their own power. As the Summer Court calls warmth and fire, I call Winter — ice, frost, wind," he answered. "When I just touched you with my magick, I could feel the heat in your core. As you said, my touch is cold, yours is like standing too close to a fire and I'm covered in propellent. If ever you were a court, I wouldn't know where you came from. I wouldn't know your line."

"You should feel it when it's out of control," I answered and avoided the hanging question. I was Wildfey. I was a Soul-Eater. We were a court of our own. If he stepped any closer to the fire, I'd burn him to ash to protect my secrets.

"That is how Zephyr is coming? Because he once had a piece of your soul?" Oisin asked.

"He still has a piece of my soul. I gave him another, for protection, weeks ago. But to answer your question, yes, he can always feel me and find me, no matter where I am." I left out the part about his shadows, my ability to call them and the fact that it wouldn't matter how many of my pearls I stuffed into him. I was Finis, and I called to him from across worlds. "When I'm scared or in danger, he comes. And I don't think there is anything that could stop him from getting to me."

I didn't know why I needed them to know that Zephyr would always find me, but I felt safer knowing they were aware. I had withheld so much from them about myself — those I loved, the Horn — and although I felt guilty for lying, I also felt smarter for it. I kept Zephyr's secrets to myself simply because they weren't my story to tell. They already knew more about him than I had thought, and it made me uneasy. The feeling of restlessness was back and had settled in my chest like a sickness.

Oisin leaned in. "Zephyr is not the most powerful here, Perdi. I don't think you should count on him to always reach you."

Although Faolan flinched at the hint of Solene, I didn't. I leaned in to meet Oisin. "Do not doubt Zephyr or Solas' determination that I come out unscathed. And they are very much not alone in their stand. Things, Oisin, are not as they seem, and the sooner you realize it, the longer you'll live."

Oisin nodded suspiciously but finally dropped it. "We'll talk ourselves into riddles. Let's move on."

"Zephyr has said two days. Why two days?" Faolan asked.

I shrugged. "I don't know. When I asked him, he said there were things we still needed to do and included me in that."

"Do you have any idea?" Faolan asked.

I shook my head and rubbed my chest. "No, but I plan to find out."

I watched worry flash across his face for the briefest of moments. It made me want to splay his mind open to the birds and take what I wanted. Instead, I let it go. I understood the fear he carried. Wearing his mask was no different than me wearing my own. I glanced around at the tables full of his people and understood why he did what he did, for it was the same reason I sat in enemy territory. We each were saving those we loved, those who counted on us to become monsters.

# Chapter Eight

Time was running out on a clock I couldn't see. The Horn was quiet once again. The warning had gone unnoticed by everyone but me, and what would come next could no longer be avoided. Soon, every soul in Elphame would wage war upon their neighbors, and all I could think of was how badly I didn't want to be there. I didn't want to see it. I didn't want to hear it. I didn't want to be responsible for it. I couldn't bring myself to leave my tent or let another in. We were all pawns, and those who knew it couldn't do a thing about it. We moved around on a board that wasn't our own. It wasn't fair, and as childish a thought as that was, I was angry for the unjustness of it all. I was hurting that I was a world away from my home, from Solas. The field that divided us felt like a realm between us.

I paced, I knelt, I curled into a ball and cried. I couldn't breathe and knew Zephyr wouldn't come to me now. He wouldn't leave Solas. Although I knew he'd feel my fear, my sadness, I was alone. I had to face this without my family, and it terrified me. I was not born to war. I wasn't raised for battle. I was born to be a Crow, and this was no place for a scared little Crow. Sitting on the edge of war was not a place for born Crows. This was a place for warriors, and I very much did not feel like one.

Around my tent, the men were torn between fighting a war they didn't think they could win and fighting for a Crow who only brought death on her wings wherever she went. They whispered my name as if I were a disease on the lands, and the very mention of me would curse them to hell. There was talk of what would happen if they just killed me. Would the war stop? If they sacrificed the Crow, would the Gods finally smile down on them? As tempted as I was to scream that Solene wasn't a God, I swallowed my words. I felt like I was a child again, in the mortal realm, hearing the other parents whisper about killing all halflings to stave off another Taking. The fear and the hate all ate at me as if I had no value.

I could almost feel Zephyr's touch against my sadness, the pull within my stomach. He couldn't come, but he was there, even if it was through my pearl. But the longing for home was too much. I finally whispered to the shadows I knew were never that far away.

"Take me home…to the island."

Shadows peeled off the walls like paint and grabbed me before I could see them form around me. I was gone, faster than ever before, tucked into a familiar blanket of calm darkness. They had been waiting for this moment, for a call they could answer. As I had stood in my tent, I now stood on the grass with the warm sun on my face.

I turned in a circle and could have sworn I was back in Whitwick, in the lands behind my family home. My lungs filled with familiar smells and a sense of rightness, of home. The noise was finally gone. Gone were the swords and armor clashing. Gone was the mention of my name and the wish I had died at the hands of Aelfdene, a death that would have saved them all the trouble I now brought. I was finally calm once I cleared my lungs of war, replacing the air with flowers and fruits and ocean and Zephyr. It felt like every time Zephyr lifted me into his arms. The sun felt like every time Solas had tucked me against his body, warming my very soul. It wasn't just home. It was a place for souls to safely stretch and recover from a world that was harsh and brutal.

Here, at the birthplace of Soul-Eaters, a place that should be terrifying, was nothing but peace and freedom. There were no wars to prepare for. Just the sound of birds and water, surrounded by creeks and the ocean, and a million miles away from the gates of hell. It smelled of calm and the promise of safety. I knew I could stay and never return if I wanted to. No one would ever come and force me to the frontlines of death. No one but Zephyr would even know where to look for me, and he had been right. His home was a completely different world, frozen in a time when there had been peace. Here, where Zephyr had been born, I could be reborn, if I wanted, and not come out all twisted and cracked like before. Or, I could stay and never have to leave. I could pretend here, and nothing would chip away at the façade. I could be Perdi, and not a Crow, not a Soul-Eater. I could just live and not have to fight for each day. The chance of pure freedom made my eyes water.

I took in every sight, twirling in a slow circle. It was a treed world within an island. Around the edges, the trees were of every shape, size and type. Each held rich colors and textures that reminded me of Whitwick. In the middle, Zephyr's white house stood. It was small and everything I thought it would be for someone like him — one story, one deck, a chimney to the right, and fading red shutters for the windows. It was as simple as Zephyr was complicated. I walked a small path from the sandy beach and was thankful the gravel was just rock — no bones, no death to guide my way to his home — just lush grass, wildflowers, wild shrubs and stones. It was a path of welcome, not of warning or threat.

As I stepped inside, it reminded me of the cabins I had gone to with my father — everything you needed without the extra bits that collected dust. The smell of Zephyr rolled over me as I stepped inside. The living room looked lived in, with books on every subject he could get his hands on stacked in every spare space. Elphame history sat next to mortal, art next to the stars and the sky. Gardening leaned against war and baking butted up against the death rituals of lost civilizations — math and alchemy, magick and myths. It was like looking into his deepest secrets, the parts of him I didn't know — the Zephyr that I didn't think anyone knew. Here, in his cabin, he could be Zeph and not war spat from the bowels of hell. Here, he could be free. Even without seeing this island, I had always known there was a world hidden within him.

The walls were covered in paintings of the world as seen through his eyes. Some were old and looked like they had been there since the house was built. But some were new. Small sketches and watercolors of Solas and me, Nix and Orrian in a garden, pixies chasing a butterfly, Zephyr and me, his men at war... Glimpses of his memories, pieces he held dear.

There were two bedrooms in the back. The first was Zephyr's and held racks of leather and armor that sat close to a small mug of flowers, which I knew were from my garden behind Solas' manor. He had bits of me, Solas and Nix. Small pieces of us littered his bedroom like decoration. A glove belonging to Nix sat on his nightstand, a mug from Solas' house sat with flowers from my garden and a little hand-carved crow hung above his bed. His entire life, his life's purpose, could be found in the smallest details. On his dresser were plans for a garden and hut, something only a gnome could fit in. I now understood why my accusation of him killing Nix's line had stung so much. He cared deeply for Nix, and I had suspected him of slaying the people of someone he cared for. A small swirl of guilt sent me out of his bedroom.

The other bedroom was for guests who had never come or never been invited. But it was still clean, as if he had expected company any day. But the only guest he had ever expected was me. I knew it was arranged for a Crow, right down to the sheets I loved—white cotton, with tiny yellow buttercups stitched to the hem. I had a similar set in Whitwick, and they reminded me of Nix and his hunger for the small yellow flowers. Although the room was as plain as the rest of his home, it was also full in some way, with love and hope and wishes we all wanted to come true. The foot of the bed was the only place that wasn't perfect. The blanket was wrinkled as if he had sat there recently and hadn't straightened it back up. I wondered how often he had sat there, thinking of me, of war, of Solas, of how to protect those he loved more than life.

Out of the back window, I saw his garden and smiled. He had brought fresh vegetables to Solas' house before, but I had always assumed he'd bought them in one of the villages. I hadn't realized he grew them himself until now. But I should have had his tips when I had built my own death garden to needle Solas. Looking out over his yard, I couldn't help but picture him selecting his prized fruits and vegetables, spending hours burning daylight, trying to forget the demands of a world that feared his people. In the back of my mind, I could almost see him out there.

I stepped from the rear of the cabin. In Zephyr's small orchard, I picked berries and an apple and took a seat with a book under what looked similar to a peach tree but smelled more like strawberries. Nothing here smelled like the rest of Elphame. It was a mixture of every court, every smell and every energy I had passed through. From lavender to mint to the scent of berries I had picked from the Summer Court filled the air around me. The energy flowed naturally here, as if it were being pushed in with the wind, drawn back with the tide — with no struggle in the middle. There was no fight for more, no drain, just an even breeze of calm. I imagined all of Elphame had once been like this before wars ruined it, as they did everything else. Breathing it in somehow cleansed the bad memories I had of similar smells. I could see why this was his secret — a place untarnished like the rest of the realm. I'd have protected it as fiercely as he did, and I would, until my last day, however soon that might come.

I took my time reassuring my soul, grounding myself and focusing on putting my pieces back together. Being here, in a place so close to where I had come from, gave me the same sense of purpose it had given Zephyr. I understood, right down to my now lazy soul, why he returned home whenever the world pressed in on him and he struggled to find his way. When I could think and was no longer bombarded with the very anarchy that was Fae, I stepped back inside and left a note for Zephyr. He'd know I had come, but I was grateful for the invite and wanted to leave him with the same peace he had just given me. It wouldn't be much, but it would mean everything to him.

*Zeph,*
*There may not be room for greatness in Elphame, but you are as close to it as they will allow. I am a better person for having known you.*
*You have all my love, now and forever.*
*Little Crow*

I placed the letter on the kitchen table and left through the front door. I turned and slammed into the chest of a familiar scent and feeling.

"Solas," I whispered his name and forced myself to eat my smile. "What are you doing here?"

"I could ask you the same thing." He glanced around. We were not free from the ears of others, no matter what my eyes told me. They might not have been with him, but the holder of oaths didn't need to be near for them to be enforced. I didn't risk it. I couldn't. I pulled my mask on tight and hated that I had to.

"Zeph said no one comes here." My words shook from the hammering pulse in my throat.

Solas smiled. "I'm not *no one*, little Crow."

"That's not what I meant, and you know it."

He smiled. "What, pray tell, would *you* be doing here?"

"Zeph said... Well...because..." I chewed on my lip, and my words fell out nervously. But I had nothing to be worried about, not here. Zephyr had said I was safe on these lands, and I trusted him with my life. The wars of Fae would never reach his shores, although I was still cautious. The games could still be played, no matter where we stood. Rather than explain I was Finis, and this was my home, I'd keep my secrets from being carried in the air to Solene. "Zephyr said I could be here. It's my home, too. I'm going to be between homes shortly, so I thought I'd check out where I'd land if it all went to hell. That's what I'm doing here. He isn't around, if that's why you've come."

"Your home?" He looked at me, a quizzical smile on his lips.

"Yes. Mine and Zephyr's home," I answered. "Population, two...not three."

He smiled again, thoroughly amused. "I see. I wasn't aware."

"Now you are." My answer was short and clipped... and awkward.

"Good thing he gave me a key as well, not ten minutes ago," he answered and looked around. "I've never been here. Hell, I didn't even know about this place until this morning. I knew Finis were born somewhere, just not where. To be honest, I thought it would look like the pits of hell and less like...this, a peaceful cabin in the woods."

"If you've never been here, how did you get here?" I asked, then stepped into his path before he could move any farther up the stairs and into the house.

"He dropped me off," he answered.

"Zephyr!" I screamed. Solas stepped back with his hands up to show he hadn't come to hurt me. But I hadn't yelled out of fear. I was angry. And when Zephyr wouldn't come by the fifth time I called out his name, I tried for his shadows. But they, like him, weren't answering my calls. "Damn it."

"Are you...okay?" His voice was barely a whisper. I nodded. "I..."

Both of us breathed past the tension that flickered between us like static. I reached out on instinct to touch Solas. The urge to calm him was intense. My heart and soul wanted to fix him, to stop his hurting. But before I'd allow the contact, I dropped my hand. I knew if I touched him, my heart would break open, and I'd never be able to leave. I was already so close to falling apart. I couldn't risk it. He saw the pain on my face and stepped back. It wasn't out of cruelty. It was because he understood how close to the edge I was and did what he could not to push me over it.

"Are *you* okay?" I whispered back.

He nodded. His smile was pitiful, but he tried. "Do you need a lift? It doesn't look like Zephyr is answering your calls."

"No, thank you. I'm fine."

"Very well, but once I'm gone, you're stuck here until he returns. Is this where you want to be when the war begins?"

"No, it isn't. I don't have many options left to choose from. I'm at my final move, Solas. And what's left to play out is going to hurt something fierce." I hoped he understood. "I can't stand and watch men go to their deaths, and I can't go to the mortal realm and wait for this to bleed out into their world. As much as I want to go and help Whitwick, I can't, because it hurts and makes me sick."

"You get used to it," he replied.

"I've been told."

"If you're not leaving, do you want me to bring anything back to you? I could bring you something to eat. I can't imagine eating carrots all day would be satisfying. Perhaps some potatoes?" He huffed a laugh.

Standing this close to him, without touching him, hurt something deep inside. I couldn't breathe with him this close. All I could smell was home. I couldn't think beyond it. I stepped forward to push past him and froze. The hum of the Horn held me firm. I couldn't leave, not yet. I had come here for a reason and hadn't even known it until I had finally calmed down and let my soul relax in the safety of Zephyr's home.

"I can't leave, not yet. I'm not done here," I answered.

"As you wish."

He was gone in a wisp of darkness that dissipated like fog. I almost regretted not leaving with him. But this time, my anger and frustration were not why I was stranded. I had come looking for answers that Zephyr may not even know he had. Here, on the island, I let my Malice free. She scoured every inch of the land while I moved from one end of the house to the other. She returned empty-handed. This place was as it looked — Zephyr's freedom from the courts and the chaos. I leaned against the bookshelf and stared out over his life. Nothing stood out. There were no riddles to unwind, no puzzles to piece together. This was the only place in these cursed lands that didn't come with a game attached.

"Why tell me of this place?" I muttered for only my ears. "What's here that I can't find anywhere else? What do you have that no one else has? What truths, Zephyr, do you hold that no one else would have?"

I mulled it over and over. Zephyr could have told me of the island so I'd know I had a safe haven to go to, but I could call on him at any minute, and he'd come. Why tell me of a place that wouldn't make a difference in the end? If I failed, we'd all die, and this island wouldn't matter. Was this all for Solas and me to see each other? I doubted it. It had been torture on my soul to see him.

I stared, long and hard, at every piece of art, but saw nothing beyond fragments of his memory, his history. I glanced back at every book. It reminded me of Solas' library, with almost every book the same. My Malice had already dug through every page and found nothing. The answers were right in front of me, like a missing word on the tip of my tongue. I just didn't see them yet. But this house was part of the answer. I looked back at the books beside his couch, the ones I knew he had just touched. They had been explicitly placed as if to hint at the answers I was seeking — the written records of the mortal world, the entire past of Elphame. I paused but didn't risk the words out loud. I stood within the history of Zephyr.

"What does Faolan have that no one else has?" I asked out loud and almost staggered at the answer that rolled through my mind. He had the entire history of Elphame. And that was where I'd find what I was looking for. That was why Solas had sent me there. The end of this all was at the beginning, with Faolan. Faolan, too, had given me the answers without saying the words. They had both knowingly given me the tools.

*"All the records of Elphame are here. Family lines, treaties, births, pledges, titles, you name it. Everything you could ever wish to know about any family, line, magick, is held in here."*

I called for Zephyr again, and nothing. I called on the shadows until the veins in my neck threatened to burst if I kept at it. Solas had been right. This was not the place I wanted to be when the war started. I had things to do, and staying on this island was not one of them, although it was tempting. Here, I could ignore it all. But I knew that eventually, I'd have to face what my fear had left for dead in both realms. If I stayed, I'd sentence them all to die, and my life wasn't worth the death of countless innocents.

\* \* \* \*

I smoothed down my wet hair, pulled my conniving ways tighter to my chest and knocked on the door. Solas opened it and stared at me, surprised as I was that I was there. I tried for a smile but failed through chattering teeth.

"I'm sorry for just showing up. The shadows dropped me on your step. Before I could tell them it's the wrong place, they left and won't come back."

He looked outside and saw it wasn't raining, nor had it. "Did you just knock on the door?"

"Yes. That's the polite thing to do," I answered. "The shadows dumped me here, and I still can't reach Zeph. Do you know where he is?"

"He's on the battlefield, preparing," he answered and fought the smile forming. "What could possibly bring you, sopping wet, to the door of the man who is waging war against all of Elphame?"

"When is there not war, and when are you not in the middle of it all?" I asked.

"I could say the same thing about you, little Crow."

"What an uncomfortable truth that is." I turned to leave, then back around to face him and groaned. "Nix taught me some of the protocols for Elphame when wanting to cross over someone else's territory without dying. I'm too damn tired from swimming to run through your territory without asking if I can be here. Can I have safe passage? Please."

I watched him try not to laugh. "Swimming? Why were you swimming? No one swims the waters of Elphame."

"Yes, swimming. Zeph didn't come back, and the shadows didn't arrive until I had already gotten to the bloody shore."

"You swam back?" Now he laughed, which made me blush. "How was the water?"

"Cold and freaking scary. And I think I'm going to get an infection from whatever chewed on me." I sighed and showed him the small teeth marks on my arms. "I don't even want to look at my legs. Those bites were much bigger. Have you ever gone into the water? Holy hell, that was terrifying."

"No. I'm not that stupid. None of us are." Still laughing, he finally nodded. "Sure, I suppose you've earned safe passage. You don't look like you can cause much trouble in your current state."

"Thank you," I said and leaned against the entrance wall. My arms and legs thanked him as well. I wouldn't have gotten very far had I tried to run. I didn't have a single muscle that wasn't drained and feeling like jelly. Each movement was an effort.

"Do you want to rest first?" he asked.

"No, but thank you. I need to get back. I have some business to attend to. Thank you for the safe passage." I turned from the door. "I don't have much time. I'm on a clock."

"Aren't we all?" he asked. "Where are you going?"

I paused and turned back to him with a defeated sigh. "I thought you said I could have safe passage?"

"You won't make it on your own, Perdi. For one, my lands are crawling with creatures not even you have seen. It is the night before the war. You'd be a fool to think you could make it alone—even more stupid if you think you could go *anywhere* in Elphame, my lands or not, and not be running for your life. Secondly, you look like shit. You won't make it under your own steam. And I'm not kind enough to let you call Faolan to rescue you. If he were to step into my lands, for any reason, it would start the war long before he's ready, and he'd die at your feet."

"Then why even bother giving me safe passage?" I asked, annoyed.

"Because you asked for it," he replied, as if that were answer enough. "But you can't do it alone."

"Then make Zephyr come back and carry me. It's his fault I look and feel like this."

"That, little Crow, I can't do. He is busy," he replied, then stepped outside. "Let's go."

"Where? Are you putting me in jail?" I asked and started to panic. "I didn't break any laws. I knocked on your door and asked, and you said yes. Tell me if I did this wrong, and I'll correct it."

He laughed and shook his head. "I think you drank too much water on your way across, and it poisoned your brain. No, not to jail. To the border. I have granted you safe passage, which includes being safe from me…for now."

Solas set out, and I followed behind him. I struggled to lift my heavy feet and shuffled across the lawn. My feet dug up grass as they dragged. I was tired and grumpy…and hungry. Each movement irritated the wounds on my legs. He stopped not a dozen or so feet from his front door and waited for me. I tried to move faster, but I hadn't a drop of energy left.

"I feel like we've done this before." He laughed softly. "Every day with you is longer than the last."

"Sorry… My clothes weigh more than I do," I called out to him. "It feels like I collected all the sand in the sea and am carrying it in my pockets."

"I wouldn't mind if you wanted to take them off. You know, to speed yourself along."

"I'd rather walk alone and take my chances," I countered but smiled. When I got to him, he picked me up. When our bodies touched, I melted into his arms as if I had been made specifically for him to hold. "I don't need to be carried like a child."

"Are you sure about that? At the pace you're going, the war will be over before we even leave the yard."

"That wouldn't be such a bad thing."

"If I'm not there, it would be a very bad thing indeed, little Crow."

I rolled my eyes. "Oh, I'm sure Zephyr will slaughter thousands in your name. Don't you worry."

"That is not what I worry about," he replied.

"I suppose it's not the same, not being there to see what destruction has been caused by your hand."

"You know, this reminds me of the day we met — you dragging your feet, arguing with me, and making it really hard not to strangle you." Solas breezed through his territory. Even if I couldn't say it aloud, I knew he was right. I wouldn't have made it.

"What I wouldn't give for a knife," I replied.

"And like the first time, you won't win."

I shrugged. "Like my father used to say, it's never too late to get the job done right."

"Are you going to do this the entire way?" he asked.

"Most likely," I answered.

"This is exactly how I wanted to spend my evening, listening to you remind me of how vile I am."

"Come now, Solas. I'm not saying anything others aren't brave enough to say to your face. The only real difference is that when I say it, it hurts," I replied.

"Who needs friends when you have enemies," he muttered. Before I could point out that we both needed friends, he squeezed me tighter. I wasn't as good at pretending that I didn't care. I prayed I'd never become as good as he was. "No, Perdi. Right now, I need an enemy that will stand against us all."

"You know, you could have saved yourself the trouble of carrying me across your territory and called Zeph." I pulled my head back from his chest with a smile. "Since you won't, let me list everything I dislike. We can start with the bloody potatoes you mound for every meal and finish with your lies, both of which I've had to choke down for months."

"Although I've missed you in my arms, you can walk the rest of the way." He opened his grip and dropped me on the ground, jarring my bones and smashing my teeth together. "We're here, and this shit isn't worth the risk of carrying you through Winter territory."

"And here I thought there were no horses in Elphame." I smiled from the ground. "Who needs friends when I have enemies like you?"

"Call Zephyr. You're not safe in the Winter Court, either." Solas stared at me, and I got the message. I wasn't safe, no matter what I thought.

"I know." My voice was less than a whisper, but he still saw the hurt on my face. It matched his own. Before I could call, Zephyr's hand slid into view. "About time you came," I snapped at him.

"You rang?" He pulled me to my feet.

"Yeah, about ten hours ago."

"I was busy." He grinned.

"Get her out of here before I choke the life out of her, revive her, only to strangle her again!" Solas barked.

"Thanks for the lift," I called to his back as he walked away.

He turned and gave me the finger and a wink. "Anytime, little Crow...except for tomorrow. I have warmongering to do, and I'm booked solid. I'll see you soon." He walked away and said no more.

I turned to Zephyr. "Well, he certainly knows how to end a conversation."

Zephyr lifted me off the ground and started walking. "Alone for under an hour, and the man wants to kill you twice. That's not what I would call progress. Before, he only wanted to kill you once." He stopped and gagged, turning his face to the side and swallowed whatever threatened to come back up. "Oh my God, why do you smell like you just crawled out of a sewer?"

"I had to swim back. Thanks for that, by the way."

He started to laugh, just like Solas had. "Why would you swim? Why didn't you just come back with Solas?"

"Really? Did you really think sending him there would magically make things better?"

"Yes. It is the only place I knew he could be Solas, not the king. The only place in all of Elphame you could speak freely and not be seen or heard. And you squandered that precious time."

"I didn't know that last part," I answered and regretted wasting that time on the island.

"War cannot touch our home, Perdi. It's why I go there," he replied. "And you both wasted those moments playing games."

Zephyr tugged me through the shadows and into my empty tent. It was like no one had even noticed I was gone. He dropped me on the ground, just as Solas had.

"Bastard," I muttered. The word wasn't all for Zephyr, although he would have deserved it.

"I know, but you still love me," he answered.

I nodded. "I do, but I can love you and be angry with you at the same time."

"And you still love Solas, regardless of what you both say or threats you make out loud." I looked up at him and didn't reply. "The question is, do you love him enough to save him? Do you love him enough to risk your own life for him? To risk it all for him? Because that is what it'll take."

"Good night, Zeph."

"Tick-tock, little Crow. We will see each other tomorrow, and it will not be a good morning. I suggest you hurry up."

Zephyr was gone in a blink. I cleaned the grime from my body and let Orrian slather my wounds with salve.

When I told Nix what had happened, he wasn't impressed, but also wasn't angry. He understood and laughed at my taking a dip in the waters of Elphame, muttering how foolish I was.

# Chapter Nine

Time was up. I had to act now or die in the valley with the rest. I stood on the edge of Unseelie territory and watched as the battle to save the mortals began. It was not with swords that the first soul fell. Magick coursed through the lands and picked off those too weak to protect themselves. One by one, I watched men on both sides fall to their bloody knees and die before their faces touched the earth.

I could feel Zephyr and found him standing at Solas' side on the field. He was dressed to kill but stood perfectly still, waiting. Behind him, the Aos Si waited to be commanded. The Sluagh crawled on their bellies and glided in the clouds, waiting to be unleashed on those who fought against their king. The only court to not join Faolan had been the Autumn Court. King Parrish and his men were being slaughtered, on Solas' side, as we waited for the magick to run out, but that could take days. Until then, troop after troop would fight for an inch of ground — small victories in the grand scheme of things.

The Court of Less was covered in fresh blood and the last breaths of young men and women. The dead fell over the soggy earth like garish red flowers. It was both beautiful and brash, life and death meeting in the middle. There was no greater force, fighting for life, with no greater rewards to a soldier of Elphame than dying in battle or living in victory. But only fools made romance out of death, made it into something handsome and worthy of grasping. From where I stood, there was no greatness to be found, only brutality and cruelty. Leave it to the Fae to toast their wine to suffering.

I had once been at peace with the thought of leaving this world — at peace with my death. But there was no such thing. I wouldn't lie down and take it willingly, not after seeing men run toward it to protect the rest of us from facing that same fate.

Where Solas stood and watched, Faolan, with Oisin at his side, cut swaths through Parrish's men. With powers that radiated through the lands, I felt the cold death dealt by Faolan. He eased himself through the opposition as if they were butter to his hot knife. And when some were smart enough to run from Faolan, Oisin struck them down before they could escape.

I wondered, for a moment, why Solas was drawing this out. It could have been over in hours, yet, he was allowing it to run its course. But I knew Solas would wear out the opposition, then strike when they were too tired, too weak to fight back. It was who Solas was. It was how he never lost. That wouldn't come for days, but when it did come, the opposition stood little chance against all the Dark Courts would bring. He kept his best back and waited.

Nix moved to my side and whistled. "I told them Solas would wear them down and to reserve their magick...but they didn't listen."

"Why not?" I asked.

"Two reasons. One, you. Solas and Zephyr are buying you time. Two, those who stand with Faolan are under the impression this war won't last as long as it could. I tried to tell Faolan, but he seemed to think a different fate was playing out rather than his own. And Oisin, born for war as much as Zephyr, is on that field because of Faolan."

"Both sides are fighting for the same reason, but neither is willing to say the words out loud," I answered. "Solas and Zephyr are standing in front of the Gate. Faolan and Oisin are killing only Parrish's men."

"Too many secrets, Perdi. We'll all die because of them."

"No truer words have been spoken," I muttered. "Nix, how did I get here, to the Unseelie Court?" I asked and moved away from the sight of war and death.

"What do you mean?" he asked. "Are you talking about this war or here to Faolan?"

I moved yards away from anyone who could hear us and sat on a log. "To Faolan."

"You came here, Perdi. Do you not remember?" He looked up at me like I had lost my mind.

"That's not what I mean. When I sent you to investigate the weird energy and the Horn I could hear, you returned to me with Faolan. Did you go looking for him?"

Nix paused for a moment, thinking back, and shook his head. "No. I didn't go looking for him. He was already looking for me. He had been pestering me, trying to get me to agree to meet with him. When I agreed, I found him close to Solas' territory. He said he had just been to the Gate. He told me what Solas had been doing."

"Nix, I need your hand." I looked at him beside me. "I'm sorry to do this, but you must let me read you. Before I can say anything more, I need to do this."

He shuffled back as though I had slapped him. "You want to do *what*?"

"I want you to allow my Malice to read your pearl."

"I know what you meant, Perdi. Have I done something to lose your trust?" he asked.

"Not you, no," I answered. "You'll understand after why I had to. It's truly not you that I don't trust."

"Perdi, you're asking an awful lot here. Some of my memories, I'd rather you not see." He dropped his gaze from me. "I've told you before that I have done things I'm ashamed of. It would kill me for you to see them and not feel the same way about me anymore. I'm not ready to lose you."

"I know, and I'm sorry to ask," I answered. "Please, Nix."

"What if you see a part of my past that you don't like?"

"It's probably not as bad as some of the things you've seen me do," I answered. "I'm sorry, but I need to do this before I can give you truths."

For a moment, I didn't think he would let me, but he let out a shaking breath and put his hand in mine. He was nervous, not because he was a traitor to me, but because he had been his own traitor those many years ago. He, like me, carried the weight of decisions that he hadn't yet overcome. I didn't read him, but I had to know if he would let me, if I could trust him, if I felt any dark webs within him. I didn't think he'd willingly sell me out, but we were all pawns, and sometimes, we didn't even know it. I had to see if Solene had her thumb on him as she did with everyone else.

"Is it done?" he asked once I had put down his hand. He cracked open one of his eyes as if waiting for pain that wouldn't come. I nodded. "I honestly thought it was going to hurt or zap my brain. Next time I won't be such a chicken. Whatever you saw, just know that is not who I am here and now. I won't excuse what I've done, but that's not me anymore. I am not proud of who I was. Now, do you want to tell me what's going on?"

"I didn't read you, Nix, not like I do with others. Your secrets are safe within you, until you're willing to share them of your own accord. But I had to make sure that what I felt was just you and nothing more. I had to make sure *She* hasn't touched your soul," I answered. "I trust you, but I don't trust her."

He sat for a moment, silent. I knew it would have hurt to have me question him. But I also knew that he, of all people, would understand why I had to. "You could have just asked me. But I know you wouldn't have done it unless you had to."

"I'm sorry. I do trust you more than anyone else, but Solene's reach is deep, Nix. I've been reading everyone since I got here. Some don't even know that she's been dipping into their minds, watching their every movement, trying to push them to get closer to me. She's lurking everywhere. I had to make sure she's not rooting around in your head without you even knowing it."

"I'm a gnome, Perdi. I'd know. I feel everyone's power, their magick, whether they're using it or not. I'm too small not to notice the faintest whisper of energy. It's the same for all wee folk."

I thought about it for a moment and realized how foolish I was. Orrian had always known when someone else was near. I'd never thought to ask Nix if he did, as well. "Who do you feel around us right now?"

"I feel everyone, Perdi. If I closed my eyes, I could tell every soul and what court they're from. It would take weeks to list them, but I don't think I'd miss a single one," he answered. "In all the mess on that field, I can feel Solas searching through souls to find you. I can feel Zephyr's shadows split in half, readying to grab you at his word. Orrian, I can feel her eating the dead. I can hear the crunch of bones under her teeth. And beyond us, in the forest, I feel the dread."

"Can you feel *her*?"

"Yes, but she's safely tucked behind her walls. She never comes out for war. She won't ever risk her magick beyond the wall during times of battle," he answered.

"If that changes, let me know, please," I replied. "Solene is who I worry will hear me."

"I won't be able to stop her, but I'll know if she comes near."

"When we first met, did you know I was...more than what I am?" I asked.

He caught my hint, my purposely leaving out who I was. "Yes...but not right away. After a few months, I could tell you were more than a witch. It took Solas months to learn what you were, though."

"She's been looking for another like me, to open the rift in the Gate."

"Why?"

I shrugged. "I don't know. She's the reason for the Taking, and it wasn't for some tithe to their Gods. But that's only a small part of what's been going on. Get comfortable. This is a long story." I filled him in on the missing pieces, the parts I had learned since coming to Faolan's territory. I told him of all the secrets I had learned and the lies that had been woven so bloody tightly around my neck that I couldn't breathe. "I'm sorry I've withheld all of this from you."

Nix slumped. "That's a lot to carry on your shoulders. But I understand being caught in the middle. More than that, I understand the mask you've had to wear."

"I should have told you," I answered.

"I wish you would have. You wouldn't have had to carry this burden on your own. But Elphame isn't a place for wishes. I know the why of it, and we don't have time to argue about what we could have done differently. Let us discuss only what matters. What do we do about it?"

"We have always been in enemy territory. We just didn't know how far that border extended. There isn't a safe place anywhere in Elphame. I had wondered why Aoife wanted me on this side, in Faolan's territory. I now know that it was only from here that I'd be able to find the truth."

"Now, do you see why I was happy to leave this place and live in your garden, where the hell of this place didn't rule my life?" He slumped down beside me. "Those were the days, Perdi. My biggest problem was slugs and mites and the odd wee Fae looking for some food along their journey. God, I miss those days. I miss arguing over apples and protecting a yard from cats and dogs. Now, we argue over life and death and an entire realm."

"I'm sorry you had to come back here."

He patted my hand. "I'm not. I don't like what we're doing right now, but I don't regret coming here with you. You are my home, wherever that is. The only thing we need to think of is what we do now. The rest can wait. We can have our garden again, and we will. And we can have peace again. But we will need to fight for it. Nothing is free. Nothing great comes without suffering for it first."

"I can't leave Winter Court, not yet. The Gate is down, and I don't think there's a way for me to put it back up. But I do know, from here, we can stop what's coming next. Eventually, it won't matter where we're standing. All we can do right now is weed out the traitors and cut off the head of the snake."

"Who can we trust?"

"Each other." I sighed. "We only have each other here."

Nix jumped off the log and stared toward the field. "Solas is going to slaughter them all."

"Without a doubt, but if they're not going to listen to you, there isn't much we can do about it," I answered. "Do what you do best and poke around. Come find me later. I have my own digging to do."

"Where are you going?"

"I've got to find a way to get into Faolan's library, the sanctuary. I think the answers, the end of her, can be found there," I answered, then groaned. "Sneaking around here will be much harder than at home. No one trusts me here. I don't know how the hell I'll get in and out in one piece, let alone get any information I find to Solas."

"Zephyr's shadows?"

"They can probably get me in and out, but the rest, I think I'll need to figure out on my own. I can't do anything where Faolan can see me doing it. If he's ever questioned, he'd have to tell her what I've been doing."

"Good luck." Nix and I parted ways.

He and I went in opposite directions. He to the battle, me as far away from it as I could get. I couldn't stomach the sounds anymore. I gave a wide berth as I passed the tents filled with the wounded, and I knew there weren't enough tents for what Solas and Zephyr could do in one sweep. Tents weren't what was needed. Once Zephyr unleashed all he was, he wouldn't leave anyone alive to need tending to. The fact that healers were here had told me no one knew how much trouble stood on the other side of the war. Part of me, the part deep down inside that I was too ashamed to acknowledge out loud, said they deserved it. *Let the war come and cleanse the monsters from the earth.* Even as I said the words to myself, I knew I'd never let it happen. There was enough hate here. They didn't need mine. And as I stood at the edge of the trees, I wondered how so many men had shown up to begin with, how they went into battle against the very darkness of this land, how they didn't run in the other direction. I would have, if I had a choice in the matter — one that wouldn't end in more death.

"How do any of you even get up in the morning when this is what you have to look forward to?" Dread washed over me, and I jerked. "Who's out there?"

"Had you moved two more feet to your left, you'd have known," the dread replied.

I looked to my left and shivered. The crevasse that surrounded Tylwyth sat waiting for someone to fall in.

From the pitch darkness within the fissure, something that equaled the Gods lurked. I tilted my head for the briefest of moments and regretted not tumbling in. For a split second, the thought appealed to me.

"It's not as fun if you want it to be," the dread called out with a laugh.

"It's not fun when you don't want it, either," I answered.

"Speak for yourself, Perdita Darkmore, Soul-Eater, Maker of Malice, Crow of Elphame," he said.

"Is there no one who doesn't know who I am?" I asked.

"We know every Crow," he answered. "But you, especially, are well known. The rest, who you are deep inside, the parts you've hidden, those who have come to realize what you are knew only for the briefest moments before you killed them."

"How do you know?" I asked.

"Because you feel familiar. Your fear tastes like the only other in these lands. I, an eater of fear, know what I'm tasting." He breathed me in, and I heard him roll my taste around his mouth like he was chewing on something hard to swallow. "You taste of Zephyr. You taste of eaten souls."

I waited for whatever scared those away from Tylwyth to climb from his darkness and eat me whole. I could almost taste my regret when he didn't come to chew my face off.

"Why do you not fear death?" he asked.

"I do. But it won't be coming for me today, so why fret over the things of tomorrow?" I asked. "I have other worries to trouble my mind to mush. My death isn't one of them."

"Do you like caving?" he asked.

I laughed. "I think Oisin is the only one crazy enough to climb in there with you."

"Oisin fears death," he answered.

"It's foolish not to," I replied.

"I do not," he replied.

"Lucky you," I muttered. "If you're so brave, why are you still down there and not on the field helping Faolan?"

"No one has asked me," he answered.

"What do you mean, no one asked you?"

"Not many are brave enough to dare ask something of a Bodach," he said and paused as if waiting for me to ask what a Bodach was. "We are the boogeyman of the Fae and are feared by all."

"I'm surprised you don't live in the Dark Court," I replied. "Are you stuck here, warded to remain?"

"No, this is my home."

"Why is your home around Tylwyth?" I asked.

"Because Faolan gave me this home when we had nowhere else to go. No one would allow us in their territory. We were, in your mortal words, homeless," he answered. "We guard our home, these lands, from those who wish to harm us. In exchange, Faolan provides us food and warmth and welcome."

"Sounds like something Faolan would do."

"Would you not have?"

I shrugged. "You know, I honestly don't know. My first instinct would be to say yes because I know what it's like to want home and safety. But the dread that pours off you would have probably made me run in the opposite direction. I already did once. When I felt you in the forest, I ran the other way."

"As I make you uncomfortable, you, too, make me uncomfortable. You feel of things I cannot eat."

I laughed in surprise. "That's probably the best news I've heard today."

He sniffed the air, loud and long. "You smell like something I would puke back up."

"Thank you…I think," I answered.

"Sadness is not a meal easily digested. What makes you sad?" he asked.

I shook my head at the question. "There's a war going on, and you ask me that?"

"If you smelled of wartime sadness, I'd not have asked that question. But you don't smell like the others, those living to die in battle. Although you walk the grounds of the Winter Court, you haven't lost the smell of the Dark Courts. You smell of Solas…of schemes, lies, war and nightmares."

"There is more than one war going on — one on the field and one in my soul."

"And the lies that bridge them pain you?"

"What lies?" I asked.

"Sadness has many flavors and tells the truths we wish to hide. Yours tells me of the lies you have told yourself, lies you tell others and something yet to come."

"You've just explained life in Elphame," I answered.

"Will you fight in the war?" he asked.

"Faolan doesn't want to risk me. If I go onto that field, the others will kill me."

"We both know he would risk you if forced to choose between you and his people. But I'm not talking about the war out there. I am speaking of the war in your soul."

I released a long, hot breath. "It feels like that's all I've been doing. Some days, I'm tired of fighting."

"I doubt that greatly, or you would have taken those two steps to your left," he countered. "You are rolling choices around in your mind and trying to find the safest way through."

I nodded. "You're not the first to point that out."

"If you want to survive this place, you must adapt," he answered softly, but it still made my stomach clench. He reminded me of monsters hiding under the bed, trying to convince a child to hang their foot off the edge. "You will not find your answers by taking the safest path. That is not the way of Fae."

"I'm not walking a safe path, trust me. It is you, dread and all, that I have to get past," I finally answered. "I can't move through this land without you warning Faolan, and I can't risk him knowing what I'm doing or others will know quicker than I can act on what I find. There isn't an inch of land in Tylwyth where I don't feel your presence."

"Have you asked for my silence? Have you asked for my aid?"

I opened my mouth to say there wasn't a point and stopped. "I didn't think it would be that easy."

"Very few things are. Tell me what you plan to do, and I will tell you if I plan to let you."

"I want to go to the sanctuary, Faolan's library."

"Just the library?"

"Yes."

"Why do you need this to remain a secret?"

I smiled. "Knowledge is power, and this is power I should likely not have. What I'm searching for, others are sworn not to tell."

"Will it end what is happening?" he asked.

"Yes. I mean, I hope so."

"What are you looking for in the library of no entry?"

I glanced around the forest, feeling the heaviness and risk of speaking out loud.

"Worry not, Crow. Not even Blood and Bones will stand this close to me."

I nodded but lowered my voice to nothing more than a faint whisper. "Solene's end. How to take her life."

He smiled, and I cringed. It made him smile wider. His grin reminded me of Orrian and how terrifying she looked. "I do not know if that is what you'll find, but what would you give me if I were to help you?"

"What do you want for your help?" I finally asked. "Know I will not give you any person or my own life."

"If you make it there and back alive, you will come caving," he answered. "If you win, I will keep your secret. If I win, I watch you all fall and eat the lives lost. Both come with a cost, and the costs are yours to carry and yours alone."

I shivered at the thought. "You will not cause me lasting physical or emotional harm. I have to be well enough to fight when it is time."

"Deal," he said.

"But, if I best you in the caves — not just escape, but win — you must help me tonight. You will bring whatever I give you to Zephyr, on the other side of that field. There will be plenty of fear for you to eat along the way."

"Best me?" He laughed hard enough to need to take a knee. "I've never been bested. As long as what you give me brings no harm to Faolan's people, we have a deal."

"You've also never invited the blight of Elphame into your caves, and you just did," I answered and stood. "We have a deal."

I didn't pause or wait. I bolted. I knew the boogeyman wasn't the only thing to fear in the lands of the Winter Court, but he was the only one I didn't want to face. As I ran, I called for the shadows. I begged for their help. The moment my plea went out, I sensed them in the back of my mind, crawling across the ground before they wrapped me inside. They were alone, which meant they could be pulled away at any moment. Without needing to say the words, they whisked me through the forest and to the door of Faolan's secret, his library. I expected the library to be locked, but it was open. I could feel Faolan's magick in the air. He knew I had come. He, like Solas, would know my every movement. Part of me was surprised that he'd let me root around in the room locked away from every other soul, but another part of me knew that he counted on my arrival.

"Find anything to do with Zephyr," I called out to them. I didn't know if Faolan would come to see what I was doing or let me be, but I wasn't willing to waste my time waiting. I couldn't risk the shadows being pulled away when I needed them most.

"Why him?" They paused.

"To track the history of his people. I need the history of the first Fae, the Seers. Zephyr's people come from the original court," I answered. "I need to know how to stop this, how to stop them. I need to know how to kill a Seer, how to take Solene's life."

I let go of my Malice, and we all blew through the room, books and pages flying through the air. When the shadows shoved a book to the floor, I picked it up and scanned page after page. The shadows slammed down on the text and sprawled it open to the Seers. I read line after useless line until the end. More riddles I didn't understand. To end a Seer was next to impossible.

"I need a blade from blood and bone? How the hell do I make one of those?" I whispered. "To take the life of a Royal Seer, I need the lifeforce of three of her kin, taken by the blade of blood and bone, to spell the blade to full power? I have to kill three of them just to get it to work? I can't kill three Seers to get the damn thing to work."

"A knife from her court, Perdi, not literally made of blood and bones...and the lifeforce. You do that all the time when you work a spell. It's just blood."

"But how do I get blood from three of her kin?" I asked. "And how the hell do I get into Blood and Bones for the damn knife?"

"We need to leave, Perdi, *now*." The shadows echoed through the room. "Time is up. Zephyr is calling us. Just take the pages, and let's go."

I ripped the pages from the book as the darkness wrapped around me, and we were gone. I was dumped back where I had started and landed on my back. It took several tries to breathe again before I rolled over and dropped down into the caves. This would hurt, but I hadn't come this far to die in the tunnels of the Winter Court.

# Chapter Ten

Faolan and Oisin stood by the fire, still in their bloodied armor. Faolan's smile twitched when I got to them. I knew he would have looked for me and would have worried once he didn't find me. I had been gone since the sun rose. He breathed in the scent that rolled from me and frowned. I dropped a brown sack at Oisin's feet and used my shirt sleeve to clean the fresh blood from my nose. It wasn't broken, but it was close enough for me to flinch from my touch.

"What's this?" Faolan asked at the squirming bag. "Dinner?"

I shook my head. "Oberon."

Oisin's mouth dropped. "What? You trapped the creature in the caves?"

"As it turns out, I'm not half bad at caving." I smiled.

Oberon burst from the bag in a fit. He stood naked with a hand on his hip and picked up his small bag holding the pages of the book. Before coming, Oberon had read them over to ensure I wasn't selling out the

Winter Court. He laughed at the impossible task but still wished me luck. Like me, Oberon bled from cuts and gashes from a hunt that had lasted the evening. I hadn't been willing to leave the caves without him, and he'd had a death grip on his home that I had to beat out of him. What started as a chase, me running from the boogeyman, ended with me hunting him through his caves and dragging him out by his ankle. And there was no amount of dread he could muster that would make me let him go. Getting those pages to Zephyr was more important than the potential nightmares I'd have from my time with a Bodach.

He pointed his long, skinny finger at me and scowled. "I said I'd help, not allow you to package me in a meat bag and deliver me to the feet of our king. Where are your manners?"

"I skinned them off on your walls." I countered and showed him my cut hands. "A deal is a deal, wee man."

Oisin stepped back. "How the hell did you get him out of the caves?"

"I lost, okay? Let's tell the bloody world of my failure and shame, shall we?" Oberon grumbled. "Now point me where you want me."

"I dragged him out by his ankles." I smiled at Oberon and lifted my arm. I pointed toward Solas' territory. "Down there, the first encampment."

"Not him?" Oberon asked and left Solas' name off his question.

"It will be as we spoke of," I replied. "You will do only as we agreed, nothing more and nothing less — or you, boogeyman, will be titled an oath breaker."

Oberon, who stood two feet and a few inches from the ground, looked up at me. "Next time, I'll remember your little tricks."

"Don't be a sore loser." I smiled. "Off you go. You have men to terrify and screams to eat."

Oberon scurried back to the trees, taking his dread with him. Oisin's legs gave out, and he landed in the mud, a look of shock still frozen on his face.

"What in the world did you do, Perdi?" Faolan asked.

"I won. That's what I did." I smiled and looked down at Oisin. "You all right down there?"

He looked up and nodded. "It appears I may have bitten off more than I can chew?"

"With what?" I asked.

Faolan laughed. "Challenging you to caving. Oberon has always won against Oisin. Oisin is only alive because the Bodach likes the games they play and wants him to return."

I helped Oisin stand, and we three walked to the hill that overlooked Solas' territory. We watched as Oberon made his way through the camp. Three rows of soldiers erupted in screams that could be heard from all corners of Elphame before the Bodach returned, sated. I hadn't sent him to kill. I had seen enough of that to last a lifetime. I had sent him to buy me more time. The fewer men who went into battle, the better. And along the way, Oberon would find Zephyr and deliver the pages of the book I had ripped out. Zephyr would know Oberon was sent by me and would have let him come and go without harm. If anyone knew what to do with those pages, it would be Zephyr. He would know my next move without me having to tell him.

"Thank you." I knelt before Oberon.

"We protect our own," Oberon answered. He leaned into my ear. "Even if you're a cheating Soul-Eater."

I flinched. "I'm not…"

"I am not the teller of secrets. And I suspect now would not be the time to divulge that information. Fear brings more death than anger. They already fear you. Let's not give them another reason to pray for your death."

"Thank you, and I didn't cheat," I replied.

"The debt has been paid." Oberon cursed me as he walked away to sulk in his pit of terror and despair. He stopped and turned at the edge of his forest. His words were like a ghost in my ear. He spoke them only for me. "Perdita Darkmore, there are other ways to fight that aren't on the battlefield. You just have to be willing to risk it. How much are you willing to give to protect our people, yours and mine? How much are you willing to lose? How much of your own fear are you willing to swallow? If it is as much as you claim, you will find those answers on the bones that pave their walkway. There, you will find that which you do not know how to gain. I suspect they, like you, want this to end and are powerless to stop it."

I didn't need to answer. Both Oberon and I knew I was willing to give it all. He was gone like the boogeyman he was, but his dread remained with me. I knew I would carry it to my tent, into my bed, and let it curl around me and bring me to sleep. It was the honesty of it that I didn't mind.

Faolan stood. "I'll walk you to your tent."

"Thank you."

"You didn't need to ask him for safe passage, Perdi. I gave it to you." Faolan nudged my arm with his. "Did you find what you were looking for?"

"I needed the favor more than safe passage," I answered. "How did you know I would go there?"

"Why else would I show you the one place no one else has been allowed to look upon or show you what no one else has ever known about. More importantly, how could you get in and out in one piece? Anyone else who tried would die at the door. Next time, just take the whole book instead of trashing the place and ripping up historical artifacts." His look made me feel like I was being scolded. "We're all dancing around truths that cannot be spoken. Please, don't give me yours. They're not safe with me. I'm glad you found what you need, what we *all* need."

"I found the recipe but don't have all my ingredients," I added. "The…umm…liquid for my recipe… I don't know where the hell I'll get that."

"You know where to find what you need. Remember who you are and how you work your own magick. Calm yourself, think it through and it will come to you. And when it does, take it without asking, or you will not get it freely. No one can simply give you what you need for this."

He dropped me at the door to my tent, and neither of us exchanged another word on the topic. Exhaustion pulled me under before I could lie awake and plot my next steps.

* * * *

My dreams twisted around me and my Malice, and I could feel Solas before I saw him. Dreams were the only place where I found the real Solas, the one who didn't have to hide behind the mask. It was both calming and unnerving to see a person as they truly were. In most dreams, he fought wars that wouldn't end and memories he'd rather not have. But on rare occasions, I found him, the man I loved with all my soul. It was those dreams where I didn't know who owned the dream.

*"Solas," I said his name as I stood before his desk. I was smiling before I even realized it.*

Although I knew it was a dream, I could almost swear it was real—like the terrors felt by those who had seen war and death, like the filled arms that haunted a mother who had buried her child. It had weight to it, the heaviness that only truth and regret could bring. The scent of the Dark Court wrapped around me, and I remembered it as if I were still there. At a desk sat Solas, leaning back in his chair, reading a book that was older than he was. The walls were filled, floor to ceiling, with books. I could smell their ink. The fireplace crackled, and I could feel its heat. It was as if I were mere feet from him, so close that I could smell his soap and shave cream.

*"I told you we'd see each other soon." His words rolled over my arms, and I sighed.*

*"Why are you here? Whose dream is this?"*

*He glanced up from his book with the smile I had grown to love and cherish, the same smile I always found myself thinking of. "You are the one that comes to my dreams. You're always here, whether you know it or not...sometimes for only a moment, or only the faintest smell of your hair, other times for the entire night."*

*"Perhaps it is you who comes to mine or pulls me, in some way, to yours," I countered.*

*"I've never once come to your dreams. And I don't pull you into mine. Not even in sleep could I force you to do something." He motioned around the room. "Perdi, this is my office. Have you ever stepped foot in here?"*

*I thought for a moment. I had walked by and ducked my head in the door to speak to him but had never gone inside.*

*This had always been his one place I wouldn't enter. Not because I feared his reaction but because this room was war, and I couldn't bring myself to feel whatever emotion had stained the walls. "No. I don't remember ever coming in here."*

*"Then it is you who has come to me, not the other way around."*

*"How do I always find my way into your dreams?" I asked. "And how do you know you're dreaming when most don't."*

*"Like Zephyr, you likely come to those you have the strongest bond with. It is why he finds his way into yours and mine," he replied, then paused as if to think of his response. "To answer your second question, I only seem to know I'm dreaming when you're in them. They are usually some of the more...troublesome dreams I've had, when I see you or Zephyr."*

*"Ah, I see," I answered. No one was safe from a Soul-Eater, not even when they slept. This, me standing in Solas' dream, was why Zephyr had warned me to be careful of what I wished. Asleep, my deepest and darkest and bloodiest wishes would come true. "I still need answers, Solas. I feel like I'm running out of time."*

*"Don't we all?" Solas set his book down and pushed back from his desk. "I cannot give you the answers you need. Whether you come to my door knocking or stand in my dreams uninvited."*

*"You let me in," I replied. "You may not be able to fight against Zephyr when he comes, but we both know you can send me packing and have before."*

*"This is the only place, Perdi, where we are safe. This is the only place we can be as we are, without others hearing us. Although, I'd still caution you on what you're willing to say out loud." He smiled fondly, like he was remembering days*

*he was desperate to have once again. "But even here, even though I want to give you answers, I cannot."*

*"Am I close? Here, with Faolan? Is there someone else I could ask that could tell me?" I asked and thought of what I was asking. "Will I find what I need where I am? Or do I need to go elsewhere?"*

*"I see Zephyr has taught you this game, well." Solas grinned and stepped around his desk to lean on the front, inches from me. His knees grazed my nightgown, and I fought not to lean into the touch. I was scared that I wouldn't let go if I touched him. "You will find more answers with her than with me. But I suspect you're smart enough to know that already. The arrival of your Bodach friend told me you found the answer I could not give you freely."*

*"What do I do?" I whispered as if Solene could hear me. "Do I go back to the Court of Blood and Bones?"*

*"That, I cannot tell you," he answered, but the look on his face said differently. "Perdi, I am bound to Solene as Zephyr is bound to you. You're not listening to what has been said. You're not asking the right questions."*

*"I hate these games," I groaned. "If you were me, what would you do?"*

*"Knowing what I know? I'd use my Malice. I'd use who I knew myself to be. I'd stop fighting who I am and would strip away the answers from those who held them from me. I'd sooner die with the truth than live with the lies."*

*"I've tried to get the truth from you, but you push me out before I can. It is the same with Faolan. He felt me digging around. At the Golden Court, I could only hover and get snippets of information. Even then, Parrish could feel me, and I had to stop."*

*"Because you are clumsy and heavy-handed. You come with desperation and far too much anger. I close you out because I know you're there. If I know you're there, I have no choice but to protect the secrets that bind me," Solas*

answered. "But you could find the answers with others if you are willing to chance getting caught. You've done it before. Remember, Perdi, you bent the will of Aelfdene for months, and he never noticed. You have forgotten who you are and have accepted who others tell you to be. Utter calmness, certainty and an understanding of the other person's desire is how you do it. You must have the willingness to die for your cause. That was how you bent Aelfdene. You must play to your audience. It is how I win every battle, by understanding the weaknesses of others and being willing to act on those weaknesses. You cannot come as a threat and not expect to be treated as such."

"You've lived for centuries, Solas. I haven't even lived for two full decades. I am not nearly as crafty as you," I replied. "Though it feels like I've been here for millennia."

"Centuries of battle, Perdi. But I've not lived those centuries. I've fought for every single day. Like you, my fate was decided upon my birth, and nothing I could do could stop it."

"You've won every war. Will you win this one, too?" I asked.

Solas nodded. "I will. That is not ego. That is simply the truth. The others are prideful. And Faolan thinks he'll be saved. But his savior won't come – not for him, not for me. When she comes, it will be for the spoils of war and not to protect her people."

"I don't think he's counting on her as much as he thinks he'll be saved by me if all else fails." I laughed at the thought. "What a strange twist of fate."

"Yes. You're a tool to Faolan. He will take what he can use. You cannot blame him for that. I'd do much worse to protect you, to protect my people. But he, like me, is bound in silence. He is doing as instructed to save his people, just as I am. I fear that when push comes to shove – and it will – he will put you in the front to take the brunt of it. And as much as I dislike him, I don't blame him. He is doing what he can to save those he's sworn to protect. He is one of the only other kings in Elphame who takes that oath seriously. The rest would and have sold out their people for more power."

I nodded and thought of questions I needed to know, but asked what my heart wanted to hear, instead. "I need to know, will you kill me on the battlefield? If I come, will you be forced to kill me?"

"Never," he answered and reached for my hand. The warmth of his touch rolled across my entire body. "I was not the one who wanted you dead, and it will not be me who takes your last breath. On that, I swear to you. I'd rather die a thousand deaths."

"One of us is close to that death. I can feel it as clearly as any truth I've ever choked on." I thought out loud. Behind Solas, the dream darkened. "I'm scared."

"We're running out of time." He sighed. "You're not alone in that fear. Trust that Zephyr will do what I could not. He will protect you. Trust him and only him. Call on him when it is time."

"Where is Zeph right now?" I asked. Solas smiled and tapped his nose. "Is he in Winter territory?"

"He is wherever you are, always. He's there whenever you sleep and are at the mercy of others. He fears for your safety, as do I."

"From whom?"

"You know the answer."

My groan came out strangled, frustrated. "Enough beating around the bush, damn it."

Solas gripped my hand tighter and breathed his cool calm through me. "I've missed that temper of yours."

I smirked. "You didn't seem too thrilled with it earlier while you schlepped me across your territory."

*"I would carry you across worlds, little Crow. I love you. Always remember that. Whatever you see me do or hear me say, know I'll die before I allow her to harm you."*

*"I wish I hadn't run," I whispered. "I love you."*

*"I told you to run, and I meant it. I did everything I could to make you leave. And now, you're still not safe. Go to the forbidden place and find our answers. Take your truth from their path. It's the only way. You will find the answers we need there. I have ensured you will find all you need. I have spent every favor I have for you to get what you need. Trust that you'll find it. Trust your gut. Trust mine. Now, Perdi, we're out of time. There is only one move left, and it's yours to make."*

*"I know," I answered.*

*"Find Zephyr. When the war is over, go to him. No one is brave enough to take you from him — not me, not Faolan and not even Solene. Zephyr and his men will protect you until their last breaths. You are their people. They'll die for you. When in doubt, the Aos Si will stand against all for you." He looked beyond me as if someone else was there. I could hear them faintly, telling him it was time for war. "Perdi, you know how this comes to an end. I need you to let it end, no matter the cost. I am ready for the cost."*

*"What cost?" I asked.*

*"Freedom. Death. The usual. Go and find your answers before they find you and you're not ready. It would be a shame for both of us to die."*

*"Wait! Is Zephyr considered her kin?" I asked.*

*He nodded and smiled. "As am I."*

*"I might need to stab you both." I grinned.*

*"It wouldn't be the first time you've stabbed me." His laughter made me smile. It had been so long since I had heard a genuine laugh fall from his lips. I wanted to put it into my pocket and carry it into the forbidden place and choke his*

sister with it. Prove to her that she could do her worst, but we were so much better at it.

"I love you. I miss you." A warm line of tears rolled down my cheeks.

"I will love you until my last breath," he whispered and lifted a tear off my cheek.

"Screw it," I groaned and grabbed onto him, pulling him into my chest. I gripped his hair and kissed him as if I would never get the chance again. I knew it would hurt more to taste his love when I couldn't have it for real – when I'd wake up alone, without him, without the smell of lavender on my skin.

He tried to pull away once, but my soul was desperate. "Please...I miss you, Solas. Even if it's not real, I need this, just once more."

"Damn my soul, Perdi." He spun me and pushed me against his desk, clearing it off and lifting me to sit with my legs wrapped around his waist. He held my face with both hands and breathed me in, filling his chest, shuddering as he exhaled. The kiss felt like it had lasted an eternity.

Pulling back, breathless, I motioned to the corner of the room to a flicker of shadows rolling down the wall. "I think someone is worried I'm eating your soul in here."

"Zephyr is close by." Solas laughed. "I think he heard me saying your name."

"I'm surprised he hasn't come into our bedroom to check on you before."

"He used to send his shadows to check on us." He laughed. "Never trusting me with a wicked little creature like you."

I rolled my eyes and stood. I glanced around the darkening room. "If Zephyr is nearby, you will wake up soon."

"I can feel it," he whispered, sitting on the edge of the desk and pulling me into his chest. "If you want to get where you need to go and leave alive, ask those who have been there but owe no oaths."

"Who doesn't have a goddamn oath to her?"

*"You're focusing on the wrong part of the riddle. You already know most have an oath."*

*"Who has been there?"* I asked and turned to face him.

He tapped his nose. *"You will need to figure that out on your own, but you've already met them."*

*"Them?"* I whispered, and he nodded.

*"I love you. I'm waking up."*

With one last kiss, the dream slipped from my fingertips. The heat of Solas' hand lingered in mine, and I tasted tears in my mouth. I cursed him for leaving...then cursed myself for believing neither of us had to go.

# Chapter Eleven

I jolted awake, the night still pressing down over Elphame, my pulse in my throat. My first thought was why I would jerk awake and reach for the blade under my pillow until I could see the shadows rolling around on the foot of my bed. My second thought was of Solas and my dream. Had it been real, my conversation with him? The lingering feel of his lips upon mine told me it just might have been. Waking up in the tent left me painfully aware that his lips hadn't touched mine.

"It was just a dream," I whispered, disappointed.

The shadows crawled up to my side. "Solas is nightmares, and you're a dreamwalker, Perdi. There's no such thing as *just* a dream between you and him."

I pulled off my night clothes and put my black leather back on. Less and less, I felt comfortable in anything but leather. After being dragged over the sharpness of this world on more than a few occasions, I'd learned that leather was the only thing that held up to the abuse of Elphame and running for my life.

"I need a knife of Blood and Bones. Solas mentioned that if I wanted to get what I needed from Blood and Bones, I needed to find someone who has been there but has no oaths to her. Is there a group of people you know that fits that description?"

"There are only two groups who have been there, who have no oaths to her, but they have oaths to those who are oathed to Blood and Bones," they replied. "The Sluagh have been there long ago, but they're bound to Solas. We feel they would be moot since Solas has the tightest oath to her. The Aos Si would be our next guess."

"They're bound to Zephyr so ridiculously tight. Solas would be able to get out of his oath with *her* before any of them."

"Indeed, but not his trainees. They're not full Aos Si, but they're trained as if they are, and most of them have been to Blood and Bones. We would be remiss if we didn't warn you that Zephyr would be displeased if you brought them into this. He's worked hard to keep you from his world."

"Why? He wants this to end as badly as the rest of us."

"If she caught them helping you, they're not strong enough to stand against her and win. She'd take them to control Zephyr and kill you because she wants you dead. Together, you all are a target too hard to pass up."

"She's going to kill me anyway if I don't get what I need. Where do I find them?"

"The Court of Shadows. The entire lot of them are resting in the caves of the Sluagh. They're in the last band of cliffs, overlooking the water."

I twisted my hair into a braid and pulled on my jacket. "Can you get me in there?"

"As long as there are no side trips, Zephyr won't call us back. We always check on his men throughout the night and report back any issues. Solas, however, will feel you step foot in there."

"I think he's expecting me to," I answered.

The shadows wrapped around me, blotting out the light. In a blast of wind and the rush of darting through the courts, I was carried to the caves of the Sluagh. It was the first time I had been there without Solas. My stomach dropped to my toes as I landed on the ledge of a cave, armed with one blade, into the mouth of warriors. Trainees or not, even the weakest was one of the strongest soldiers in Elphame. The moment I stepped forward, I could hear the faintest of steps and the unmistakable glide of blades being drawn from a home I bet they rarely saw.

"I don't think Solas will take kindly to you killing his little Crow," I hollered down the tunnel. "Not to mention what Zephyr will do to your bodies when Solas is finished."

"Perdita Darkmore, what brings you to the gates of hell?" a man's voice called back.

"The usual, war and death," I replied.

With a nudge from the shadows, I walked down the stone passageway, once built for monsters. But what sat at the end were monsters, only these played tricks on your eyes and mind. They only looked less vicious than the sky beasts, but they weren't. The hall opened into a massive room similar to Elda's home. Inside, I scanned over three dozen men in various undress, lounging on pillows, beds and blankets and drinking enough wine to kill the memories the day had given them.

I kicked a pair of pants out of the way. "I love what you've done with the place."

The one closest to the entrance held my stare like Zephyr did. "I could say the same about you and everything you've set your eyes on."

"Finn, don't be an asshole." The one beside kicked Finn's shoulder. He stood, still wearing his leathers, and extended his hand. "Miss Darkmore, I'm Cas."

I shook his hand, firm but polite. "Just Perdi, please."

"Can I offer you a drink?"

"Please," I answered and glanced around for something to sit on. I pulled a pillow from under Finn's arm, making him jerk forward. I dropped it on the stone floor and took a seat. Finn grinned and passed a glass from Cas. "Thanks."

"What brings a Court of One to the door of a Court of None?" Finn asked. "Respectfully, of course."

I drank my entire glass of wine and handed it back. "One more."

Cas grabbed the entire bottle and handed it over. "The bottle may be more fitting."

I poured another glass and drank it. I closed my eyes and heard nothing. No war. No armor clanging. No swords. No cries. Just the night and the sound of water crashing against the cliffs.

"It's peaceful here."

"Did you crash our party for a little peace and quiet?" Finn asked. "If you weren't the harbinger of war, there would be peace to be had for us all."

"How are you even still alive?" I rolled my eyes. "You must love pain with a mouth like yours."

"We all have our kinks." He winked.

"It's been touch and go his entire life." Cas interrupted before Finn could say another word. "What can we do for you?"

"First, do any of you have oaths with Solene of Blood and Bones?"

"We know who she is," Finn answered, and I groaned internally. He was a mouthpiece. "No, we don't. The only Aos Si that does is Zephyr. Full ranks are bound by his oaths, but we're not full Aos Si."

My heart began to beat a little faster. "I need something from Blood and Bones."

The room fell silent.

"I'm not here to ask any of you to go there. I need to know how to get in there without sounding off every alarm the Seers have."

Finn was the only one to laugh at my comment. "You must love pain with ideas like yours."

"We all have our kinks," I parroted.

Cas' mouth dropped open. "Wait, what? You actually want to go in there and steal something?"

"And get back out."

"There's no way in," he answered. "Anyone who has tried hasn't come back out."

"I've already been in there once and made it back out in one piece," I corrected him.

"If you can get Solene to come out, you could get in," Finn spoke up, to my surprise, without cockiness. I had expected his opinion to be laced with more attitude. "When she steps out, the wards on Blood and Bones drop—but only while she's outside. You could send someone to a doorway and have them wait for you until she goes back in. The wards take thirty-four seconds to roll all the way back down. But, once you go in, you have to find a way to get back out. Like Cas said, no one comes back out."

"Fuck." I groaned.

"Indeed, you would be," he replied. "Royally. And that's not even the hard part. You have to move around inside without being detected. The Seers, her sisters, patrol every square inch around the clock. There are dozens of them, and they're almost as strong as the Aos Si. They train as we do."

"Not to mention the theft," Cas added. "Get in, move about, steal that which you should not possess, leave, get away and have them never know? I've never heard of someone accomplishing that task before."

"Not the hardest thing I've done, but the odds are a little lower than I'd like," I replied. Finn grabbed my bottle and poured us both another glass. "Do any of you know where I'd find a weapons room? I need a knife from there."

"I do," Finn answered. "I'll draw you out a map. After that, you're on your own, and I'll lie about helping you. If you die in there, I'm not hanging for it."

"If I die in there, it doesn't matter. Everyone dies after that."

"Hence why we're drinking the rest of our wine stock." He toasted the room. "To final wars and early graves."

I lifted my own glass in salute. "At least we won't care. We'll be dead, and the dead don't care about a damn thing."

Finn tapped my glass with his. "Small mercies."

Cas passed Finn a stack of papers and a pencil. Finn began sketching out a small map of Blood and Bones, detailing the doorways from the outside and halls on the basement floor, where I'd be going in.

"That's not all I'm here for." I dropped the other shoe. "If I do make it out…"

"That's a mighty big *if*," Finn interrupted.

"Just the same. If I make it out, I need to ask you all for help." I cringed, knowing what I was about to ask of them. "The final moments on the field, I need to ask you not to kill me."

The room erupted in laughter, so pure that it made me smile.

Cas leaned forward and patted my hand. "Who the hell told you we'd kill you? Do any of us look like we could get through Zephyr or Solas?"

"I know enough about the Aos Si to know once she steps out of her little slice of hell, she could command you over Zephyr," I answered. "I plan to…make her see things my way. I'm making sure no one gets between her and me. I'd really hate to have to kill one of you guys in the process."

"The Seers will get between you and her. They're sworn to protect her. We're not," Finn answered.

"If the Seers try to stop me, are you all strong enough to stop them from getting to me?" I asked.

"That's a big ask, little Crow," Finn replied, and I smiled at the use of the name Zephyr and Solas used as a term of endearment. I knew, right then, they may not be able to help me, but they wouldn't make my job harder.

"I know. But I'm not asking you to do anything I wouldn't do," I answered.

"And if you fail or get hurt, Zephyr will skin us," Finn replied.

I smiled. "If I fail, let him catch you. At least you'll be one of the first to die. Because those who didn't help will die shortly after you."

"We cannot fight Solene. We can hold back the Seers, but if we stay, Solene could use us to block your path. It's best if those of us who can leave do so, the first chance we get. If we're not there, we can't hinder you. But Zephyr will have the full-rank Aos Si there. They will do as they're commanded, bound by oaths we don't yet have. Though, I doubt even the Gods could order them to kill the little Crow," he replied and handed me the map. "I circled the two rooms that hold their weapons. You'll be safer if you stay in the basement. Once you're in there, you'll have to figure out how to get the hell out of there on your own."

I eyed the dogeared page. It looked like a maze of twists and turns, dead-end halls and more rooms than any other manor I had been in. "Easy-peasy."

Cas lifted his glass. "Here's to your last night alive."

I clinked my glass against his. "This is going to hurt so bad."

The Horn hummed lightly in the background, and I watched Finn's face. Our eyes met. He could hear it. He groaned and drank his entire glass. "If you get caught in there, we'll run a training lap around the cursed place and hope someone steps out to see what the hell we're doing. We'll hold open a door for you. And if Zephyr beats the shit out of us for it, we're taking it out on your hide."

"Thank you." I smiled and breathed a sigh of relief.

"Don't thank me. If you think I won't beat the hell out of you because you're a woman, you'll be sad to hear that I don't give a shit. For this, he's going to come for blood—a pound of flesh, for a pound of flesh."

"Get in line." I stood and tucked my map in my pocket. "Thanks for your help. I'd keep this between us."

"None of us are volunteering to have this conversation with Zephyr or Solas."

"Thank you for your help." I drank the remaining wine in my glass and left them to drink their memories away.

I stood at the mouth of the cave and closed my eyes. The Horn hummed in the background, as it always had. The pressure of it tonight built in my ears until they popped. I was on the edge of a decision that could end it all. I pressed my hand into the middle of my chest, and instead of trying to rub out the tension, I pushed against the pounding of my heart.

"That feeling in your chest never goes away." Finn stepped up to my side. "We all have it on the eve of war. It's your heart searching for other answers that will never come."

I opened my eyes and tried not to roll them. "Thanks, Finn, for whatever the hell that advice was."

"What I mean is, you're not alone in how you feel. We're all feeling it. What you're about to try has been attempted dozens of times."

"Yeah, you're not very good at pep talks. I didn't need to know dozens of others have tried and failed to do what I'm about to do."

"I'm only telling you what she'll probably tell you herself. She gets into your head in ways that crush your courage. She digs it out and leaves you with nothing. But if you already know, she can't scare you with her words. No matter what is said or done, remember, those who tried before you were not *you*. She has never faced the last Crow."

"If you know her so well, any pointers? No one else seems to be able to talk about her."

"Neither can I, but by the time it makes it back to her ears, you'll have either killed her or the world will be over, and it won't matter what that bitch wants from me," he replied. "I can't speak to what she'll do, but if I were her, I'd go for whatever will hurt your heart the most, since you're the only one in this fucking realm who has one left. I'd take everything you loved and destroy it. Once you remove who someone is, there's not much fight left."

"She's no different than any other Fae, then."

"True enough," he answered. "I'd advise you not to let Solene touch you. It hurts both your mind and body. If Solas is nightmares, she's the horror you feel when you're stuck in those dreams. She will drain you of your energy and magick, while you scream at shadows not really there."

I nodded. "Walk in the park."

"If that park was in hell and she was the devil."

"If I don't make it, Zephyr will end this world."

"He'll be stuck with her at the end, then. Because he won't be able to kill her without you."

"How did you hear the Horn, and no one else does?" I asked.

"I'm not hearing it as you are, just an echo from you. I'm glad I'm not the one to hear it. It's a fate that'll drag you into hell and leave you there without a way back."

"Pretty much sums up my experience so far," I replied. "Thanks for the tips, Finn. See you at the end of the world."

I stepped out of the entrance and wrapped myself in shadows, jumping off, and my stomach climbed into my chest as I fell. With a tug, the shadows pulled me back to my tent, where I dropped into bed, dizzy from the wine and exhaustion of war—both in my soul and on the field.

\* \* \* \*

Dawn came with sadness. I could already hear the camp preparing to fight yet again. Faolan was in my tent, dressed in armor, and nudged me awake. I jerked at the smell of Christmas, if the holidays rang in with war. My hand was already around the knife I slept with under my pillow but I willed myself not to draw it. I calmed once the panic I had awoken to from someone touching me in my sleep had faded.

Even with a new plan, I woke flustered, angry, tired of Elphame and the games it played with everyone. I was tired of not knowing how to play. Unlike the Fae, I didn't know the rules or the moves I could make. And because of that, I was pushed from one place to the next. Fear overwhelmed me at every move, and I ran. I always ran. Solas had told me to run from danger, but I managed to find my way back into the center of it each time. My human heart didn't understand that it was the only one here, the only heart in the middle of a world of hate. Fae had endless time to shed their naivety. Years of games had stripped them of their ignorance. I couldn't run until the end of time. I couldn't survive if I didn't take the chances I knew I had to take. I didn't want to live if this would be my life—used to start and end wars, used to rule, used to kill. I'd sooner die today than be back here in a few months, fighting for another day.

"I'm going to the Court of Blood and Bones," I said to Faolan's obvious surprise.

"Don't take this the wrong way, but why? They closed their doors to Elphame so long ago. We don't speak of them anymore," Faolan asked, his voice raised but not out of anger. He was scared. He understood what the potential cost could be — my life. But he didn't know what I knew.

I had read Faolan's part in the mind of Solene. "When she came to you, she tried desperately to goad you into invading Solas' territory to kill me, the Crow who shamed you in front of Elphame. And when that didn't work, when she couldn't get you to kill me, she threatened to take your land and your people. She is, after all, an original Fae. The lands are hers to take."

His face flushed. "I refused."

"You risked your people when you refused," I added, and he nodded. "And when the Gate closed, she bound you, as she bound others, to oaths so old, not even you knew they were there. All kings would maintain the Gate. And all kings would be trapped within those oaths. Caught in a game you couldn't win, you did the only thing you could think of. You came to me. Bound by oaths and fear, you told me just enough truth to get me here and showed me the path the best you could. And for that, I've seen your punishments, the lashes you suffered at her hand."

"Any lash I've taken after my father's death, I've taken willingly," he answered and thought of what he could say next without breaking his oaths. "To know I suffered lashes for doing what is right made them worth it, made it hurt less in some way."

I didn't have to like the choices he had made, but I could understand the reasons for them. I even understood his lies, for I had spoken enough of them to survive, myself. I had wormed my way through every court to get the truth. I couldn't really throw stones now, when I'd have done so much worse.

"Don't take this the wrong way, but why are you going there?"

"I've been there before," I answered.

His eyes grew wide. "I'm surprised you made it in and out. No one else has."

"I'm going to try again. I need to…" The look on his face told me not to overshare, that my truth was mine to carry alone.

He put his fingers to his lips and shook his head. "Whatever your reasons, I'm sure you believe you must go."

I rolled my words around in my head, trying to piece together a truth within a lie. I wasn't as skilled as he was. "If I'm not back by dinner, get a message to Solas. He'll know what to do."

Faolan didn't try to talk me out of it. He simply nodded. "Solas isn't going to let you just walk across his territory. How will you get there?"

"Alive," I answered. I didn't bother telling Faolan that Solas would let me live because he loved me. I was not the enemy of the Dark Courts, but I wasn't willing to say that out loud. The masks we had worn, for all to see, would stay on until the bitter end.

"I don't like this. I don't think you should go."

"You don't have to like it, but you won't stop me from going," I replied. My voice was angrier than I had intended. "Faolan, your people, my people, all of Elphame, need help. Solas' army is bigger than imaginable. What do you think is going to happen when he releases all the Dark Court on Elphame? There are thousands of Sluagh, and they aren't even who I'm worried about. Aos Si may only be in the dozens, but each one fights like his own army. They pale compared to Zephyr, but even a shadow of who he is should terrify you. You have no idea what is standing on the other side of that field. There are at least two dozen to every one soldier you have."

"They are not what scares me, Perdi." Like me, he knew what stood beyond that field, and it wasn't Solas. "Solas could release hell, and I still won't tremble nearly as much as when the very pits spit out the last demon. When *she* comes, I'll tremble. Until then, this is a dance I do not fear. As uncomfortable as it is to say, I've grown used to this."

"At least you understand that no one — and I mean no one — is coming to save you. All of this, you and your people will face it alone without any higher power to save you from what's left to come when this is over." I felt pity for him, for once. "You all will fall, and I'm trying to stop it from happening."

"And you think they, Blood and Bones, will listen to you?" he asked. "Why? Why would *she* listen to you? I'm sorry, but *she* doesn't care about you. Going there is not where you are safest. It is where you face the most danger."

"Because I know the truth, Faolan...all of it." I glanced up at him while I pulled on my boots. "But here is not the time or place for us to speak those truths. I pray there will be a time when I can be angry about this."

"Things are... I've no control over it." He swallowed hard enough for me to hear it. "Things are so different now with you. I wish you didn't have to be here. I feel your yearning for someone else, and I never wished this for you. I wish I could change the part you play, but this was the only way to save you, to save my people, your people. It was the only chance any of us had."

"There is no room in Elphame for wishes," I replied, parroting the exact words Nix had said to me. "Things are out in the open, Faolan. And no, things aren't different now. They are as they have always been. Only now, we *both* know what the other has been hiding. The lies and schemes are unsaid but understood." I left it at that. "The words do not need to be spoken for me to hear your truths and you to hear mine."

"Perdi...I wanted to tell you the truth, but I couldn't." Faolan's voice held enough guilt that it made me step back, but not before I rolled his soul in the hands of my Malice.

"You couldn't, or you wouldn't? Did you hang me out to dry, Faolan? Is that why I'm here?" I asked and slinked into his deepest and darkest secrets. "I've run out of time to do this the nice way."

Without having to hold back, I finally got inside without having to fight him for his truth. I had tried so many times before and had hit a brick wall. This time, though, I didn't care if he caught me. I didn't care if I left him a shriveled husk of a man. I had nothing left to lose — no more lies or masks. There were thousands of reasons to lie, all of which were the same reasons I would have done the same. But there were thousands of souls who depended on the truth. On both sides of the Gate, countless innocents needed me to become the monster I fought so hard against. And I knew it would hurt like any other monster would.

"I wouldn't fight it. I'll shred your mind before I leave the truth in there. I said I'd protect your people, but I didn't say I'd protect their king. The oaths protecting you died the moment this war started. We're at the bitter end now, and I don't have time to dance with a fool."

"Stop…please." He winced at the claws I dragged across his soul.

I knew he'd have to try to stop me. I felt those oaths as I picked and pulled what I wanted from his mind. But those oaths didn't bind me, and I didn't care for the pain I caused. I didn't care if I left him a bowl of jelly. There was no time left to tiptoe. But where I thought I'd find a fight in him, I found an open door. When I readied myself for an attack of frozen magick, I found him finally giving up. He had done all he was willing to do to stop me, but hurting me was not something he had oathed himself to do. I stepped back and shook my head, disappointed in us both — him for being so weak and me for being so cruel. I had never forced someone's soul to twist in terror for me, to spill its secrets unwillingly…never like this. And I'd suffer for it later. I pushed the disgust I had in myself into the pit of my stomach and swallowed the vomit that threatened to breach.

I watched his life play out like a book I had memorized, from childhood to this exact moment. The pain I swallowed was enough to turn my stomach. His childhood had been horror in every sense of the word. He had been born to rule with an iron fist, but because he was raised under one, he tried every day to be a better version than the previous day. He had many faults and flaws and cruelty in him that rivaled Solas. To protect his people, he'd have killed me on the spot. If he knew my beating heart would save them all, he'd carve it from my chest. It would hurt him, and he'd carry that shame, but he'd do it just the same. It was the way of Elphame. It was the only way to survive a world that bet against you. But unless he absolutely had to be ruthless, he was who he had always shown himself to be. And I hated that bitch all the more for forcing him to leave his kindness at home.

"I'm sorry," he whispered. "I tried so hard to do what was right."

"I know you did," I answered. "As did I. But it doesn't take the pain away when we're forced to be who we don't want to be."

"No, it doesn't. It makes it even worse when we don't want to be monsters," Faolan replied. "And now it's too late to stop this from happening."

"I may not be able to stop what's already started, but I can be there for the end," I answered. "From the moment you came to me with your twisted truths, I knew you'd be the one to give me the answers I needed."

"Just as I knew you'd find them here," he replied. "I did everything within the oath that bound me to ensure you'd find the path you needed to be on. And I kept every secret of yours I could along the way. Do you really think I don't know what you do when I'm not around? Do you think I don't know what you've been up to? I've said nothing because I've been waiting for you to act on it, waiting for you to help me save us all. You are the only one in this cursed mess who isn't bound to some oath that'll kill us all. And as much as it pains me to say this to your face, I could live with your hate again. I could live in that wound for eternity if it meant Tylwyth was safe. I could suffer a thousand deaths at your hand to save them. I want to be sorry. I want so badly to feel something more than relief that you're here, but I don't. My curse has been and always will be to do everything in my power to shield my people from the horror of Elphame, no matter the cost. Those in Tylwyth depend on my willingness to suffer in their place. I can't be sorry for protecting them over all else."

I nodded. I'd do the same. I was, in fact, doing the same. I'd kill them all to protect Whitwick, and I wasn't sorry for it. "Why? That's all I want to know. What reason could you have for risking the lives of all of Elphame, including my people? To do this, to let this play out as it has, why would you allow this to happen? Oath or no oath, there were ways to bring the truth to me, but you didn't."

Faolan's careful control slipped, and he screamed wordlessly until there was nothing but a sagging king. "*She* will kill my people—those who depend on me, depended on my willingness to sacrifice everything for them, including you. I had nothing to lose with you. I couldn't lose you twice. You were already gone. But my people? For them, I'd do worse things to better people. I wish that wasn't true, but it is. I don't want to be a nightmare for anyone, but I'd be much worse than that. It kills pieces of me every day, to do what I must. I'm sorry for hurting you, but I can't be sorry for saving everyone else with that hurt."

"I know. I would become the same monster for my people," I answered. "But you did have a choice, even after I was dragged here from my home in Whitwick. The truth was already out. You still could have come to me and told me what was happening. I would have helped you. I wouldn't have sacrificed your people for mine. I do not trade one group of people for another."

"No, I don't think you would have helped, even if I could have come to you." He answered. "Not after everything that happened. You would have watched me burn."

"That's where you're wrong, Faolan. I wouldn't have let your people suffer because you broke my heart once. I would have fought for them and for you. I wouldn't have let your people die for what you did. We would have had a fighting chance, but you took that chance from us all, including your people."

"The oath bound us all, including Solas."

"But he found a way, so could you have."

"I did love you once," he whispered. "You must know that."

"No. I don't think you know what love is. I've seen inside your soul," I answered. "I think you only know what you want it to mean, but you don't know how to show it in any way that doesn't hurt. You don't do this to the people you love."

"I did this for my people!" Faolan screamed inches from my face.

"And I did this for us all!" I returned his anger with my own. "You best remember this moment. This was when I decided your life has more value than it should, the day a Crow burned the world for you and yours. Because it will be the very last time I lose a drop of blood to this godforsaken place. If you fuck this up, if you tell Solene a damn thing" —I leaned into his ear so that only he could hear my words— "your soul will be the first I collect."

"What have you done?" Oisin stepped into the tent and grabbed Faolan's arm, forcing Faolan to face him. "You have killed us all, Faolan...and for what?"

"I did it to save us," Faolan answered.

Oisin laughed. "If we win, *she* will take everything. Solene will drag her claws over our land. You lied to me. You lied to us all. You have sentenced our people, *my* people, to death, for an oath I knew nothing of. You tied my hands, the hands of our people, to a sinking ship."

"Not if I can help it." I stepped back, toward the door. "Oisin, I'm going to Blood and Bones. If you don't see me by dinner, find Solas. Tell him what I've done. He can save me or be there while I draw my last breath."

Oisin followed me outside the tent. "I didn't know."

"I know," I answered. "But that's the crux of following a king blindly. You never see what's coming. Get your people to safety."

Oisin ran his hand down his face as if trying to pull the fear away. "Our people will die for this."

"Your people were only ever at risk if we failed. Look out over that field. None of your people are fighting Solas. I won't defend Faolan or his actions, but I will say that he's done everything he could to protect as many as possible," I replied. "You, now, must do the same for him. Trust no one who wants to stay and fight. They've already given their fealty to Solene. Solas and his army are the only things standing between Elphame and the mortal world. Many of your men have already sworn themselves to fight in her name and invade Whitwick. Understand, they will never leave that field with a pulse."

"We never wanted that, Perdi, to invade the mortal realm," Oisin replied.

"Truth between us. Those who try will fail, and there will be no survivors." I gave him a firm look. "Do *not* let Faolan onto that field until this is over or we will all die together for this."

"I don't know what to say." He ran his hands through his hair.

"That you'll save as many as you can," I answered for him.

"I would have had your back the day we met Solas in the Wildelands. I wouldn't have left you there."

I leaned in and hugged him — not because I needed one, but because I knew what it was like to feel scared and uncertain and how a hug sometimes forced all the pieces back together, just long enough to face that uncertainty. I left him with a chuckle and a new world of worries. He could hold Faolan's hand. I hadn't the time nor the desire. I had bigger things to worry about than how either of us felt. I didn't have time for old wounds, not while I was preparing to create new ones. I was heading into the place of no return. I wasn't foolish enough to think the Seers would help us fight this war, but I wasn't going there to ask for them to fight a war that shouldn't be happening. I would be going for two reasons — truth and death.

I found Nix a few feet from the tent. I knew he would have heard us. Nix's ears were tuned to any mention of my name. He always heard everything that involved me. On his shoulder, Orrian stood. Both looked like they had been through hell but still stood on their own two feet.

"I'm going to the Court of Blood and Bones," I told them.

"*We* are going to Blood and Bones," Nix corrected me.

"I'm not ordering you to go," I replied. "I'd never do that, Nix."

"As I said, *we*. And that, Crow, is an order." Nix winked. Orrian nodded her agreement from his shoulder. "How do you suppose we get there?"

"Follow me," I answered and led them from the tent to the trees. "Seth?"

Seth dropped from the branch like the heavy rock he was. Only in my dreams was he graceful. His landing shook the ground under my feet. "Blood and Bones?" he asked.

I nodded. "Can you get us there safely?"

Seth's wings rose and fell with his sigh. "We'll need to wait until the battle begins, when the Sluagh aren't looking for a fight, or they'll pick us out of the sky, then pick us out of their teeth, out of sheer boredom."

"I won't risk you, Seth. If you think they'll pick you off, I will go without you," I said.

He smiled, and it looked as awkward as it always did. "We will make it to Blood and Bones. I do not doubt that. But I'd rather increase our odds by waiting for the war to start."

We left the camp and walked to where we would cross, near the Autumn Court, who had been slaughtered on the field. There was no one left to guard the Autumn territory, no one to try to stop us. The band of land between Autumn and Court of Less was small enough for us to run it. As sad as it was to know Parrish's court had been decimated, I was also thankful. Parrish was a traitor, and I knew it. I'd felt it the moment I first met him. He would fight for whoever could give him more power. The man was a coward and had sold his people down the river for that power. Everything about him told me he would kill his mother if it meant he would rise another rung. With his army down, it would clear the path we needed. Fighting a war within a war would keep us from getting to the Seers, so I didn't mourn the loss of those who would stand in my way — not today, anyway. Hopefully, I'd have enough tomorrows for regret to settle in.

Along the way, I told them of my plan. Nix and Orrian laughed until they realized I had every intention of going into Blood and Bones, stealing what I needed, then trying to find a way out. The last part wasn't perfect, but I'd spell if I had to. Nix would go to the doorway to hold it open. It was as good of a plan as ever. We crossed through Unseelie territory and over the Autumn Court's border. Nix stopped and inspected the earth, burned and turned and still smoking. It looked as if a path had been cleared this very morning. Nix rolled a handful of rocks in his hand and looked up at me with a frown.

"Zephyr?" I asked.

Orrian spoke to Nix, who translated. "Solas. She said it smells like Solas."

"Why would he attack the army that was helping him?" I asked.

Nix translated for Orrian again. "Parrish sought revenge. It's why he joined Solas' cause. He was going to try to kill you, specifically. When you killed King Aelfdene, you cut the Autumn Court off from a great deal of wealth and power. Parrish was one of Aelfdene's favorites. He earned this fate."

"Solas put them on the front lines," I said out loud, but more for myself, as I slid another piece of the puzzle into place.

"They fell quickly, and I suspect those who ran back were killed," Nix answered a question I didn't know I had. Orrian's pitch called my attention back to the battlefield behind us, and Nix translated again. "Look at who is stepping onto the field. Faolan has sent only those who are traitors but none of his own men to the front lines."

"Why?" I asked.

"The same reason, I suspect. Solas has only fought those who want to take the mortal lands. I think Faolan is killing off those he knows will stand with *her*, those who would enter the Gate."

"Interesting. It must be why Faolan's not listening to any of us when we warn him of the Dark Court's power," I answered. "He told me he wasn't scared of Solas but of what would come after the war."

Seth motioned that it was time to go. Violence erupted behind us. The war had started and we ran. Seth took to the air and lifted the rest of us with him. Nix and Orrian were tucked in my jacket as we maneuvered through the trees. Seth would remain hidden for as long as possible. As soon as we cleared Unseelie territory and sailed over the Court of Less, Seth flew wildly. A small contingent of his people glided at our sides.

I watched the gargoyles fall from the sky one by one as winged beasts from Blood and Bones dragged them from our flank. I chewed my lips to keep the screams trapped inside. The wind whipped my hair across my face like tiny knives. My lower body dangled below, jerking with each quick movement Seth made. Every muscle in my body screamed as I twisted in the air.

I stared below and saw Solas, Zephyr at his side. Zephyr had the nerve to nod and wave, clearly amused at my stupidity. Solas, on the other hand, shook his head. He lifted his fingers to his mouth and whistled. His Sluagh lifted off the ground and took to the air. A small scream escaped my mouth as I watched two dozen beasts lift into the sky. But they hadn't come for us. They fought against beasts I had never seen before. They had crawled from Blood and Bones and fallen dead within their lands. Seth was bombarded from every direction. All sides slammed into us. Beasts began fighting each other over the scraps of meat in the sky. For the briefest moment, I wondered, did the Sluagh come to help us or fight over our dead bodies?

Arrows flew through the air, taking down what the Sluagh couldn't grab in time. In the tree line, I could see Finn shaking his head and readying his bow once again, aiming right for me. His arrow took down two beasts at once, their bodies hitting the rock below. The sound of their impact was a mix of broken glass and soggy things. To his left and right, Aos Si were shooting down the creatures of the cursed lands, not an arrow sent without purpose. If I lived through today, Zephyr would kill us all for this. Solas, on the other hand, would grin.

Seth dropped us down to the rocky path of bones and tumbled after us. I rolled through the rocks and bones and felt as though I became the namesake of this cursed place — blood and bones. I curled onto my side and fought the burn in my chest as I struggled to take back the air that had been knocked out of me. I heard Orrian's high-pitched squeal and knew something was wrong. I could feel it. Seth was covered in blood and gouges. Chunks of his leathery back were missing, his wings torn to bits. He'd gotten us here as he had said he would. But now was nothing more than blood and bones.

"Seth!" I yelled and ran to him.

"Find the truth and go home. End Solene, Perdi." Seth's voice sounded like it was rumbling in his chest like rocks in a cast iron pot. "I told you it would be glorious when one of us fell, and by all the Gods witnessing, it is magnificent." He curled his wings around himself and hardened.

"No, Seth!" I tried to pull him to me, but he wouldn't budge. His weight was more than I could manage.

Nix tugged at my pant leg. "Perdi, we have to go."

"I can't just leave him here. They'll kill him." I sobbed. "I have to protect him. He would never leave me like this."

"He's already gone," Nix whispered. "I'm sorry, but he's stone. There is nothing we can save. He has moved on to his next life. Goyles do not linger."

"He'll wake up. He has to," I cried. I put my hand on Seth's wings and tried to stir him, but he was as hard as any rock had ever been. I stood and scrunched my face, trying hard to hold back the torrent of emotion behind my eyes. "But he said we'd make it. He told us."

"We did make it. Seth got us here, as he said he would," he replied. "He did not say it would be without cost."

"But I wouldn't have... I didn't ask this of him." My voice squeaked as I tried harder than ever to hold back my sobs.

The pain in my soul hurt more than ever before. It hurt more than coming to Elphame as a Crow, more than every death I had caused and every hurt I had suffered. Nothing could amount to his sacrifice. Nix pulled me again. I didn't want to leave Seth, but I also knew I couldn't stay with him. I turned from him and felt our connection snap into a million pieces. He was gone. I hadn't known before, but I knew now that my soul had always sensed him. Now that Seth was gone, there was a void inside that would never fill again.

Nix scurried to the right, and within a blink, he was out of sight. I followed Orrian to the wall. I was numb and felt everything at once. My heart fluttered in my throat, threatening to come out as a scream that would never end. Nothing came for us. Nothing tried to eat us. They were either hiding or too scared to face the angry Crow. If I were them, I'd be tucked as far away from this angry Crow as I could be. I'd kill them all. I'd drain every drop of pearl from their terror-filled bodies as payment for Seth.

At the wall, the sliver I had used before was closed. That didn't stop me, and I didn't leave. I banged on the blood-stained wall. I kicked, and I screamed. My fists were covered in old blood that mixed with my freshly skinned knuckles. I hollered until it was nothing more than cries.

"This is *your* fault!" I hollered for all to hear. The wall would do nothing to silence my voice. "*You* did this! You all have watched and have done *nothing* to help your people!"

But they didn't care. If they had, none of this would have happened. The war wouldn't have even started if there had been a single care about anyone. I sank to my knees and curled forward. My forehead touched the ground-up bones of those who had begged before me.

"You knew this would happen, and you did *nothing!*" I screamed again, my rage finally letting loose. The burn inside my stomach roared to life and poured from me in waves of fiery heat and hate. But there was nothing here to burn, and it faded on the bones. "You did *nothing* to stop this."

From the wall, Solene stepped out, dressed in pristine white garb. She looked as if she had never had the hand of war touch her pretty cloche. But I knew better. Her filth was under the unspoiled exterior. Her guilt tarnished her as it tarnished me. I thought for a moment that she would burn. I could burn her and eat whatever was left of her dirty soul. I would gladly drag her around for all of eternity, just to see her suffer an ounce of pain. As much as I wanted it, I knew I'd never burn her fast enough for me to win.

"You knew the Gate would open and mortals would be Taken. You cannot tell me you didn't see that coming. But you watched, from your walls, as innocents were marched into Elphame to die. And now *this*? You have the power to end all of this, and you choose to do nothing." My words carried the heat of my fire, but she didn't flinch. She didn't say a word. "Answer me!"

"This is not our fight." Solene finally spoke. "We are not responsible for the wars of others."

"*You* did this. This is *your* fault," I replied.

She lifted her hand to silence me. "War is most difficult to witness, but we are not the cause of this."

"*You* saw this. You saw it all coming those years ago when you closed yourself off from Elphame. How dare you say you didn't cause this. The day you banished Fae from your court, you sealed my people's fate. You killed us. Your hands have as much blood on them as the rest of this cursed world."

"I did *not* see this day," she replied. "I cannot see the path that binds me to Solas' future."

"Please, help. I'm begging you." I risked it all and grabbed her hand. If she knew what I was, what I really was, she didn't move away as quickly as she should have. As I held her hand, I pleaded for her help. I played to her ego, the great Seer she wanted all to believe she was. And for the briefest of moments, I felt all I needed to feel. She was the puppet master of Elphame. She plucked the strings of all. She always had and always would. Kingdoms rose and fell on her word. Communities, people, children, all burned on her whim. She held power over every king, every royal and every Fae. There was no corner in this realm that didn't stink of her touch. The worst part was that no one else knew of her machinations. She pitted them all against each other. It was the reason the Horn wanted us all together—a war the Horn cleared a path to happen. All of us would pay for the broken oath, together.

And now, she used me as her golden pawn, an unknown hostage in her games. But Solas knew, and he was waging war against the very men who would use the Gate to invade. Now that he had fulfilled the debt to Solene, he would protect the mortal world. And for this, she would kill him. Once he was dead, she would lead the invasion into Whitwick, aided by kings and courts who had pledged themselves to her long before I had stepped into Elphame the first time. They would raze the human world for Crows and take them all in one grab, looking for a Soul-Eater.

In the very back of her hatred for mortals and Fae, Solas was there. He had waged war after war and brought down her followers. With every step she took, he had been five ahead and cut her off at the pass. Her hate for him was the strongest emotion she felt. As much as she tried to wear him down, he still held out hope that I would stop her somehow. It was one of the reasons she toyed with me, to make him suffer. But in truth, deep down beyond what any other knew, she wished for my death because I was a threat to the Gate. Her disgust and rage for me were as bitter as her love for her brother. Flashes upon flashes moved before my eyes until she pulled back, but not before I saw her standing in the background, watching me close the Gate and knowing she could force Solas into helping her destroy it. Me closing the Gate had set the rest in motion. Once I closed it, she enforced an old oath on Solas and onto the others. But when it was all said and done, she would kill me as quickly as her own brother. Her hate for me was as rich as any other.

Under the blankets of lies, the shadows she weaved, stood my answers. It wouldn't matter if all of Elphame stood against her. She would win. She was just that strong. Those who could have taken her life were all dead, save one, but it would take more than one. In all of the deceit, no one had yet told her that there were two Soul-Eaters. She did not fear Zephyr, because he was only one. But she had no idea about me — the witch, the Crow. Faolan hadn't lied to her, but he also hadn't told her the truth about me. And she hadn't known I had touched her soul because she rarely used the cursed thing.

She stepped back and shook my hand from hers. "You will find no blood on these hands."

"Solene." I glared at her. "Just because you don't do your own dirty work does not mean you haven't bathed in our blood each and every night."

"The same can be said about you, can it not?" she asked. "The moment you stepped foot on these lands, you brought death and destruction. You are the cause of two wars in under a year. You've accomplished more in your short time than anyone else has in decades of worming their way through court after court. Before you stand against anyone else with your accusations of betrayal, perhaps you should stand in front of a mirror and reflect on the lives you've taken."

"You will pay for this," I screamed into the bony path. Frustration poured from me.

"No, I won't," she answered. "And I warn you to be careful in what you do next, before you are the one who pays for this all."

When I lifted my head to spit venomous words in her face, she was gone from the wall as quickly as she had come. I kicked and pounded until my fists cramped in pain. I dropped to my knees and screamed my frustration until my voice broke. I cleared the tears from my eyes and stared over the path of bones and destruction. The coast was clear. I bolted to the right and found Nix standing on the shoulder of Finn.

"After you," he smiled. "I'm not going in, but I'll hold the door until they toss your dead body off the wall."

"Thank you."

"I was never here. We are forbidden to come here," Finn added. "You owe me."

"I know, a pound of flesh for a pound of flesh," I replied. "When Zephyr peels you like a grape, I'll be right beside you."

# Chapter Twelve

We tucked in against the wall, Nix and Orrian scouting ahead. I was thankful I had shown them the map, because I had forgotten where to go or how to get there. Orrian tugged on my hair, directing me from my shoulder. When Nix slowed, so did I. I breathed slowly, trying to control my heartbeat, but it was the drum we marched to. The walls were sheets of stone, as if sliced from some unfortunate mountain. The floors were cobblestone and worn from decades of footfalls. And although it was dark, the smell was what nudged my panic along. It smelled of death. It smelled of the basement in the Golden Court and the rows of dungeon cells that housed those I had freed, but not before they suffered a fate worse than death.

I knew Zephyr would feel the surge of panic I had felt when I stepped into Blood and Bones. I wondered how long it would take for him to come and look and if he'd skin Finn alive before I could rescue him from a Soul-Eater. My fear twisted odd thoughts in my mind, like what small talk Finn and I would have while Zephyr ripped off our limbs. I tried not to laugh and pushed my morbid thoughts away.

"Someone's coming." Nix scurried from door to door, with me trying each lock. The first one to open, we ducked into it. He pressed his back against the wall and blinked several times, finally turning to face the wall and heaving as quietly as he could.

"Are you okay?"

He shook his head. "No one will smell us beyond what lies in this room, behind us."

My brain told me not to turn around. If Nix couldn't stomach it, I most certainly could not. But I never took the easy route. I glanced over my shoulder, knowing I'd stain my soul with what I saw. Nothing in Elphame that made a gnome sick would leave me with a hop in my step. I blinked, trying to will the vision from my eyes, and swallowed hard. On the table behind me, a man was tied down with leather and iron, nude. His eyes were covered with a thick black strap, his mouth gagged and his body bound. I turned back to the door and shook my head. I told myself I couldn't afford to help him. If I did, they'd know I was there. But I couldn't pay the cost to my soul if I left him there.

"Damn my soul to hell," I whispered. I moved to the table, my stomach curdling at the sight of him. Wounds over wounds. He wasn't new to the place, from the look of him. When I touched his naked body, he didn't jerk, didn't scream — not a muscle tensed, as if he had grown used to it.

"It's okay. I'm not...*them*."

"Perdi," Nix scolded, "we're not here for him."

I glared back. "If we leave him here, we don't deserve to win. If leaving him to die is what it takes to win, I'm not fighting for the same thing as everyone else. We don't do this. We don't allow this to happen for any reason."

Orrian buzzed over the table and landed with a thump, leaning over and puking on the man. Her whispers told me everything they needed to. She was embarrassed. Her small hands tried to clean what she had done, her tears making a bigger mess of it. Her voice came out quiet as a whisper, but it still pierced my ears. She looked to the door, to the plan we'd come here with, then back to the man. Her shoulders slumped as mine had. She, like me, couldn't leave him.

Orrian whispered to Nix and pointed at the man. "Aos Si?" Nix asked her, and she nodded. Nix jumped onto the table. "We can't leave him."

"Why, because he's a soldier?" I asked.

"If that was the reason, I'd tell you to leave him. He'll be missed and noticed gone," Nix answered. "We can't leave him because you're right. If we leave the innocents, regardless of what he did to piss off Solene, we've already lost. I don't want to live in a world where this is okay. No one deserves this, no matter the 'why' of it."

I leaned into the ear of the man and whispered, "I'm going to untie you. Do not make a sound, and do not run. You are a shadow in here, or we all die. At least, I hope we die, because Zephyr will kill us all for this. He's already going to be angry with me for coming here. I don't need to add more reasons to the list."

He nodded his head. Nix and I unbuckled his arms and legs and took off his blind and gag. Under his blindfold, it was much worse. His eyes were puffy and bruised. I glanced around the room for something to wrap him in. Being naked was somehow worse when you were already vulnerable. I settled on using a large sheet they'd been using to clean their blades.

"I'm sorry," I whispered when he winced at the wrap. "Can you walk?"

He shook his head, and I looked down the length of his body. His legs had been broken over and over, up and down each leg. I gripped the table when the room spun. I breathed in through my nose and out of my mouth. I didn't want to pass out or vomit. The less evidence I left behind, the better.

"We could pull him together," Nix whispered. "We're strong enough to do it."

"Okay." I nodded and looked back at the man. "What's your name?"

"Z...Zeno..." he whispered. His voice was soft. It didn't sound how mine would, had someone tortured me. It didn't sound like he had screamed even once.

"I'm Perdi," I replied. "This is Nix and Orrian."

"Did the Seers do this to you?" Nix asked.

"Solene and a few of her special sisters," he answered.

Nix nodded. "Saves me from killing them all. A few, I can manage."

"How many did you bring with you?" Zeno asked. "What court do you have?"

I scrunched my nose. "I'm a Court of One, my good friend. It's just us three."

"I've faced worse odds."

I smiled and glanced around, motioning at the room. "So, it seems. I hope we fare a little better this time."

"As do I," he replied.

"I'm going to leave you here for a few minutes," I said. "If I don't come back, could you crawl your way to safety? Finn is holding the door open. Zephyr is on the field of the Courtless Lands, by the Gate."

He nodded.

"Nix, if I don't come back, you're going to lead him to Finn, okay? Ten minutes and you all leave."

"You're not leaving me behind."

I touched his shoulder and squeezed. "I'm *not* leaving you behind. But, if I don't come back and Zeno can't crawl, you're strong enough to drag him to Finn. Then go get Solas and Zephyr."

Nix finally nodded. "You'd better come back."

I passed Zeno one of the scalpels they had used to cut him with. "Normally, I wouldn't consider delivering a person into this hellhole, but if you don't protect my friend, I'll find you and bring you back here."

He smiled but nodded.

Orrian and I left them in the room, and I followed her down the hall. She paused in front of the first weapons room. She pressed her ear to the door and nodded. We slinked in and inched through the room, looking for a knife. As quietly as I could, I opened each drawer and door. We found everything else and a few things I had no idea how to use. Orrian's squeal brought me from a cupboard to standing squarely in front of a white-clad woman. She didn't speak, but she didn't have to. She reached for my neck. I pulled back as her blade sliced across my stomach, cutting through the leather like butter and into my flesh. But it didn't hurt. It should have hurt.

Before she could take another step forward, her eyes flew open, and blood poured from her mouth. Hands grabbed the woman and lowered her to the floor. The woman who had helped me the first time I had come to

Blood and Bones put her finger to her lips. I stared down at the blade still in the woman's hand. Before I could reach for it, she shook her head. She picked it up, slid it across her hand, then passed it to me.

"We could never give you one. But now you have your blade the hard way," she whispered.

"Thank you."

She dug through a drawer and returned with a ball of white fabric. Tearing a long strip, she wrapped the fabric around my stomach. "This is the only help you'll get from me on this matter. I have paid my debt to Solas by saving your life and getting this knife into your hands. Go home with your blade."

I looked down at the lady she killed. "Thank you."

"No one will miss her," she whispered.

"Wait! Are there any other Aos Si here?"

She nodded. "Three."

"You know I can't leave them," I replied. "Are there any others who shouldn't be here?"

She shook her head. "The only ones who are still alive are Aos Si. The others die too fast under the touch of Solene."

"I can't leave them here."

She closed her eyes, releasing a groan. "Then you better be making your move now, because she'll feel them leave. She'll come looking for them, ready or not."

"Let her come. I'll be ready."

"Are you? Are you ready for her to come right now? Because if you're not leaving them behind, you'll never leave here at all." She glanced back once. "If she comes down here, I won't be able to stop her. I won't suffer for a 'maybe.'"

"I wouldn't ask you to suffer in my place," I replied. "But if I suffer for doing what is right, I'll share it with you all to stay alive long enough to kill her."

"You don't have everything you need to face her here," she replied. She breathed me in. "At least you have a gnome and a fairy. That'll increase your odds more than the three wounded."

"Can you drop the wards around the wall?" I asked.

"No. Solene controls them," she replied. "If you want a chance in hell, you better figure out how to use what you have at your fingertips. The next rotation will be down here in five minutes. Every ten minutes, Perdi, someone will be down here. If Solene feels something is off, she'll send more down even sooner. There are more Seers here than even Zephyr knows about. I suggest you kill whoever comes, because I'm not coming back here to help you again. When all hell breaks loose, my sisters and me — those who want this to end — will not come to fight against you. Don't make this all for nothing."

"How long until Solene knows we're in here?"

"About an hour. The wards around the wall are off. She'll come to check within an hour," she replied. "Heal your men and get ready for war."

"Heal them? How the hell do I do that?"

She stared at me for a moment, confused. "You don't know? You came to rescue them and didn't know how to heal them? How the hell did you think you'd get them out? Carry them?"

"I didn't even know they were here. I came for a bloody knife, not a rescue."

"Christ, you've got to be kidding me." She groaned. "You know how to pull energy, yes? Do you know how to push it out of you?"

"I've seen it done," I replied. "Is that all I do?"

"It'll work for today. It won't heal them, but it'll give them what they need to heal themselves. They're the strongest in Zephyr's army. They'll heal enough to be useful. Also, cover their mouths while you're doing it. They're damaged pretty bad. I've yet to hear them scream, but everyone has a breaking point."

I nodded. "Thank you."

"Don't thank me. I don't think you'll make it. I can't see your path beyond this room." She left me with a shake of her head.

I leaned over the Seer on the floor, the light fading from her eyes. I pulled every drop of energy from her soul, taking one of her pearls with me. I moved from the weapons room, a long bag over my shoulder, and into the hall. Orrian and I opened the door two up from Zeno and slipped inside. A man was strapped into a wooden chair. His arms and legs were held by leather belts and iron. I knelt in front of him and touched his arm. He didn't flinch, and my heart broke for that reason — to be so used to suffering that you didn't recoil from it anymore.

"Don't scream," I whispered. "If you want to leave with me, you can't scream."

He nodded. I pulled his arms and legs free. He jerked his hand up and grabbed me by the throat. I didn't scream, although I was close to it. This was what caged animals did. They didn't care who they were biting. He lifted the blind from his eyes and stared into mine.

"Who the fuck are you?" he asked.

"Perdi," I answered.

His eyes narrowed. "Zephyr's Crow?"

I tried to nod, but his grip didn't allow my head to move. "Yes."

He dropped his hold, and I gasped. "Sorry, ma'am. I'm Triton, one of Zephyr's men."

"I know. Nice to meet you. We don't have time to get to know each other. We have to move. Can you walk?"

"I'll crawl if I must."

"I can help you if you swear you won't scream from what I'm about to do, because I've no idea how to do it." I looked at his blistered legs and winced. "Do you need me to cover your mouth?"

"No." Triton smiled. "I won't even breathe."

"This is going to hurt," I whispered and pushed the energy I had taken from the dead Seer into Triton's soul. I didn't know how to control or focus it. I had only seen this done — sharing energy with another. I pushed until he gripped my shoulder.

"Jesus," he hissed.

"Sorry. It's my first time," I answered. Triton grinned, and I flushed. "Doing this, I mean."

He stood from the chair and rotated his shoulders, popping them back into place. "Thank you. I'll heal the rest on my own."

In the corner, he pulled his leathers from an old pool of crusted blood. He didn't seem to care that he was wearing his own gore. He moved stiffly but looked no worse than a rough night in a ditch. I passed him a sword from the bag I had taken from the weapons room.

"We have two more to grab, and we're running low on time." I motioned to the door, where Orrian was listening to the hall. "If we see another Seer, grab her, but keep her quiet."

He frowned. "I don't need revenge."

"No, but I'm going to need to eat her energy. One of the other Seers told me to kill whoever comes down, so I'm not chancing it."

"This isn't a rescue, is it?"

"I wouldn't call it that, per se," I replied, and he tilted his head. "No. None of us are just walking out of here."

"At least I'm already used to the place. Maybe my next room will have a view."

Orrian's wings flapped twice and brought our attention to the door. She raised one finger. Triton inched to the door without the slightest sound. He reminded me of Zephyr. He motioned for me to wait at the wall beside the door, out of sight. He put his sword down, and once Orrian nodded, he slipped out of the door. I held my breath, waiting to hear a commotion, but heard nothing over my pulse in my ears. The door pushed back open, a Seer unconscious in his arms. I closed the door while he placed her on the table.

"Quickly, they don't stay out for long," he whispered.

I stood at the foot of the bed and closed my eyes. I didn't want to watch as I drained her life. I reached into her soul with my Malice and pulled until there was nothing but empty air on the other end. I pulled her soul from her body and turned my back. The sound of her neck breaking echoed in the room.

"Can't be too careful," he said.

We left the room, closed the door quietly behind us, locking it from the inside and pushing into the next one. The man was tied to a table and didn't move a muscle when we stepped to his side.

"Dear God," I whispered, seeing the man's condition.

"Rest easy, Jare. It's me, Triton. I have Zephyr's Crow with me," he explained.

Triton helped me unbuckle the third man in our rescue. He didn't panic. Seeing one of his brothers helping me untie him had made him relax. I grabbed on to the table and breathed through the searing panic starting in my stomach. I could feel the hot blood dripping down my stomach and making the band of my pants sticky.

"Jare," I whispered, "I can give you energy, so you can heal quicker if you swear not to make a sound."

"Take it, brother. We're not walking out of here today without fighting for it," Triton added.

Jare nodded and closed his eyes. The energy I had taken, I gave to Jare in one burst. With him, I heard his bones sliding back into place as he ate down what I gave him. I swallowed the vomit that came halfway up and pulled back from him. Jare climbed off his bed and squeezed my shoulder. He pulled his leather pants on and dropped his ripped jacket in the corner. I passed him a sword, and with a nod, he palmed it. We waited with Orrian at the door while Triton told Jare of the plan to kill the Seers, save Zeno and kill Solene. It sounded like another half-baked plan created in the head of a Crow.

"Easy as pie," I replied. Orrian flicked her wings and lifted three fingers. A small groan escaped my lips. I closed my eyes and passed Triton my bag. "I got this."

"Do not let them scream," he replied.

"They won't even breathe," I answered.

When Orrian nodded, I sat on the floor with my eyes closed. I opened the door an inch and watched three

Seers walk by. With my heart hammering in my chest, I unleashed all my Malice. I didn't hold back. I reached into the hall and drank down the energy from all three in an instant. They fell to the floor, unconscious. I couldn't take any more than that. My body felt full. Triton and Jare stepped into the hall and carried them back. I stood on shaking legs while the sound of the Seers' bones crushing filled my ears. I tried to push the visual from my mind. I had to focus on the task at hand and not the deaths of those who undoubtedly deserved it.

"Can you take more energy? I took way too much, and my head feels like it's in a vise," I asked Triton, who pointed at Jare.

"He can take all of it if it's too much. He's the only one here who can take the full force of Zephyr and not even stagger."

"Neat trick." I smiled.

I grabbed on to Jare's arm and released a wave of energy. He accepted it without so much as a sway. He placed his hand on Triton, and the remaining wounds mended before my eyes. I grabbed the three lingering souls from the dead Seers and stepped to the door, thinking about how handy the magick Jare possessed was. We locked it behind us and inched our way to the room where we had found Zeno. He was unconscious on the floor. Nix was preparing to drag him. I grabbed one side of the sheet, and Nix held the other, eyeing the two I had collected along the way.

"You smell of blood," Nix said.

"Slight hiccup, don't worry," I replied. I pulled up my jacket to show my wound was almost fully healed from the energy I had taken.

"She'll kill us for this," Triton replied.

"She's going to kill us all, anyway," I replied. "Might as well die a free man."

"What's the plan, now?" Nix asked. "We're not walking out of here with three Aos Si."

Orrian pointed at the door and squealed.

"Finn is here." Triton motioned to the door.

Finn stepped into the room, dragging a Seer behind him. He dropped her on the floor and closed the door. When she let out a groan, we all jumped. Finn glared at her. "Shut up."

She closed her mouth and said nothing more.

"Nifty," I replied. "What the hell are you doing in here?"

"The shadows came to check on you. Faolan sent word to Solas. Zephyr sent his spies."

"Is it dinner already?" I asked.

"Yes." He glanced at the door. "The rest of us came in when you didn't come out. They're raiding the weapons room."

Zeno's eyes flared open, but he didn't utter a word. Once his eyes focused on Triton and Jare, he smiled. "So, not a rescue mission?"

"Get ready for some more pain," I said as I placed my hand on his leg.

Jare knelt beside me and shook his head. He held my hand and put his on Zeno. He closed his eyes and calmly drew energy from me. What he took from me, he pushed into Zeno, focusing on his injuries. Where I came as a storm, Jare was a cool breeze. The room filled with bones sliding, muscles snapping and something sloppy and awful. This time, I could feel the movement of bones across my own, and I was sick.

"You couldn't turn your head?" Finn asked, kicking his boot out and flicking vomit from his foot.

"Sorry... That was disgusting," I answered.

"So was what you just did," Finn replied.

"Don't be an asshole, Finn," Zeno replied, his voice holding no signs of having just vacationed in the arms of hell. Triton and Jare helped Zeno to stand.

Finn pulled a set of leathers from his sack and tossed the empty bag on the floor. I glanced at the clothes and back to Finn, who grinned. "You're such a bleeding heart, Perdi. As if you'd leave anyone behind. And Zeno, here, wasn't wearing clothes when he was taken. Why do you think I sent you to these weapons rooms? You didn't have a hope in hell of getting out of here on your own. I thought you'd at least have an Aos Si to help you get back out."

"Great job, Finn. But with you in here with us, we're locked in now. The ward is back down."

"I couldn't stand at the door forever. Why do you think so many Seers have come down to look? They could feel the ward wasn't grabbing."

"Zephyr is going to lose his shit." I groaned. "If we live, he'll kill me for bringing you all in here."

"Tell him Zeno commanded us," Finn replied and eyed Zeno. "Right? You're second in command. Tell us to stay and fight."

"One day, Finn, you're going to skirt the wrong rule and end up in places much worse than this," Zeno answered.

"But that day is not today," Finn answered. "At worst, I'm tied to one of these slabs. I've been in worse places than this. At best, the bitch kills me."

"That's an uncomfortable thought...worse places than this." I shuddered.

Zeno shook his head. "Zephyr can skin us all when we get out of here. It's not anything we've not endured already."

"Speak for yourself. I've only been tortured once. I've yet to get used to it," I countered.

"You never get used to it, little Crow." Finn sighed his words as if remembering more than he'd ever say out loud.

We moved to meet the others, who had six Seers dead on the floor. Cas smiled from the front and waved. I waved back. They strapped themselves with more knives and blades than anyone could need, but they were apparently planning for every inevitability. That they each felt they needed to be covered, head to toe, in weapons, told me everything I needed to know about what we'd be facing. It made me nervous. I hadn't even lived through the first and only war I had been in.

"You've seen how the Aos Si fight. The Seers fight just like us." Cas leaned over. "Keep that in mind when we go out there. Knowing how they'll fight, how they'll move, will keep you alive. You've fought Zephyr and Solas in training. Those we face are but a shadow of who you've stood against. You can do this with one arm behind your back."

"But Solene…" I groaned.

"She is not stronger than Zephyr or Solas. She's just harder to kill. All you need to do is survive long enough for Zephyr and Solas to get through the wards. Nothing more."

"Oh, only that?" I huffed a laugh.

I swallowed a rock in the back of my throat, pushing my fear into my stomach for my Malice to eat. "Without ego, who are the strongest Aos Si here?"

"Finn, Zeno, Jare and Triton." Nix leaned out from my shoulder to make eye contact. "Never doubt the nose of a gnome."

"Okay, you four with me. The rest of you empty the halls. There's a group of Seers who do not stand with Solene. Don't kill them unless you have no choice," I replied.

"How will we know who they are?" Cas asked.

"They won't be trying to kill you," I answered, and he laughed.

"Finn will go in first," Zeno added. "When he has her, he'll get her to drop the wards, then we'll bring her to Zephyr and Solas. A quick grab and dump…in and out."

I didn't ask why. Part of me didn't want to know why Finn was first up. Nix jumped from my shoulder to Cas, who tried to pass Nix a small knife. He pushed it away and laughed. Nix was his own weapon.

I tilted my head and could hear the faintest shriek echo through Blood and Bones. "The Sluagh are here."

"Well, things just got interesting. To war we go," Finn replied.

"See you on the other side," I said and turned to the door. Orrian flicked her wings, and we headed into Blood and Bones for an early war, without the armies who would have helped us. I could almost hear Zephyr's *"Foolish little Crow."* Solas' words echoed behind, *"Burn them all."*

# Chapter Thirteen

We started through the halls at a steady pace, silent as the wind. Above, we could hear the yells from the Seers, who were under attack from the Sluagh and were surprised at the audacity. They, who'd lived in their blood-stained towers, hadn't expected the rest of us to grow tired of their terror. The air held a foul yet sweet smell of uncertainty mixed with fear. I was sure the stench of terror was coming from me. I was shaking in my boots. The others ignored it, and I was thankful for that.

The sour aroma sharpened with each step forward we took. My cleansing breaths worsened the dread filling my body, as if the very air held fear enough to choke on. What had started as a reminder of the Bodach had grown into something verging on wild horror. I pushed my Malice to the surface, begging her to eat whatever hung in the air. She eased the feeling, but not even she could eat what poured down the halls and told me I could run, but I couldn't hide. I doubted even Oberon could eat what flooded the corridors.

The halls divided, and with each turn, a group would branch off and go toward a fate I didn't know. Those foolish enough to stand against us met their deaths in surprise. Their focus had been on the beasts above and not the ones crawling up from the bowels of their castle of bloody walls. I pulled the energy from them as they fell. I would need it for what I was about to do. When Zeno began to speed up, I knew it was time to run. For every one of his steps, I took three. His legs ate up the ground and forced me to jog.

When the last of the Aos Si took a different path, leaving the four most powerful with me, my arms were pumping from the jog. There was no more room for me to stay protected in the middle. I palmed two blades and readied myself for what I knew was coming...*war*. There could be no other way in this world. My hands gripped the metal handles and brought the world into expert focus. I was practiced with a sword, but not enough to save my life from an attack. I favored being up close and personal with my blades, where I could use my darker skills if needed. With my Malice swirling under my skin, I moved without hesitation. The time to reconsider had been dashed when I had found Zeno and couldn't leave him behind.

Moving with four of the strongest, we found the path had been cleared quickly. In the halls, we'd passed some Seers who'd dropped their swords. "*We're with Lily,*" had gotten a free pass from us. Within minutes, the screaming had erupted into burning terror as the Sluagh breached the walls and roamed the halls. I could smell their hot, leathery hides and found myself smiling. As if the sounds of Seers being broken in half was the signal we all had been waiting for, Zeno's pace turned into a run. We were no longer chasing the fight. It came boiling down the hall toward us. The first wound I felt, but after the first sting, there was no more pain. I moved as I had been trained. I wasn't as fast as the others, but I wasn't as slow as I once had been, either. I wasn't as scared as I thought I'd be and didn't hesitate as I once would have.

Each time I was cornered, one of the men would be there to pull them off me. When a blade dug into my stomach, my panic called the shadows, but they weren't on the other end. The wards blocked all but the Sluagh. And for the first time, I understood all of Zephyr's training. There would come a time when he wouldn't be able to save me, where I'd have to depend on only myself and what I could bring to a table of one. My Malice answered my call, reached forward and pulled the life from the woman who had tried to take mine. The rage she felt replaced my fear and panic. The hall came into hyperfocus. I darted behind the one Triton found, sword against sword. I sank my blade into her back and drained her of life. Neither he nor I stopped there. Each Seer who had tried to stop us felt the kiss of iron and the pull of my Malice. We didn't pause to count bodies, but I had pulled enough energy to know it was more than I wanted to look back at. We left them where they fell and ran toward our final stand.

We came to a long hall that I recognized. At the end was 'the seeing pool', and to the right of it was a meeting room I had only glanced at. It looked less frightening than the first time I had walked the hall. I rubbed my arms and wanted to vomit.

"What the hell is that?" I asked, wanting to peel the sticky feeling from my skin.

"Don't ask." Triton shook his head. "We don't have anything to fear."

Nix came around the corner at full speed and jumped across two sets of shoulders before landing on mine. His body was slick with blood. I didn't ask questions. I already knew he had fought his way through. "Just in time."

"Finn." Zeno's word fell from his lips like a rock.

"Fuck." His only reply before he was gone.

Finn blasted through the hall at a speed I couldn't track. We ran behind him, passed the seeing room and into the meeting room. Finn had Solene in his grip. Although she fought him, she didn't escape. From the look on both their faces, the real struggle was within. I stepped forward, my eyes on Solene. The deep pool of rage boiled to the surface, sending flashes of ways I could punish her for all she had done. I shook it from my mind. I wouldn't let her turn me into another version of her. Justice would come, not punishment.

"Take your time." Finn groaned. "It's not like I hate this or anything."

"Don't be such a baby," I replied.

Zeno interrupted before Finn could tell me where to go and how to get there. "Tell her to drop the wards."

Finn smiled. "Solene, be a dear and drop your wards. The end of the world awaits us."

She struggled, but we all felt the wards drop. When they were down, I could feel the shadows finally answer my call and blast through every crack and crevice. In one swoop, they grabbed us and spat us onto the battlefield. Finn let her go, wiping his hands as if they were coated in disgusting things, and stepped back. Zephyr appeared at my side in a haze of shadows and shook his head. He wouldn't say it, but I knew he'd have a few choice words for me. I would point out that I had saved his people, and he would point out that I had risked too much for them. Neither of us would win the argument, but we'd both get our points across and be thankful to have survived long enough to have that very talk.

The clouds opened and thunder shook the earth as screeches echoed through the sky. Winged beasts hit the ground in heaps. I looked to Zephyr, who gave me a knowing look. He tilted his head. He could hear the Horn in the distance. The real war was about to start, and it wouldn't be played out in mounds of death that littered the ground. Solene watched Solas walk through the field. He was the only one I knew who could do war casually. Solas glanced at me once and winked. *Cocky as ever.*

"What the hell is that?" Oisin stepped up to my side. The only one brave enough to stand this close to whatever the pits of hell spat out. Oisin stared at the black clouds rolling over the field.

"Solas is pissed off," I answered. "Whatever happens next, you must let it play out, Oisin. Keep everyone back. No matter what you see, do not stop it from happening."

He nodded. "This is going to hurt so bad."

"I bet being wine-drunk at home, having never met the Crow, is looking mighty appealing now," I replied.

"I'll never regret my path meeting yours. I have your back, Perdi. I always will." Oisin gripped my hand once and took a step back, putting his to mine. He would keep an eye out for whoever was foolish enough to carry out my death sentence, as already demanded by Solene.

Solene faced her brother. "You wage war against Blood and Bones? You will die for this."

"I warned you of this moment," Solas replied. Utter silence rolled through the armies. The slightest breath could be heard over the stillness. "I told you, one day, there would be someone powerful enough to take your life."

"And I will say it again… Nowhere in Elphame is there enough power to kill me." Solene laughed, still brave in the face of her ending. "Solas, you will leave, or you will suffer."

"No. I don't think I'll be leaving," Solas replied.

A collective gasp rumbled over the men. I could tell by the tension in the air, everyone feared what came over the wall from Blood and Bones.

"Do not do this, brother. I spared you once for the Gate, and this is what you do with that freedom? You squandered it on a failed invasion? I will not spare you again."

Solas looked beyond Solene and found my eyes. "We all die someday, and today looks like as fine of a day as any for an ending."

"You *will* be the one to die." Solene spat her words. Solas stepped forward, and the world slowed as the Dark Court teetered on this very moment. Solene pulled her blade. "You will not get another warning from me. You will die."

"Indeed, I will. But today is not that day," Solas answered.

Today could have started and ended in thousands of ways, but the fates had decided, long ago, that it would end with pain and death. Nothing worth having ever came easy, and I felt that truth the moment Solas met my eyes. The Court of Blood and Bones, the original Fae, stood in the middle of a war that never should have started, a war they had allowed to happen — a war Solene had caused the moment hell spat her from her mother's womb.

Each path I had seen played out slightly differently than the next. They all depended on what I was willing to give of myself. The cold iron knife, held bare in my hand, began to burn in my grasp and cook my flesh. For the first time since coming here, iron burned my skin. The Gate, just beyond, was no longer my way home. I was already there, and from where I stood, not ten feet from Solas, my home was already being invaded. I let the knowledge of it sink in and blister my soul along with my skin. Solene had come into *my* home, *my* lands, threatened *my* people and would dare hold a knife to *my* family. My face went utterly blank.

A world of truths brought me to this minute in time, but it was love and honor that demanded I act upon it. The Horn blasted in my ears, and I staggered. I glanced at Zephyr, and he nodded. In the blink it had taken for Solene to utter her death threat, the ground crawled with darkness, and I dug my nails into my already bloodied hand. The time had come. The ending was here. I whispered to my Darkmore line, pleading for its strength to end Solene's reign of terror. But it was Elphame that answered. The Horn gave me everything I needed.

"Your tricks will not work on me, Solas," Solene said, glancing at the shadows. "You are not strong enough to stop me."

"Oh, dear, foolish sister, those shadows are not mine." Solas smiled. "It was never *me* you should have feared. I was not who you should have been watching so closely. You are the one who squandered their time and missed the threat that you invited into your very home, into your very soul."

"They belong to me." I moved with liquid speed. Solas held out his hand for my blade to drag across his flesh and gather the third drop of lifeforce from Blood and Bones.

I slid to Solene's back and pushed the knife, gifted to me by her very people, into her back to its handle. It would not be a killing blow, but I hadn't planned on killing her...yet. The iron, made of blood and bones, crafted in the depths of despair she'd crawled out of, was coated in the blood of three kin. The knife cut her off from her magick. I took that moment and pushed my Malice into her bones and stilled her to her core. Her power faltered as she gasped and tried to pull on her magick. I pushed her soul back into its cage and ate her fire that threatened to burst from within.

As one, Solene's sisters landed on the field of the Last War, oathed to protect her until their deaths. In their wake, the sky crackled with thunder and power. With his sword drawn, Zeno stood between the Seers and Solene. The energy that rolled off him nipped at my legs. It felt like two cats fighting across my skin. Behind him, the entire Aos Si army landed, from trainee to full rank, spreading out around us—ready. Triton caught my eye and winked. Jare had eyes only for Solene. Had I the chance, I'd have given him the pleasure of taking her life.

"You will die before you reach our little Crow." Zeno's voice cut through the air like a knife. His eyes landed on the Seers. "I offer you one warning, take it and your life, because it will cost me nothing to kill each of you. My oath died the moment I was stolen into your court." He eyed the one who'd helped me. "Lily, make up your mind before I do it for you."

The Seers stepped back, to Solene's surprise.

"Do it." Lily looked beyond Zeno to me. She nodded her head. "Do it before I can no longer stand back."

"What have you...?" Solene muttered, and I cut off her words with a twist of iron in her flesh. Her body shuddered against the blade.

"Did you really think I'd stand here and let you kill Solas? You have come to *my* home and threatened *my* family. You threaten our neighbors and friends. You have taken our family and tortured them in the basement of your hellhole. Did you think we wouldn't come for them?" I screamed into her ear, vibrating with rage at what I had found in her dungeons. "You killed our people for power? You forced them into servitude and held their lives in your hands. Did you think we'd just watch? Did you think us that weak, we'd allow you to step foot onto *our* lands and kill *our* people? Your court is not the only one made of blood and bones. You willingly stepped foot into the land of fucking nightmares. Allow me to give you a tour."

The world around us burst into shadows, like hundreds of bats taking to the air, and tore away the war-torn lands around us. I unleashed all my Malice on her mind and held nothing back. I didn't care if I left anything in my wake. I tasted every desire, horrific honesty and fate she had cast from her tower. Little by little, she had chipped away at Elphame, turning it into her vision of ultimate power. She craved it as desperately as I did my freedom. And, like me, she'd do anything to satiate her cravings. I rolled her thoughts in my mouth like sweets. She had seen everything but me, who had been carefully hidden by Solas and Zephyr. No one ever expected the Crow to rise up — not the Golden Court and not her. But I had already killed one king to prove I couldn't be owned. I'd kill just as quickly to prove it again.

"You, Solene, are an oath breaker. The wild hunt calls your name, and we are here to answer the call." Zephyr stepped through the shadows. I pushed her from my front, and for a moment I hoped she would run.

"I did no such thing," she sputtered. Her eyes danced between us both.

"Your own sisters knew of your treason." I held the knife I had driven into her back and tossed it end over end. I knew she recognized it when her face paled. She shook her head and stepped back.

"I've done nothing to bring about the wild hunt." She spoke as if her words would be enough to convince the Gods to let her live.

Zephyr stood at my side, his body readying to chase her should she try to run. "I have owned one of your pearls since the beginning of your life. Given at your birth, to guard you, it allowed me to always feel you. I may not have read you like all other pearls, but it allowed me to follow you and watch you come and go, turning Solas into a man who needed to be slain. You turned him into the man all of Elphame would need to kill. You urged Solas to kill Perdi before she found out what you were doing, before she could ruin your plans. But you didn't count on Solas choosing her, a Crow, over you. You tried to force him to allow her death at the Gate, or you'd call him an oath breaker and would own him. But you couldn't control me any more than you could control Solas. I brought her back, and as punishment, you tried to ruin *my* king for it. You tried to take *my* king from me. You tried to take *my* people from me. You tried to take *my* Crow from me!" His scream was a lash across her face, and she jerked under its hot touch. The ground shuddered under his anger. "And when you thought you won, the wild hunt called on the only one who would find your truth at any cost, the little Crow you, yourself, have been trying to kill at all costs."

"Are you willing to pay that cost now?" I asked her, then leaned into her ear. "For everything you've done, I'd kill you because you took Nix's family from him. But I'll make it hurt for what you did to my people."

Zephyr's shadows flared to life, closing off her remaining chance to run. There would be no escape for Solene. Her eyes darted wildly. The shadows rolled around us like thunderous clouds. They crackled with hate, edged with my own Malice, that starved for her death.

"What are you doing here, Soul-Eater? You will pay for this. You all will pay." Solene spat out the last word. "You cannot stand against me and win."

I moved with the speed I had seen Zephyr move with. Elphame radiated through my soul, the energy propelling me to Solene's front. I grabbed her, pulled her toward me with a jerk, and whispered into her ear. "We are called Finis. We come at the end. And today, we've come to eat your cursed soul."

She struggled against my grip. "No. You can't be."

Zephyr smiled. "Population two."

"Oh, but I am. The one you've been searching for has been here all along, hidden right under your nose. Now you will pay by my hand or at the hand of the wild hunt. Either way, you'll be just as dead."

She laughed. Even in the face of her fate, she laughed. "You're wasting your time. You will be sentenced to death for this. You can't prove I've done a thing, Soul-Eater. But the world will know there are two of you now."

Zephyr joined in her laughter until it spooked her into silence. He leaned forward with an unfriendly smile. "You're as foolish as you've always been. You will find no friends on the battlefield, only your death."

"The Gods will not allow this!" Solene screamed.

"Your God isn't here," I countered.

"No! You will all die for this."

"No. You are the only one left to die," Solas countered as he stepped through the shadows. "You either die for what you've done, or you die to protect Perdi's secret. Either works for me. I'm not picky today."

"But..." Solene screamed as the fate she was never powerful enough to see played out.

I cut off her words as I pushed cold iron into her heart and twisted the blade. "But...you shouldn't have touched a Soul-Eater's family. Did you truly think two Soul-Eaters would allow you to touch a throne under their protection and live to tell about it? You are an arrogant bitch."

"No! This isn't how it was supposed to end," she pleaded.

I whispered in her ear. "You are the Curse of Blood and Bones. The songs of your court will forever sing of your disgrace."

"The songs of *my* court," Solas corrected me. "I am the heir to her throne and claim it now. And I sentence you to death."

I screamed in her face as I reached toward her soul with my Malice. I felt her need in the very pit, hidden from the world. The reason my death was on the lips of every king, at her orders. She would end my life to keep the Gate open, to keep the rift between worlds open. She'd called countless Crows to their deaths, waiting for a unique little Crow to come, a Soul-Eater. She hadn't known what I was but would have hunted all the mortal world in search of another to rip the rift wide open. Solene was doom for all. She would have been the death of countless. She'd have bled the mortal world dry for the only other Finis standing before her. What surprised me was that she hadn't done it for hate. She had done it for love. Of who, I didn't know. I didn't care, because they were gone from her.

I snaked through her fighting body and found Zephyr's touch deep within. I followed the path he blazed and gripped Solene's soul in the pit of her stomach. The power that radiated from deep within Solene would take both of us to extinguish. He had said, once, that I had been born to come here and would find myself standing at his side one day, where I would understand why. And now I knew. It would take two Soul-Eaters to end the Taking of the Crows. As Oberon had said, no *one* person would end this. It would take both Zephyr and me to finish it. It burned every inch of my body as I pulled against her fight for survival. Both Zephyr and I screamed in pain until Solene's final breath rattled from her chest.

"This was why," he finally spoke, his forehead wet from sweat. "Why we'd be standing together."

"To end it all," I whispered and wobbled on my feet.

He smiled and helped me stand straight again. "We eat worlds, little Crow."

"This is what two pissed-off Soul-Eaters look like," I answered.

Solas grabbed my waist and pulled me into his arms, and I shrieked in surprise. "I've missed you, little Crow." When I froze in his arms, he still didn't let go. "For one day, please, Perdi, let me just live one day and suffer for it tomorrow. Call it a dying man's last request."

"You're not exactly at risk of dying anymore." I laughed and hugged him back. "I'm glad to have you back, Solas. I'm so sorry for the horrible things I've said."

"We'll have time for that later. There are things that need to be said and cleared, layers of lies I've told. But right now, let me feel you once again. I finally found my way back to you. Let me just have today," he whispered into my mouth. "I knew you'd find the truth, and you'd find me buried under it."

"I'll always find you," I whispered back. "There will never be a day I don't find my way back home to you."

The shadows faded with me in Solas' arms. The others would know exactly what we had done, and that was whatever we could to save us all. We stepped away from Solene, limp on the ground, and watched with the others as her blood seeped into the earth. It was a fitting end to be left on the ground, nothing more than blood and bones. In the time it took to take her life, the Aos Si and Seers had brought the war to a close.

Faolan was on the field, next to Oisin. He was the first to move, to stand next to Zephyr. I stepped as far away from the still-warm body as I could without running for the hills, and stood between Zephyr and Solas. One look at Solas, and I knew he was still in war mode. Even with his sister dead mere feet in front of him, he wouldn't show the rest of Elphame any weakness or remorse — not now, not ever. He'd save it for later, tucked safely away from the eyes and ears of those outside of his trusted circle. Solas kissed my temple and, with a nod, began barking orders in true Solas fashion.

I squeezed Zephyr's hand, a silent thank you for always coming back for me. Zephyr's entire body shuddered as he ate another pearl. With my hand in his, I felt it as he took more of Solene's soul, trapping her in his shadows for all times. She, unworthy, would never feel the touch of the Gods or Goddesses. No one cared to move her body, not even her people bothered to look at her.

I found Zeno standing with his men. He looked healed but aged and tired — exactly how I felt. He tipped his head. "Thank you, little Crow."

Finn stood at Zeno's side and grinned. "And here I saved you a seat for nothing."

"Maybe next time, the world *will* end." I smiled. "I'll keep a seat warmed for you."

Zephyr pointed at Finn. "You, go be somewhere else."

"You know where to find us, Perdi. We can finish off the rest of the wine." Finn winked and casually walked away.

"Stay away from that one, little Crow," Zephyr said. "Not him. Anyone else, just not him."

I laughed at how protective Zephyr was. He'd fight the moon if I hated the night. My smile faded along with the light. Little by little, I watched as the world grew a little darker around the edges. I lifted my hand off my stomach and stared at the blood. It was brilliant in the sun, brighter than I remembered blood to be.

"Worth it."

Zephyr caught me as the world tilted. He breathed me in and cursed. "Where is Jare?"

"I sent him to Elda to help heal the injured," Zeno replied.

"Tell Solas I'm taking her to the caves." Zephyr picked me up at tucked me into his darkness.

I lifted my hand to his face and smiled. "It doesn't even hurt."

"Foolish little Crow," he answered and landed on the lip of the cave.

"I'm tired, Zeph."

He shouted for Jare, who pulled me into his arms. "She's bleeding pretty bad."

My eyes tracked slowly to Jare. "Hello, again."

He smiled and carried me into the cave, to the corner, away from the others. He rolled a metal room divider out from the wall and pulled a curtain across. He helped me sit up, peeled my bloody jacket off, and cut my shirt off, gently pulling it from my sticky wounds. I watched his face as he worked. Not a single emotion betrayed him.

"You're a man of few words."

"Yes, ma'am," he answered softly. His voice made my bones relax into the bed. Every worry leaked out of me, along with my blood.

"Your voice is beautiful," I whispered. "Say something else."

"But I am no one to you."

I tried to lift my hand to his face but struggled against the weight of it. Watching me struggle, he cupped my hand to his cheek. "Don't ever let someone take away who you are. You're not no one, not to me."

"Thank you. You're everything Zephyr said you'd be." He breathed me in, a shudder leaving his body. He pulled back and cut the rest of my clothes from my body, hissing at the sight of me once I was stripped down.

"How bad is it?" I asked.

"You're dying," he answered.

I frowned. "But it doesn't hurt that bad."

"The path to death is what hurts us, not the act of death," he answered. "The path back will hurt even more. Are you ready to pay for it?"

"Nothing is free."

My scream ate up every space within the caves. Jare's hands brought my pain into brilliance. How Zeno had stayed still while Jare had healed him was beyond me. I felt the first wound close, knitting my muscle, tissues and skin. I could hear it the same way a bone breaking could be heard. I turned onto my side and was sick. I strained against the pain to move away, even though I'd have died unless healed. I pushed at his hands each time he tried to touch me.

"No more," I choked out.

"I cannot take the pain away, but I can make it happen fast enough that you'll go to sleep." He kept talking while he worked. It didn't take the pain away, but it kept me from running.

"Don't be such a baby." Finn's laughter rolled across my broken body as his hands gripped my shoulders and held me down while every inch of my flesh burned as it knitted back together. Finn's eyes met mine. "It's almost over, little Crow."

I could hear the skin pull and grip and seal. Wave after wave of pain came until the world darkened and

I passed out. I had never been so thankful for passing out.

# Chapter Fourteen

Zephyr lifted me from the bed. I opened my eyes to him sitting on the grass, my head in his lap, with him softly combing my hair. I didn't know how long we had been there before I woke up, but it had been long enough for the lines around his eyes to ease. The woman who had stood on the hills, blowing the horn, was gone. The sound of it, which had driven me crazy some nights, had left with her, and it was almost deafening.

"What did I miss?"

"Besides your death?" He glanced down and shook his head. "Solas is still on the field in the tents. He has told them all the truth of Solene and the Horn of Elphame. He's giving them a way out of their mess — or it's war, as usual."

"How'd they take it?" I asked.

Zephyr lifted his brows and rolled his eyes. "As any king would, insulted that we hid the truth from them. None of them are willing to admit their own parts in any of this. Fools. We could be at peace, once and for all, but they'd rather argue. I'm so tired of this shit."

"I'd do it again." I smiled. "To get here, I'd do it again."

"I don't think I could, little Crow. I felt each time you cried, each time you longed for home. I knew, even before Solas came to me and told me to help him find a way to get you back, to bring you home, that I'd eat them all to get to you."

"When did he tell you to bring me back?" I asked.

"When was he not scheming to get you home? You ending up in his dreams didn't help. A few times, he asked me to go and get you, and I had to refuse. You kept asking me to leave you in Winter Court, that you had these grand plans. More times than I can count, I had to pin him down to keep him from going to Tylwyth and getting you, himself. And again, this morning, he made me oath myself to him. If he failed, I was to grab you and leave. He made me swear I'd return for Nix, Orrian and your father, so you wouldn't be alone."

"And here I thought you didn't make oaths?" I smiled. "It was worth it in the end."

"I don't know. I've never felt that pain before. It hurt so bad, Perdi. I never want to feel it again. I watched Solas go mad without you. I felt it. I watched you fade without him, and it killed something inside me. I watched your dreams. It was the good dreams that killed me, when you'd dream of us and your laughter that filled the halls." Zephyr interrupted my bravado. "I mean it when I say that the world almost burned when I thought you'd left us. When I thought you'd left me."

"You don't own me." I opposed the very notion that he could control me in any way.

His shadows flickered behind his eyes. "I will stop you, and you will fight me every step of the way, but I will not watch you both burn from stubbornness. If you had told each other the truth, rather than trying to protect each other, putting me in the middle, this wouldn't have happened."

"I'm sorry, Zeph. You know I never meant to hurt you."

"Don't ever do this again." Zephyr's voice turned stern. "I will drag you back. I swear on all I have. This can never happen again."

"We both would have died," I answered. But one serious look from him and I backpedaled. Now was not the time to argue with him. "I will only run again if I'm in danger."

"Talking to you is like talking to Solas. Both of you are headstrong and have mastered the riddles of Elphame."

I shrugged. "Solas is the cool touch to my flames."

Zephyr huffed a laugh. "No, Perdi, you eat the souls Solas has ripped from lifeless bodies. You both are war and death."

It was an ugly thing to say...but true.

"I heard the Horn of Elphame. I felt it in my bones."

"It's a frightening feeling," I answered.

"It was a call to arms, a call to your cause. The call of an oath breaker is a powerful feeling. I felt compelled to help you, not just because we're bound, but because of that horn. I couldn't have walked away, even if I had wanted to. None of us could. It is why the Aos Si returned, and the Sluagh dropped from the skies. Fae I have not seen in centuries crawled from the sea and slithered from the mountains. We were ready to fight another war, both sides as one." He answered and shivered. "It is why Lily helped you in Blood and Bones. Like the rest of us, they felt the call and wanted it to end."

"Well, isn't that nice, all of you coming together over a broken oath. Here I thought you'd never find a common enemy," I teased. "Thank you for coming, no matter the reason."

"When you came from Blood and Bones, your blood dripping from your body, I couldn't see beyond my rage. It was a darkness I've never experienced. The Horn pulled me from the dark. I knew what you were about to do, and I didn't want you to face her alone. Even though I felt compelled, I would have come to the call of a Crow."

"What happens now?" I asked. "Now that the Last War has been won."

"We go home." He motioned toward the table of kings. "I don't care where the rest go. They're Solas' headache, not mine. I'm so thankful we don't have thrones, little Crow."

"I want a throne," I teased. "Plunked down in the living room, at home. A big one. With gold Crow wings and diamonds. Solas owes me a crown, the one from his head, for this."

He laughed and pulled me a little closer, as a brother would before pulling your pants up too high. "The best I can do is a chair from the dining room. I'll paint a Crow on it if you want?"

"Why are we out here and not on the field?"

"I must speak to you in private before we go on."

I cringed when I saw the serious look on his face. I sat up and faced him. "What bomb are you about to drop on me, now?"

"You'd deserve it for the bombs you're always dropping on me. But right now is not for surprises. Little Crow, I have invited you home to the island. And now, today is the day you learn of my truths as I have learned yours. And from there, you'll decide what the next steps are and where we will go from there, because I don't see anything beyond the ending of Solene. I can't see my path with you anymore."

"What truths?" I asked. "Why can't you see us together?"

"I can't see our paths any longer because choices need to be made," he answered, and I relaxed a little more. "Perdi, I felt your birth. Even from a world away, I felt your first breath. It is that way with Finis. We can feel each other always. I knew before any other knew of you, before Aoife knew of her own fate, you would come to Elphame, and you would carry a cost on your broken wings that I would gladly pay. I gave myself to that prison for many reasons. The truth is that I gave myself willingly, so I could be near you, so I could help you and love you. I had hoped if you felt that, just a little piece of home, you wouldn't give up fighting. You wouldn't let them take your will to live. Even if you hadn't released me, I was willing to die there for the chance of you staying alive. I felt you every moment of my life. And from the very moment you freed me, I have done all I could to steer you toward this moment."

"You steered me?" I asked, surprised.

"I didn't make your decisions for you, but I always made sure you knew of all your choices. I have sent my shadows for you, always. From the beginning of my life, every shadow I chose, I chose for you. I selected only the strongest, those who would challenge and protect you. Everything I have done, I've done so I'd be strong enough to protect you. I've done it because I love you."

"Did you have the shadows guide me, as well?" I asked. I trusted Zephyr with my life, but I couldn't hide my unease with being pushed down a path that had rubbed my soul raw.

"No. And you're not listening to me. You're hearing the words and cobbling together a truth that is not mine. I didn't force you to do anything. I helped you. As you can see, from the fires I put out as you walk the path of your choosing, you've made every decision you've wanted, as have my shadows. With you, I've given them complete freedom. They spoke to you without my influence and helped you as you requested, not as I forced. Because I knew that one day we would stand here together, and I wanted to be at your side. I merely made sure you got here in one piece," Zephyr answered. "When you came to me about Solas, I'm sorry I didn't act in the way you wished, but I couldn't. Not only because he is my king and my friend but because I knew that if I tried to save you, you'd never save yourself or your people. Sooner or later, I knew you had to find your own way, as much as I hated the route you took. But I was always there, in case you fell. You are still but a wee Soul-Eater."

"Tell me the truth, Zeph. Did you ever force me?" I asked.

"No. I never have and never will. But in those moments of fear, when you gained courage, that was me. When you didn't want to get back up, I pulled you to your feet. When you wished for death, I whispered fearlessness and will to live. And when you faced off against your enemy, new to this world, it was me who gave you my energy to fight. The nights you wanted to world to burn, I came and held you and ate your sadness. I guided you, little Crow. I didn't force you. Your choices are still your own."

"I knew you were there but didn't know you have *always* been there. Thank you," I answered. I was okay with knowing Zephyr had steered me from danger, from the brink of death, to ensure I would stand with him in the end.

He held his hand out. In his palm, a pearl. "This is yours to have."

"You're giving me back my pearl? But, Zeph, why? I'm sorry. Please don't give it back." I asked and felt instant sadness and panic. I looked up at him through tear-coated lashes. My heart hammered hard enough to feel it in my throat. I could see the pulse in my sight. "I gave that to you." I gripped his arm and shook my head. Tears rolled down my face. "Please, Zeph, don't leave me. I know I'm a pain and make you angry, but I can't lose you. Don't go, please. I love you. If you go, you have to take me with you. Solas would come. I know he would."

"What? Calm down, little Crow." He huffed a small laugh and dabbed my cheeks. "This is *my* pearl. I'm not leaving you. We are the last. We must protect each other. But for us to be truly Finis together, you must have mine as I have yours. But if you take this pearl, know you are tied to me until death. There will be no power in any realm that could keep us from burning the world to get to each other. You can never leave me. I can never leave you. Only in death can we part," he answered. "And, if we're being technical, you didn't *give* me your pearl. You suckered me in with an oath to protect you against everyone, which ended up also being my king."

I swallowed back my sob and hugged him. "I thought you were leaving me. I thought I wouldn't see you again. I don't know, I panicked."

He held me tightly against him and stroked my hair. "I can't leave you. You were born to eat souls. How could I unleash that on both realms? I'd be the laughingstock of hell."

I pulled back and he placed his pearl in my hand. I opened my mouth to ask him what I would do with it and watched as it melted into my palm. Zephyr gripped my arms as I shuddered, filled with all of who he was—his pain, his joy, his rage, his laughter. Flashes of his entire life, from his first breath to this very moment, flooded my soul with memories. And when it edged too close to being too much, his calm control filled me. He, like me, had relived it all, every gory detail. I felt his fear that I'd see who he was, all of him, and would leave him in the forest alone. Zephyr thought he deserved to walk his path alone and was ready to let me go if I couldn't face who he was—a fate earned from decades of war. I looked up, met his eyes and hugged him once again. This time, simply because I knew he needed it. He needed to know I still cared after all I had felt. I did, as he always had for me. I hugged him until all his pieces were pushed back together. Nothing he had shown me had made me think less of him.

"You're not alone anymore," I whispered to him. "I'll always come."

"As will I, little Crow." He breathed out a shaking breath of worry. "When first I came to the Dark Courts,

I met with Elda. She told me of the wars I'd fight, the victories I'd have and the lives I'd take. She told me of the suffering I'd endure, but the pain and hurt would be for something. She said I'd save a Crow, the same Crow I had dreamed of my entire life, and it would be at the expense of the life I had known. She said I'd stand in the middle of a war, and I'd choose to stand beside a Crow rather than a king. That I'd pick a Crow over everyone else. I'd protect a little Crow over Solas. I didn't believe her until your soul called out to my shadows, the day you were born and every day in between.

"When I was locked in my cage in the Golden Court, I still felt you. If I closed my eyes and concentrated hard enough, I could feel you in Whitwick. I could hear your laughter, taste your tears, listen to you and Nix argue over how to bake an apple turnover. I lived every day through you. But it was your first day, when you stood against Solas to protect Orrian, a Fae, someone you were supposed to hate, that I knew you were the one. It was then that I knew I'd do whatever I could to save my family, my little Crow."

I pulled back. "Family?"

"My line is your line. We are the same. We are kin."

"You always felt like home." I smiled as his shadows wrapped around us.

"As do you," he answered. "Now that you've seen my truths, where do we go from here? I would understand if you need time to process it. It's a lot to swallow. Trust me. I live with it every single day. But I wanted you to see my truths. I will bring you wherever you want and give you as much space as you need."

"Home." I smiled. "Zeph, you come home with us. I could never stop loving you."

"Thank you." He kissed the top of my head. "I love you, too. But Perdi, if you ever fucking lie to me again, I'll hurt you in ways that only someone you love could."

I pulled back and chose not to argue. "I'm sorry."

"I know, and I know why you did it. But just the same, do not *ever* lie to me or try to hide your scheming from me. Know that I will forgive you once, for you are new to the games of Elphame, but not twice. Twice will come at a cost."

I hugged him tighter. "And I will kill you the next time you lie to me."

"You and what army?" He laughed and brought me back to the tent.

"I have people. Haven't you heard? I make friends everywhere I go." I laughed back. Did I think I could kill him? No. But I knew I could make him hurt, which was just as bad.

Our feet touched back down outside of the tent. Inside, Solas and every other court sat, arguing over the fate of Elphame and the mortal world. I didn't want to go inside. Lily, the Seer, smiled as she stepped around me and into the tent. The look of relief on her face said she had hated Solene as much as the rest of us. I'd had only a taste of the woman and killed her for it. I couldn't imagine what her own sisters felt.

"Perdi?" Faolan came out of the tent before I could go in. "Could we talk in private? Oisin is in there. He'll speak on my behalf and has more patience for these games than I do."

I stared at him for a long moment and finally nodded.

"Faolan, I see you've fared well in this." I finally spoke, cutting the uncomfortable silence and his pacing.

He stopped me from saying anything more with a gentle squeeze on my arm. "Wait, Perdi. There are so many things I've wanted to say but never had the chance to say them. We were always being watched. I was always under the close eye of Solene or her people. Please, allow me just once to say what needs to be said. I'm finally free to give you the truth. I know you've been in my head, but I feel like it matters whether I'm willing to say it out loud or not."

"Okay, you have the chance now. This chance will never come again, Faolan," I answered. I fought not to cross my arms and glare at him.

"Honestly, I still can't believe I'm alive, that any of us lived through this or that you'd even let me live after finding out I had been under Solene's thumb. Perdi, I never wanted you to be Taken. That's the God's honest truth. I never agreed with it, the Taking. But I also didn't want my people to die for your freedom. It was a position I didn't know how to get out of. I felt my choices were between two things I didn't want to give up.

"On the one hand, my people. On the other, someone I cared deeply for. I told you the truth when I said I tried to save you. I really did. Even when Aoife told me you'd come here, I still tried. But after you were Taken and I watched you run to Solas, I burned with so much anger and hurt. I had a choice then, and I still made the wrong one.

"But once I got over the pain, it was too late. The damage was done. I had already sentenced you to a fate you didn't deserve. I didn't want to play a part in doing it again. So much hung in the balance, so many lives, and it had been going on for so long that I couldn't protect the person who needed me the most. I came to Solas' land and told you what was happening in the only way the oath allowed, whether you see that or not—and suffered Solene's rage for my warning to you. Every time I guided you, I suffered so you wouldn't. I thought if I could save you from her, even from one lash, you'd see I tried in the only ways I knew would save as many people as possible."

Rather than attack him, which would have been easier, I tried to understand. "When you came to me in the forest, I tried to hear you, to listen with more than my hurt. But my heart knew you weren't telling me the whole truth, that the truths you brought were what Solas wanted to world to see. I couldn't fully believe he would hurt me in the ways you said. It's why I couldn't bring myself to get closer to you, but I could use the tools I had. And that's what I did. I chose to stay in your lands to find the answers I needed—to find a way to stop this."

He nodded. "I know. I felt it. You were thankful to be in my territory but not to be with me. I figured if I could help you, even a little bit, it would set things straight. They were the saddest and happiest days of my life, if that even makes sense. For the first time, in a long time, my soul was happy, even though my heart broke to know your love was with him. But I still tried to give you the answers you needed, even with tied hands. I tried to show you where to find the truth when I was bound not to say the words."

"I know, and I'm grateful," I answered. "Fao, what the hell would you have done had this not worked out? Had we lost?"

A sharp laugh burst from his lips. "I was never going to win against Solas. None of us would have. But I knew if I protected you the best I could, he'd let my people live. It's why I only sent those who would sell you out the moment they could onto that field. Not even in my maddest state did I think I'd ever win against the Dark Court. I think the only reason he's never invaded my lands is that he doesn't like the cold. But more than that, I knew you wouldn't fail. You wouldn't lose. You're the last Crow. You'd save us all. I was willing to hang the fate of us all on you because you were the only one not oathed to her."

"I could have died out there."

"Never would you have died out there," he countered. "I knew, even if I had failed, Solas would protect you. He could do what I never could."

"What's that?" I asked.

"Die for you."

I nodded. "Solas would have. If I couldn't stop her, he would have died today."

"I wouldn't have risked it as he did. Zephyr would have brought him back. Zephyr is never that far from either of you for that reason. But there was always the risk that it wouldn't work. I wouldn't have taken that risk, not even for you. I love you in my own way, but not enough to risk my life like that or my people." Faolan sighed. "I'm sorry, Perdi. I'm so sorry for all of this."

"I don't know what to say," I finally answered. "I understand. I don't want to, but I do. I know firsthand what this world forces you to become. And I know what I was willing to do to protect my people and those I love, so I don't blame you for that. But I'd be lying if I said I forgive you—because I don't, not yet."

"I don't deserve to be spared, but I thank you. I can't thank you enough. Because of you, my people are safe."

"Go home, Faolan, and start over," I said. "I won't be as civil next time we meet on rocky ground. I meant what I said. Your soul will be the first one I'll pick."

"It doesn't seem fair. I get what you fought so hard for...home. And you're still here."

"I am home," I replied.

"Will he forgive you?" Faolan's voice cracked. "Do you want me to talk to him, to tell him what I've done?"

I let go of the anger in one breath. Faolan wasn't worth me dragging his memory around. "You weren't the only one to lie. I came to your territory for the truth, not to be with you. Solas and I did what we had to do to get to this moment. In some twisted way, you helped get me here, alive. In truth, Solas forgave me before I had even left and fought to keep me alive every day I was gone."

"Do you love him? Really and truly?" he asked.

"Yes, very much," I answered and felt that love to my core. "I cared deeply for you, Faolan, and a part of me always will. But with Solas? He's my home. He's...part of my soul."

"We're all looking for a home, Perdi, and I'm thankful you've found yours." He breathed in and smiled. It was a smile I was used to, that I remembered from a time when life didn't make you earn each hour. "Thank you. Like Solas, I knew you'd end it all. If anyone was going to do it, it would be you. Even as I made oaths, I knew they'd mean nothing in the end. When you knew the truth, I knew you'd still do what was right. I knew you'd do what the rest of us couldn't and end Solene's reign."

"At least one of us knew." I smiled. "You didn't make it easy for me."

"But I worked to not make it harder than it had to be. Nothing worth having is easy or free, but I tried to pay your costs to get you back home. When our paths cross again, I hope they cross in kindness." Faolan paused before stepping back into the tent. His entire body shuddered in disgust. "What the hell is that sound?"

I glanced at the bush behind the tent. "That's Nix and Orrian. They're with the leprechauns, eating someone, I imagine."

"They're always eating someone." Faolan shivered in revulsion. "Did you know my cat is missing?"

"The wee folk aren't feared without reason. If I were you, I'd leave soon. If they come asking questions, you'll know real anger." I walked in behind him. "I'm not joking, Faolan. You're not high on the list of people to trust. I am grateful for your help and what you endured to give it, but the wounds are still fresh, and I need time to let them scab over."

Solas' face lit up once he saw me. I stood beside Zephyr while the others made arrangements to protect the mortal realm. The Seers and Aos Si would send their people to guard the passage between worlds. No one would cross until a new treaty had been drafted. I watched as agreements were made to protect the mortal world. I never once thought I'd see the day that this happened. Then again, Solas gave them no choice. His army was already here, and with Solas saying the day was still young enough for another war, there wasn't a lot of pushback. He had no problem killing them all where they sat, to end the suffering of all with the blood of kings.

Solas stepped away from the table to my front. He tried not to look worried and relaxed once I stepped into his arms. He wrapped me tight against his body, as if any space left between us had hurt not to fill it up. It felt right. It felt safe. And I melted into him.

"You bounced back from hell so much quicker than I do." I reached up and pulled his chin to mine. Kissing him had always felt like opening the door to home.

He smiled. "Good genes, I guess."

"Solas…" I started, and he lifted me into his arms. "Can we go…"

"Home." He finished my sentence.

We left on the heels of Zephyr. The remaining Seers and Guardians, who saw this end as clear as day, stood at the gate to Whitwick with the Aos Si. For once, since the Gate had opened, the mortal world was safe. My people would never face another Taking. When I was dead and long gone from this world, who knows what their fates would be.

# Chapter Fifteen

The war was over, and now we had to rebuild. Like the rest of Elphame, I was used to rebuilding, having grown up in a world that sat mere feet from the gates of hell. My father returned to Whitwick as Captain of the Guardians. The old one had mysteriously vanished. He would sit for the negotiations of a new oath, a peace treaty between the mortals and the Fae. He was welcome in both worlds, and unlike me, he was happy to walk between the two. I was both mortal and Fae, with nothing in between — no Gate, no force from others, no strings attached to a puppet master. And now my home was Elphame, with family stretching across both worlds. For tonight, however, I was just Perdi. And although there was a glaring monster of unspoken words sitting in the room with us, we'd ignore it for as long as possible. If we didn't learn to ignore the monsters, we'd never have time for dinner.

Zephyr lifted his glass, the three of us together again, and toasted to freedom. The dining room, in shambles from Solas' rage, still oddly felt like home. We sat at the table, caked in mud and other things, and stared at each other. My leathers were ripped, slashed and covered in blood, matching Solas and Zephyr. Almost an hour had passed without words exchanged, just the silent awe of what we had been through.

"This place is a dump. We should have gone to my house." Zephyr picked a leaf out of his wine glass that had blown in through the broken windows.

I laughed. "I agree. The caves the trainees live in are better than this. Solas, you're slacking."

"I've been busy, warmongering and carting Crows across Elphame. I'll clean it up tomorrow." Solas grinned.

"When were you in the caves with the trainees?" Zephyr asked.

"The night before I went into Blood and Bones. They drew me a map," I replied. "I felt like a bag of crap the next day. Too much wine."

"They failed to mention this," he replied.

I rolled my eyes. "Leave them alone, Zeph. Please. Just this once. Without them, I wouldn't have made it back out, and we'd all be dead. I went in for a knife and ended up starting a small war while I was in there."

He finally nodded. "One time, Perdi. But I won't the next time they step out of line. We have rules for a reason. Those rules keep us alive."

"Always the stickler for rules. You can't control a little Crow or anyone she calls on for aid. They, like her, will do what their soul commands of them." Solas winked. It was rare for him to get between Zephyr and me, for no other reason than knowing I could speak for myself. But I appreciated it today. "Breaking those rules kept Perdi alive. It helped her save three of your men and bring an end to Solene in the process. Maybe a 'thank you' is warranted? I know I'm grateful as hell."

"And that's the only reason I'm not teaching them hard lessons as we speak," Zephyr replied and turned back to me. "Thank you, Perdi. I don't like that you risked so much, but I thank you for bringing them home."

"How are they?" I asked.

"They're okay. I hear Jare spoke to you? He usually doesn't talk to anyone. It surprised us all to hear him talking to you. Like you, we enjoyed hearing it."

"What about Triton and Zeno?"

"Triton is tougher than he looks. He's opted out of going with the full ranks and is in the caves with the trainees. He's always been closest to them. As for Zeno, he got the worst of it, but he'll heal." He left it at that, and I didn't push. "Your little boogeyman was on the field today, looking for you. He said he could smell your fear from his hovel. He ate his way to us, then stayed on the field, tormenting Faolan's army, until you came out of Blood and Bones. His people chased down those who tried to run. He said he expects you to attend for caving."

I shuddered at the thought. "Great. The first time was hard enough. I think Oberon will pluck my wings the second time around."

Solas barked a surprised laugh. "I wondered how you got him out of the cave that night."

"As I said, I make friends everywhere I go." I smiled in return.

"What are we going to do about Parrish?" Zephyr asked and finally broke the silence on the war none of us wanted to talk about. But Zephyr never cared if we wanted to ignore the monster in the room. He didn't tap dance around truths. He crashed about until someone noticed. I didn't mind. I liked being included once again.

"What about him?" I asked.

"He threw his hat in with Solas, but we knew who he really served. We did nothing to protect his people during the initial battle. Some survived and fled along with him. He didn't die out there as we had hoped."

"We'll kill him when he comes," I said, my voice flat as if I weren't talking about taking a life. "If and when he comes, I'll kill him myself. I'm tired of this shit."

"Of that, I have no doubt." Solas smiled.

"The mortal realm will not be happy about the Gate," Zephyr added and looked at Solas. "Regardless of how or why it fell, that Gate was the only thing they believed they had to keep us from their realm. Now, it is gone. Generations of horror will take generations to heal. What do we do in between?"

I shrugged. "Focus on one day at a time. For today, let's just be together and worry about tomorrow's war tomorrow."

"I doubt they'll give us many tomorrows," Zephyr added.

"There are never enough tomorrows," Solas replied.

"Parrish aside, is anyone going to comment on the fact that Solene's body was gone from the field?" I asked.

"The Seers probably took her," Zephyr answered.

"All of the Seers were still on the field when we got back. Which one?" I asked.

"I have Solene's pearl. It's dead," Zephyr replied.

"Find her body, and I'll stop worrying. I don't like not knowing. It's a scary place to be."

"Someone probably took her to punish her," Solas added. The look on my face made him laugh. "As uncomfortable of a thought it is, we're a creative lot. No one will care if she's dead to exact their revenge. Honestly, I don't really care where her body ended up."

"You all need better hobbies." I rolled my eyes.

"Am I too late for dinner?" A woman's voice carried from the doorway.

I frowned at first, then shot to my feet. "What's going on?"

Solas sucked in a deep breath and lifted his hands to try to calm me down. "Hear me out." I stared at him, questioning him with my eyes.

Zephyr burst into uncomfortable laughter. "Oh, these next few weeks are going to be great. You've both told so many lies. This house isn't going to survive you coming clean. I told you both to tell each other the truth. I warned you. But does anyone ever listen to me?"

"Shut up, Zephyr," I snapped at him.

"I hid her," Solas finally said.

"You did *what*?" I asked and spun to the door. "Elswyth?" I muttered the words, not wanting to believe it.

She walked into the room with Nix on her shoulder. "Perdi."

I pushed away from the table fast enough for my chair to tip and break. "Elswyth? How? Where did you go?"

Nix jumped from her shoulder to the table and sat on a cluster of fruit, picking a grape and bouncing it in the air. He joined Zephyr in the laughter. I, unlike them, didn't find any of this funny. Elswyth moved across the room while I stared at her in shock. I pulled her into a hug and mumbled all my worries and fears, that she was supposed to be dead at the hands of her husband, that Solas had sent her to her death.

"Let me explain, please," Solas begged from behind me. "I had a good reason. Okay, at the time, I thought it was a good reason. Now, I think it wasn't a good idea."

"But you sent her away long before I had closed the Gate to begin with." I turned to Solas, confused.

"I sent her away when I brought you here, to protect her. Being close to a Crow is dangerous enough. I knew she'd be at risk if we kept her here. I had planned to bring her back after the Gate, then the oath happened. I spread the rumor that I let her die to keep her safe. If everyone thought she was dead, she wouldn't be hunted and couldn't be used." Solas stood from the table and walked to my side. "I'm sorry, Perdi. But I told you the truth, that it was too dangerous for her to come here, that she had earned her freedom. I couldn't tell anyone what I had done. You can't stand this close to a throne *and* a Crow and not burn for it," he explained. "You're a pawn when you're loved, and she is very much loved by us, which made her a tool to be used to get to us. I couldn't risk Solene taking Elswyth. If Solene got her, I would have let her die to protect you. I had to choose. I thought that lie would save you both...and it did. As much as I regret lying to you now, it kept her alive."

I nodded slowly. "We have a lot of air to clear."

"There were a lot of lies I told," he answered. "Truths I didn't want to keep from you. I thought...I don't know, that somehow, the web I wove would be strong enough to save you."

"These aren't the only lies that need to be cleared. There is also the matter of Faolan and his crimes against you and others," I answered.

Elswyth blanched. "Perdi…"

"Oh, yes, I know of those lies as well. Whatever was said to get me to the Dark Courts, you nearly sentenced a man to death for them." I didn't just look at Elswyth. I stared into her very soul. "If given a chance, I would have killed him for what his father did. I would have killed him for you…in a heartbeat. And I would have lost no sleep over it."

"Perdi…" Elswyth started, then closed her mouth. Whatever she had planned to say, she seemingly decided that now was not the time to tell me.

"That's on me, not her," Solas interrupted. "It was the truth, told in a way you don't like. I don't care what he says. He did many things to Elswyth and others. I've heard the story. He was young. He had no power. But I've been there myself, and never once did I allow that to happen. When she was kicked from his territory, I had to buy her from those who had found her. For what happened to her while she waited for me to buy her, I blame Faolan. He is responsible for doing nothing to protect her, even when he released her, just as he did nothing to protect you."

"Neither did you!" I spun and finally screamed until the walls shook. "Don't you dare say you've never fucking allowed it. You were at the Golden Court with me, Solas, and we both allowed it. We watched as innocents died by the handfuls, and we both listened to the screams that echoed in the halls each night. We, like him, did what we could to survive in a place that wanted us both dead. We listened and chose to save ourselves and let the rest die in our place!"

I picked up my chair and flung it across the room, breaking the only remaining window in the dining room. I struggled to keep the anger from boiling to the top. Everything had been a lie. There were reasons for them, but I didn't have to like them. I didn't have to feel good about it. Now that the games and scheming had ended, the truth had finally caught up to us, and it burned every inch of my heart and soul. The old wounds broke open and mixed with the salt of new lies.

Zephyr stood from the table and pulled Elswyth from the room with him. Nix was gone before Zephyr had even stood, pushing Orrian out of the room on her way in. Solas moved, but to my side. For a moment, I thought he would try to touch me, to take away my rage. Instead, he handed me the leg of the chair and motioned to the room. I grabbed it and swung. I hit the table and cleared it. He stood back and watched as I destroyed what was left of the dining room and foyer. I screamed out all my frustration. And when my chair leg broke, he passed me another, until I was using the legs of the broken table.

"It feels good, doesn't it?" Solas asked when I finally slumped against the wall.

"Yes." I breathed out hard and fast and landed on my rear. "Sorry."

He laughed and took a seat beside me. "This isn't the first room you've demolished, nor is it my first. Most of the house looks like this."

"No, I mean, I'm sorry for what I just said. I know you couldn't help them. It wasn't fair to blame you."

"Doesn't mean I don't feel that pain every day. And you're right. I know Faolan's story. I know what he endured. His father was a bastard. My father was war, but his? That man was pointless cruelty in the most creative of ways. And Faolan grew up trying to be better than his father and was punished for his reach for greatness. I see what he did and didn't do and can't see the parts where he was powerless. It took centuries for our relationship to sour, and it'll probably take as long for me to see any goodness in him, without seeing the horror of his father first."

"Tell me the truth, Solas. Did you ever truly love me? Do you still love me?" I asked and almost wished I hadn't. I was scared of the answer. "Was I ever a tool for you?"

"Never a tool. And yes, I love you with all my being. I never stopped...ever. You're the first I've ever loved and the first I didn't know how to protect," he answered, and I sagged with relief. "Do you still love me? A lot has happened, and I'd understand if your heart has changed under the pressure of my cruel touch."

I leaned into his body. "Always, with every piece of my soul."

"We'll figure out the rest. The truth between us, always. We will clear the air, and every lie told, I give you my word," Solas replied. "But we should probably have those conversations outside. I fear, little Crow, you'll burn the house down when we finally speak all our truths."

"Did you hear the Horn?" I asked. "Zephyr and Finn could, although Finn said it was just an echo he could hear coming from me."

"Yes," he answered. "I knew you could, too. Every time I heard it, I watched you tilt your head to the hum."

"What was it warning me of? The coming war? The Gate?" I asked.

"Not what...who. It started the day Solene began leaving Blood and Bones, long before you had even come to my court. Eventually, after I had ignored the call, it tried for you and finally, this morning, Zephyr could hear it. He is your other half, as it is with Finis. He was the only one who could answer the wild hunt and fight for you," he answered. "The only other time it sounded was when the Gate was created, which was also the first time Solene stepped out of Blood and Bones. It knew, long before any of us, that she'd be an oath breaker, and the Horn tried to warn us."

"It didn't sound during the war that divided your lands?"

"Not like what we just experienced. The Horn has followed Solene since birth, like a faint hum in the background."

"I saw her, the woman with the Horn."

Solas nodded. "As did I, just before you killed Solene. She looked exactly like my mother."

"Why would your mother want her own daughter dead?"

"Because we all knew Solene would bring about the end," Solas answered. "Even those of us without the sight knew Solene would be a blight on Elphame. But Solene was far too powerful, even from a young age, for any of us to do anything about it. Perdi, it took the wild hunt, two Soul-Eaters, her own people sabotaging her and the collective power of all Fae to kill her. She was unstoppable until her greed tripped her up."

"She is the reason for Crows, Solas. I saw it in her soul. She's called the halflings to Elphame in search of another Finis to open the rift."

"Open the rift?"

"Not just the Gate, but the rift, the world around the Gate," I explained. "Before the tithe to Elphame, she loved someone. Perhaps it was a mortal? She wanted the worlds to open completely. The reason for it, I don't know. Whatever the reason, Solas, my gut tells me we need to look into it. She may be dead and gone, but the horror of who she is and what she's done will never fade until we have all the answers."

"I don't know the reasons, but I'll check into it — what she's done and why — once things settle down a little. I'd rather not poke my head into Blood and Bones for a bit. I don't know how they'll feel about us killing Solene."

"I want to feel bad for killing your sister, but I don't — and neither will they. Lily gave me the knife to kill Solene and did what she could to help us."

"I don't feel bad, either," he answered. "Both of our realms are better off without her."

"Months ago, the shadows told me she would have to die to end this. I thought, though, when I felt the Gate come down, I'd have to kill you first."

He nodded. "They were right. Everything had to play out exactly as it did for us to be sitting here together. I couldn't stop it. Each time I tried to move in a different direction, I would always end up back on this path. The night you told me that you'd think of a different way, that you still had your mask, I knew the path to end it all wasn't mine to walk. It was yours."

"You should have asked me for help sooner."

"I know, but I couldn't bring myself to ask you to help. The cost would be so great. I thought I could keep this from you, that you had given so much already. It sounds foolish now, but at the time, all I wanted was for you to survive. I just couldn't find a way to make it happen that wouldn't hurt you in some way. But if I drove you away, I thought it would hurt you less than having to shave off your soil on a risky maybe."

"No more masks. No more hiding. We are in this together or not at all," I answered. "You must give me your word or we will part ways now. We can navigate what has happened, but I will not do this again for any reason. You will never leave me in the dark on any matter. It is my decision what I am willing to risk. You will never take those choices from me."

He wrapped his arm around me. "And so shall we make this oath."

"And so shall the oath be written in our blood," I added.

He picked me off the floor and carried me to my bedroom. "I destroyed mine."

I laughed as he set me on my bed. Everything was exactly how I had left it, except my bed. It smelled of him. He had slept in my bed after I'd left. My room, the only link he had to me, was cared for.

"I'm sorry, Solas. And before you tell me we can talk about it later, I need you to know how sorry I am for any pain I caused you, and we caused each other."

He positioned himself around me and pulled me against his body. I tucked my face into his chest. "So am I. Never again, Perdi. There is nothing I wouldn't give to protect you, to save you. But I thought, if you hated me enough, you would survive Solene. If you were gone, she couldn't get to you. I was wrong. Even after I watched you walk away, I knew you wouldn't give up."

"I love you."

"You came to my dreams, Perdi. Each time I wanted to end myself, you stopped me. Seeing you, even in my dreams, was enough to keep me going."

"I missed you more than I was willing to admit out loud. I had to see you, even if it wasn't real."

"It was real enough for me." He kissed my temple. "I tried to find a way to get to you, to bring you back."

"Zephyr told me."

"Zephyr voted to just kill Solene and let the cards fall where they may."

I laughed. "Zephyr votes to kill everyone. He's a Soul-Eater."

"We wouldn't have suffered so greatly if I had let him find a way to do it."

"He wouldn't have succeeded. Both he and I had to do it together," I replied.

"Soul-Eater." Solas pulled back. "I think I should have just sent you both."

"If there is ever a next time, we're doing it the Finis way. I've had enough of the games to last me a lifetime." I smiled and pulled him back into my chest.

"What a terrifying thought." He laughed softly.

"I think you love me more for how terrifying I am."

He lifted my chin and growled into my mouth. "Yes, I do. I'm finally not the only nightmare of Elphame. I like the competition."

Solas placed his hand on my stomach and waited to gauge my reaction. His hand slid to my hip and paused again. I could hear his heart pounding in his chest. He was nervous. I thought it was the first time I had experienced Solas uncertain of himself with me.

"It's okay," I told him and placed my hand on his chest. "I want this."

"I can wait," Solas answered. "We don't have to... I mean... I don't know all of what happened to you in the Unseelie Court. I know nothing happened that you didn't want, or Zephyr would have leveled the place. It's currently standing, so... I mean, I don't want to force you..."

"Nothing happened there. Close, but I couldn't bring myself to cross that line. Kissing while I strolled through his mind was all."

"Zephyr told me."

"Does that make you uncomfortable?" I asked, blushing.

He lifted my chin, drawing my eyes to meet his. "I do not own you. I'd be lying, though, if I didn't say that I'm not glad you and he weren't together as we are, but I would have no right to be angry with you had it happened. We each had a path to walk, and I knew, when you left, that your path would hurt my soul."

I nodded but couldn't shake feeling uncomfortable now. I would have told Solas all of it. I wouldn't have lied about it. But I didn't think I would feel so guilty. Solas drew his lips to mine and ate the guilt from my soul.

"I love you," he murmured.

"I love you," I whispered back and released a moan as he finally gripped me and pressed our bodies together.

He whispered my name over and over as we kissed. At first, I was ravenous, but soon, the craving was gentle. I pulled back and braced my hands on his chest. I wanted to see his face. I had to see his eyes. I needed to sear his eyes onto my mind, my heart, my soul. I wanted to never forget who he was, who I knew he was when no one was looking — the man who would let the world see him as a monster but hated when he had to do the monstrous things that were demanded of him.

"I love you," I whispered again.

"And I love you." Solas picked little twigs from my hair and laughed.

He scooped me off the bed and into the shower. Tired, we washed the grime from each other. Another fight for the Gate washed down the drain, taking with it the doubts and wounds we had lived in for months. I had to slap his hand away several times as I tried to clean blood and mud from my hair. After sending him out of the shower so I could finish, I dried and pulled on shorts and a shirt. Solas sat on the balcony with food and drinks. I sat beside him and drank a glass of wine before settling in. My body was still on edge, ready to run at a moment's notice.

"I can't believe we did it." Solas sighed. "But I'm more surprised you let Faolan live."

I shrugged. Faolan wasn't the person I wanted to be thinking of at that moment. "I've asked myself why, too. What he had done to me was one of the cruelest things I thought I would ever experience. But I've been here long enough to know that isn't true. I know what this place does to you, what it forces you to do to survive. If we killed everyone who had become a monster when backed into a corner, Elphame would die out. As for this last dance between him and me, he didn't do anything you or I didn't do. I guess, in his own way, he tried to give me the answers I needed without risking the lives of his people. I can't really blame him for that," I replied. "Although, Zephyr will probably hunt him down if he so much as sneezes in our direction. No oath or power in this world will keep Zeph from raining fire down on Faolan."

"I think that's the first time you've referred to Fae and mortals as *our* people," Solas pulled me into his arms and kissed me. "The Gate is open now. Are you going back?"

"I don't know," I answered.

He grabbed my hand. "Can I come to visit you if you do?"

"I don't think I can, Solas," I replied. His pulse quickened at my words. He was scared and didn't try to hide it.

"You'll get used to the feeling of being there. It goes away over time. And with the Gate open, you'll still feel Elphame," he replied. "I don't think you'll go mad if that's what you're worried about. You haven't been here long enough."

I curled into his chest. "I don't think I can leave you."

"But your home, Perdi. You've wanted to go home since the day you left it. I love you, but I'd never keep you from your home."

"I *am* home," I replied. "I'm right where I want to be, where I fought to get back to."

His body softened as if he had been waiting for the pain of me leaving again. "Stay with me for always."

"Technically, I still have about six years left on my tab."

"You'll always be my little Crow."

"And you'll always be the nightmare that comes for me. I pity those who stand between us," I answered. "I expect your crown delivered to me by tomorrow morning."

His laughter rumbled in my chest. "Queen Perdita."

I felt the nudge of fate and welcomed her in. Oath or no oath, Solas was mine, as I was his. He shivered against me. He, like me, felt fate at the door. And when neither of us pulled from the other, we knew we had invited her in and set a place for her at our table.

"Perdi," Solas whispered into my mouth.

"Welcome home, Solas." I held him against my heart, for him to hear it beat, just for him.

The path home was not the Gate. I was where I needed to be, where my soul could stretch out and heal all the broken pieces. I had walked this path willingly, hauled over the sharp flints of horror, and dragged my will to live through every ditch in these cursed lands. And along the way, I had cut off everything good and pure and robbed myself of all the glue and twine that kept my heart and soul together. But once I stepped into the front doors of my home in the Dark Court, my heart, held together with twine, was healed in the arms of Solas.

Together, we'd silenced the Caller of Crows, but not before fating us all with the chaos she left behind from beyond the grave. I had crawled through glass to come home and stood between fire and ice to get back, and I didn't fear doing it again. I was a Soul-Eater. I'd have done worse to better people to win. Gate or no Gate, I would be the last Crow, or the world would burn for having tried to pluck another from their nest.

# A Cursed Crow:
# A Curse So Dark and Twisted
## Lanne Garrett

### *Excerpt*

We are comprised of a junk drawer we carry around in our souls. We're made of baggage we can't let go of. Some of us pack light, while others drag around every memory they've ever had or thing they wished they'd said. Some, more than others, hoard every regret, slight, tear or unwilling parting in life like a troll under a bridge with his precious trinkets. We all have odds and ends hanging off our souls. Some of us just pack it differently. The trick is learning to carry that baggage the best we can while figuring out how to unpack it and face what we've towed around from place to place, person to person. That's what healing forces a person to do — dump it out, sit on the floor with all the broken pieces you haven't been willing to face or throw away, deciding what to take and leave behind. Sometimes we do the same thing with people or places we once loved. We let them go. We move on. We choose to become better versions of the person who had a death grip on all the junk that kept us in the moments of yesterday.

Unpacking my baggage was what coming to Whitwick was supposed to do for us all. It would let us look into the black hole we all carried on our backs and take pieces out, brick by brick, using them to build the foundation of a new future…a new beginning. Instead, we used those bricks to beat each other bloody. No one was safe from the anger or blame, and everyone was at fault. The Guardians of Whitwick hadn't protected the people, only their own children. The children marked for the Taking didn't leave fast enough and caused the deaths of those who didn't need to die. The Fae tormented more than they needed to. A Crow, in their mind, had broken the Gate, and now Fae could roam as they pleased. It didn't matter that I wasn't the one who had done it. I was still responsible because, somehow, I hadn't stopped it. It was easier to unload the bricks of the past onto someone else than to let go of them. And every time I came to Whitwick to repair the wounds, it felt like new wounds opened, fresh reasons to bleed for Whitwick Gates.

"I'd rather be holding my own guts in with my bare hands while I crawled through the caves of the Winter Court, being ridden like a pony," I muttered to Nix and motioned to the room. "Anything over this."

"There's no place like home," Nix whispered from my shoulder as we watched the arguing unfold before us, as though we weren't even present. We were currently back on the topic of recreating a Gate that was no longer there. It always came back to the Gate. "Remember when I told you I wanted to return to our garden after the war? I take it back. I don't like being here any more than you do."

I nodded my agreement. I didn't want our garden this bad, either. I leaned back in my chair and tried to sigh past the anxiety this place brought me, but I could never get a deep breath in the mortal world. Jare, one of Zephyr's men, stood behind my chair. His eyes never stayed still. He scanned the room, his legs apart, arms folded casually but ready to grab any unfortunate soul who reached for me. He looked terribly out of place, towering over us all. But he was pretty relaxed under the Fae threat that was rolling off him. A decade in the bowels of Blood and Bones, tortured and broken daily, made everything else look like a walk in the park to him. Coming to Whitwick was supposed to heal wounds, but neither Zephyr nor Solas felt comfortable with me going anywhere by myself, let alone to a different realm. Jare glanced down once with a smirk that said it all. He saw this for what it was — a game of blame, an endless talk in circles. And by the time we were done each time and I returned home to Elphame, I was weaker, exhausted, drained of magick, and it seemed like we hadn't done anything more than find new wounds.

"I feel like I've been cursed to suffer, first as a mortal and now as Fae," I whispered to Nix. Hearing the words come from my mouth made them feel more real, heavier and sharper.

I rubbed the cramps that had started in my thighs from having sat in one position for too long and watched a dozen red-faced mortals attack each other with venomous words, each meaning more harm than the last. They were no different than Fae around a war table, who haggled over whose threat of bloodshed carried the most weight. Here, they argued over who had suffered the greatest and who held the most blame for it. Mortals could be just as hateful and vengeful as the Fae, if not more.

I had watched for hours and added nothing more than a head shake or nod. Nix hadn't bothered to say a single word. They didn't like him any more than they did me. I was too Fae and Nix was too small for either of us to matter. Why I was there had nothing to do with what I could offer and more about what they could blame me for and demand I do — both of which were ridiculous. It had been like this for weeks and only worsened with each visit. I hadn't expected my homecoming to be celebrated, but I certainly wasn't expecting the hate my arrival had caused. They had no idea what I had given up and endured for their survival. Nothing I said would change how they saw me. I was Fae. I was one of *them*, part of the problem.

Whenever I tried to speak, to add to the conversation, they accused me of lying to protect *them*, the Fae. I was either too Fae to care about man's plight or too young to understand. Or, as I had been told to my face only moments ago, it was because I was the whore of Elphame. They had conveniently forgotten I had once been dragged through the Gate and that I'd given my life to save Whitwick from the plight they accused me of not understanding. Crows in the mortal realm had about the same level of respect as they had in Elphame...*none*. It had taken the death of a king, escape, wars and killing of a Royal Seer before anyone in Elphame had looked at me with anything more than contempt in their eyes. I wondered if the same would apply in the mortal world. I didn't want to do here what I'd had to do in Elphame to earn an inch of regard. Mankind wouldn't survive how Fae gained respect.

When I signed up to help mend the fence between realms, the scared butterflies in my stomach told me that coming here would become the war of broken souls. While no one remembered I had taken the same walk of fate that so many before me had, that I'd survived and was living there was all that mattered around this table. No one cared that I suffered whenever I came to Whitwick, only that I chose to stay with the Fae. And after our first meeting weeks before, I would rather be in the middle of a bloody battle on the fields of Elphame than this. Out there, in the trenches, I had a better chance of winning. Here, the four walls around us felt like a prison, where the captives fought each other to the death for scraps of meat. I was the meat, and I didn't like the look on their faces.

My eye finally started to twitch in frustration when the same question was asked of me. "For, quite literally, the hundredth time, I *can't* bring back the Gate. I can't repair it. I can't bend it back into shape. I can't glue it or tie it. It's *gone*. I tried to fix it, but it's gone." My voice raised over the back-and-forth arguing. "I don't know how else to say it in a way you'll understand. It. Is. Gone."

"Try something else." The man to my right nudged me. "Maybe we can help?"

"I appreciate that, but it's actually gone. I don't mean that it's so broken I consider it gone and of no use. I mean, when we pass between realms, it's not there. It's an empty patch of grass. It's gone and isn't coming back," I answered. "We only still call it the Gate because there is no other name we use for the point between worlds. But rest assured, there is *no* Gate to speak of. It no longer exists. It rusted and blew away in the wind."

"Can you do a spell to bring it back?"

"No, I can't. I can't call one from thin air or build one from scratch. I don't even know how or if it's possible." I looked to my father, who sat at the end of the table and shrugged. "I'm sorry. I will do what I can to help, but I can't do what you're asking me. I'm not powerful enough. It took three Darkmore witches to build it and an original on the other side, who is dead, to sing a Gate to life with Elphame magic. I am *one* Darkmore witch and can't sing to save my life. Bring me an idea that can work, and I'll be more than happy to help. Until then, we're beating a dead dog."

"I bet you'd do it if Elphame wanted it," another spoke up.

I whipped my head to face the comment and glanced down the table. "No, I wouldn't, and I couldn't. You're not hearing me. I'm not saying that I don't want to do it. I'm telling you I *can't* do it. I'm not powerful enough. And quite frankly, I don't care who is asking. The answer will remain the same, no matter what."

"You're the reason it's gone. Fix what you did!" he yelled.

I wanted to snap back and tell them it wasn't my fault, but I didn't. The silence was easier. If they knew Solas had played a part in breaking the Gate, this would stop being a conversation and move straight to pickaxes and shovels. Solene, Solas' sister, was given all the blame, and they couldn't ask for her head because she was already dead. Soon, I feared, it wouldn't matter what I said or how hard I tried to keep them from marching into Elphame with war on their minds. They would spill blood eventually. Fear would drive them to stupidity. It did that to all of us, mortal and Fae.

"I'm sorry this has happened," I finally stated. And I was. If I were in their position, I'd be terrified right now.

"It's easy to be sorry when you're not the one at risk. You have no idea what removing that Gate has done. While everyone else fears what will come next, you sit in your castle."

"The Gate didn't save any of us...ever. It didn't do a damn thing to protect mortals. It certainly didn't keep me from suffering. And it didn't save me in Elphame, where I fought every day to keep you all alive. Now, there are oaths to protect you, Fae armies that will protect you," I replied. "Arguing isn't going to solve any of our problems. We need to move forward. It was never the Gate that saved us. It was oaths. Now, there are new ones, and the Taking of mortals, for any reason, is prohibited."

"What about those who are not protected?" he asked. "You can't save everyone."

# About the Author

Lanne Garrett writes books. Considering where you're reading this, it makes perfect sense. She lives in Vancouver, here she spends her days getting lost in the beauty of reading and writing and can be found behind a mountain of books on any given Sunday.

Lanne loves to hear from readers. You can find her contact information, website details and author profile page at https://www.finch-books.com

Sign up for our newsletter and find out about all our romance book releases, eBook sales and promotions, sneak peeks and FREE romance books!